Catherine Feeny wa[illegible] undergraduate degre[illegible], she spent three years at Vanderbilt University in Nashville, Tennessee, teaching and studying for her MA. On her return to England she became interested in alternative politics and, with her partner, Raymond ffoulkes, restored and set up a radical theatre in Canterbury during the 1980s. After spending many years in a small village in rural Burgundy, they now live in Brighton, where Catherine was Writer-in-Residence at the first Brighton Fringe Festival. Her previous novels, *The Dancing Stones, Musical Chairs,* and *A Matter of Time*, are all available from Hodder & Stoughton paperbacks.

Also by Catherine Feeny

The Dancing Stones
Musical Chairs
A Matter of Time

Making Do

Catherine Feeny

FLAME
Hodder & Stoughton

First published in Great Britain in 2000
by Hodder and Stoughton
First published in paperback in 2000
by Hodder and Stoughton
A division of Hodder Headline

A Flame Paperback

10 9 8 7 6 5 4 3 2 1

All characters in this publication are fictitious and any
resemblance to real persons, living or dead, is purely
coincidental.

A CIP catalogue record for this book
is available from the British Library

ISBN 0 340 68259 0

Typeset by Hewer Text Ltd, Edinburgh
Printed and bound in Great Britain by
Mackays of Chatham plc, Chatham, Kent

Hodder and Stoughton
A division of Hodder Headline
338 Euston Road
London NW1 3BH

This is dedicated to my sister, Sarah Feeny Welch,
my sweet Es.
Wheresoe 'er we went . . .
Still we went coupled and inseparable.

ACKNOWLEDGEMENTS

Many thanks to Sara Menguc and Carolyn Mays. To my partner Ray ffoulkes for his truly wonderful support, especially financial, during the writing of this book. And to my dad, Paddy Feeny, for his expert advice on Muncher's memories of the ring.

CONTENTS

CHAPTER ONE

An Enormous Presence

Clara Hood was a woman who knew how to get away with wearing pink, green and crimson combined. And much else besides.

Around her short dark hair – which she cut herself, using two mirrors for the back bits – she wore a rose-coloured headband, found on a bus, to which she'd sewn a cluster of puce feathers plucked from a feather duster. A red logger's shirt in brushed cotton topped a full, silky skirt, sprigged with jade leaves and coral flowers. Her shoes were covered in glitter the colour of candy floss. They had very thin heels and were sharply pointed at the ends. Clara's height was on the short side but she'd have liked to have been tall, and she'd worn stilettos for so long now that she was as speedy on them as on bare feet. Which was just as well.

Although it was June the evening was chilly, so Clara had lit the gas and left the oven door open to cosy the kitchen up a bit. This had disturbed the mice who lived in the warm drawer, and they'd come out for a night-time potter. Every so often Clara spotted a little brown form making its way up a curtain or along a shelf. Because of the mice every bit of food in the house had to be stored in the refrigerator, which could prove tricky, especially when Clara had sweaters in there as well: chilling was the best means of refluffing old wool and angora.

Not that fridge space was a problem at present.

Traditionally, this moment of the day was toast time. Thick buttered slabs, which Clara sprinkled with cinnamon and brown sugar and ate with rum and pineapple juice – ratios dependent on the current roll of the dice. But there was no toast today. The bread had all been eaten up, and the grill-pan could remain on the floor, fulfilling its secondary function as a reminder that there was a hole in the floorboards underneath it, which was best avoided. This wise precaution had been inspired by the night Clara's uncle and lodger, Muncher Barrow, had slipped on something to do with Sassy, the since-deceased dog, and got his leg stuck down there, and Clara had had to make the hole bigger with her chainsaw in order to get it out again: Muncher was an ex-welterweight and it was still quite a leg. It was from Muncher that Clara had inherited her slightly crooked jaw. The large mouth and shrewd brown eyes she had apparently conjured up for herself.

There wasn't any pineapple juice either, and rum was only a distant memory. Clara put some coffee on to brew in the battered metal pot. A watery second pressing of used grounds, barely sepia, though she drank it jet black given half a chance.

Half a chance? Pushover! Clara Hood could make something out of less than a quarter.

On the kitchen table was a pile of money-off coupons cut out of discarded newspapers she'd found on the Underground. Beside them, spread out and grouped according to date and hue, thirty-seven bills, flanked by a gleaming line of a dozen or so credit cards. Also, a shopping list, the items ranked in order of importance.

Even now, with things so much tighter than usual, it was hard to survey the whole without a sense of relish.

This was Clara's canvas. The war map from which she hatched her battle plans. In this realm she was juggler, tightrope-walker and trapeze artist; the cunning fox, the running deer, the one that got away. With her credit cards at her side, Clara could cut a perilous and winding path between this month and the next and in due course the one after that. These weren't Clara's only allies either. In addition, there was her own resourcefulness, which knew how to make the most of any good fortune that might turn up, and also the rent from her four lodgers. The rent couldn't be counted on in quite the same way as the other assets (partly because there was always the risk the landlord would get wind Clara was subletting; partly because its payment was erratic), but whenever one of the lodgers landed a good month – when Muncher got a lot of washing-up work, say, or Si scored plenty of tricks, or tips were unusually lavish down the drag club – nothing had the power to appease like a little bit of cash in hand.

Clara poured the coffee into her favourite, sky-blue mug, then pulled the dope drawer clean out of the table. Mainly it was a tangle of empty plastic bags, but by upending them all and tipping the drawer at an angle Clara managed to gather about half a teaspoon's worth of gritty fragments, some of which might just conceivably have been marijuana. She rolled them in a Rizla paper, along with some of Muncher's tobacco, and lit and puffed, holding the joint between the tips of her fingers: she wasn't very good at smoking. Until it had burned down to nothing, Clara indulged herself by not doing a thing, except thinking how nice it would be to go in an aeroplane. Immediately the joint was finished, however, she drained the mug, opened the window a chink to disperse the smoke and buckled down.

Absorbed in her task, Clara didn't notice when rain started, or hear the sirens and car horns on Shaftesbury Ave. She did register the smell of Cantonese roasted duck coming up from street level, though.

Twenty minutes later, 'So it's going to be like that, is it?' Clara exclaimed, leaping to her feet, startling the mice and causing them to scatter. She checked out the kitchen door, which led on to the sitting-room. Knobless. Clara rifled through the pile of tools in the old bicycle basket under the table until she found a big screwdriver, then she ran up the stairs and along the second-floor corridor to her bedroom.

There were fewer doorknobs than doors in the building, so the ones there were moved around a lot; the lodgers constantly got marooned outside their rooms, or discovered someone had borrowed their handle while they were inside and they couldn't get out again. By jiggling the screwdriver in the hole where the handle should have been, Clara managed to open her bedroom door a small crack which, by pushing against the wooden panels with all her force, she was able to widen enough to allow her to enter.

It had been a while since Clara had been in there. One day the room had got too full of stuff for easy access, so she'd simply stopped using it. (Though looking around now, there was much that could be put to good purpose and it was probably time for a clear-out.) Since then, she usually slept in an armchair or on the sitting-room sofa. She rarely needed more than a three-hour stretch anyway, and even with the bedroom out of action there were plenty of other places to put the rest of her belongings. The house was a warren of cupboards, from jack-in-the-box size right through to stand-up. Clara had clothes, shoes, scarves, jewellery, eyeshadows and lipsticks squirrelled away in most of them. Frocks and dresses she hung up in the sitting-room, and from the bathroom shower rail and the spare bit of washing-line in the attic. T-shirts, blouses, scarves and jackets were draped over the backs of chairs or piled in corners.

What Clara wanted at the moment, though, was a calculator. After a lengthy search she found one under a cushion. It was dusty, and the batteries were dead, but she managed to coax some new life out of them, downstairs again, by warming them slightly in the oven.

Not that Clara was convinced a calculator was any better than her own brain when it came to multiplying, adding, subtraction and division. She just needed to check. And to be proven wrong, ideally.

Among her bills and her credit cards, Clara's quick fingers tapped arpeggios on the large, old-fashioned keys, trying to make both ends meet. But however much she squeezed, squashed and strained, still they wouldn't quite.

Eventually, Clara pushed her chair away from the table, its legs making an exasperated noise against the wood. She knotted her fingers behind the back of her neck and raised her chin determinedly towards the cobwebs.

'Knickers!' she muttered, echoing the word that was written at the top of her shopping list, where it represented only the tip of a very big iceberg. 'Times seven,' she added more loudly.

And not long till Muncher's birthday.

With one room effectively unoccupied, it really was craziness not to take on another lodger. Barely an option right now, in fact. Clara's mind flitted around her abandoned bedroom: boxing and bagging up; evaluating and pricing, with a view to touting and flogging off. Emptied and tidied, it wasn't a bad room at all. Depending on how the flogging-off went, Clara might even be able to slip Si a few quid to tosh it over with a bit of emulsion, and clean the windows. She could throw in a cupboard in the corridor as well: extra storage space was always a hook.

Get someone in there quick. Specify a month's deposit. Perfect, except for one major drawback. In Clara's attic, hidden there with the complicity of the lodgers, was the individual who was in need of those seven new pairs of knickers, and who in other ways also had stretched Clara Hood's budget beyond its limits: an illegal immigrant, named Bethany Smile, on the run from the British immigration authorities.

There was no way Clara could take the risk of letting a stranger in on the fact of Bethany Smile's enormous presence.

CHAPTER TWO

The Calaluan in the Attic

There was no time like the present, and Clara hated to be idle.

Packing and sorting in her old bedroom, she listened to the streets fill up with people flocking out of the West End theatres and the cinemas round the corner in Leicester Square. She loved the clamour and excitement of it all. It made her veins feel as if they were filled with neon; the nuances and undercurrents of her own patch of London seemed to rush through the tunnels of her brain. Soho tonight wore an air of expectancy. It fizzed with the kind of rush you got when you knew you had had a very good idea.

Hurrying feet made spongy, plashing noises on the rainy pavements. Chinese voices shouted. 'How many? Five? Upstairs, please.' 'We get you a table. You wait. Ten minutes.' In her mind's eye, Clara saw the damp queues in the restaurant doorways; through their steamy windows she saw curls of orange pigs' tails and mahogany rows of lacquered ducks. Because of the downpour, the food smells had got muddled in with a pong of wet rubbish bins, sodden newspaper, and the dense, swampy stink of the fishmonger's in Newport Place, where they sometimes gave her free carps' heads.

Blocked cabbies leant angrily on their horns. An argument broke out among a group of drunks outside the White Bear, accompanied by the sounds of kicked cans and rolling bottles.

'Sorry, mates, private party,' insisted the Aussie barman-cum-bouncer with the mermaid tattoo.

Clara's circle of bare carpet got bigger. A row of bulging carriers stretched along most of the corridor.

From the scrape of wooden crates and the rattle of awnings, Clara guessed that the oriental supermarkets were starting to close. One of the White Bear's Aussie bar staff yelled time. Flummoxed American accents discussed the availability of taxis and the best ways back to hotels. There were the usual boozy disputes outside Clara's building, and then there was that brief, simmering period, the short breather when Soho drained of this particular influx, before being flooded with clubbers.

Soon the house would burst into life. It always did late at night, which was when most of the lodgers knocked off work – the reason why it was at its quietest early in the morning.

Now, sure enough, the front door opened and a whoosh of draught raced up the stairs and along the corridors. The door slammed shut again. Clara heard the sound of footsteps making their way up to the first floor. Not Muncher's plod. These were the scampering feet of a young person. Exactly how young Clara had always thought it wisest not to ask – Si would have lied about it anyway, and a person's age was their own business. Fifteen was her guess.

Food was held in common. When Clara entered the kitchen Si was examining the watery bags at the bottom of the crisper.

'Any bread?' he asked, straightening up and letting the refrigerator door swing to.

'Only if you've got hold of some. I tried earlier, but they were watching the monitors.'

'Bastards! Starving.'

Si was slight and wiry; half East End, half Chinese. In his work clothes – skin-tight jeans and a jerkin – he radiated a certain girlish eroticism. The effect faded, however, when, abandoning the hope of toast, Si chucked the jerkin to the floor and replaced it with a Superman sweatshirt that was lying there, then pulled his wet, shoulder-length hair into a pony tail and secured it with an elastic band.

'Sodding rain. Y'know what? Nobody – like *no*body – cruising.'

Si grabbed a comic off a shelf and sat down, tipping the kitchen chair back on two legs, one of his feet on the ground, the other braced against the edge of the table. Like that, few would have guessed he was a rent boy.

Clara poured some more water on the coffee grounds and put the pot on the gas again.

'Y'know what, Clara?' Si often held conversations from behind a comic.

'What?'

'I reckon Bethany Smile eats too much.'

There was a pause.

Clara said, 'It isn't that Bethany eats too much, the problem is that we haven't got enough. But I'm going to remedy that.'

'Tonight?' Si's voice took on a note of interest.

'Soon.'

'Ah!' In a thought-as-much tone.

'I'll tell you about my plan once everyone's back.'

But Si wasn't interested in plans.

'Y'know what, Clara? I still don't get why Bethany couldn't stay where she was and just hide out or scarper.'

'There's nowhere to scarper to on Calalu Island. It's the size of the Isle of Wight.'

Though this didn't mean much to Clara either. It was hard to imagine a place where there wasn't a drain you could disappear down, and she'd rarely ventured beyond the limits of the District and Circle. But then, on the other hand, it wasn't a whole lot easier to understand how Bethany Smile had managed to traipse around London for a whole twenty-four hours before finding Lisle Street, and more especially without getting caught. She was, it must be admitted, a woman of sizable proportions.

Which was why she was so heavy on her underwear.

And Clara never had, never would, buy second-hand knickers. Not for herself, and not for anyone else either. Nor could she tolerate the market-stall, three-for-a-oncer variety. The underwear she favoured was the kind that came in boxes, in colours such as champagne, peach and claret. Clara was wary about what she let close to her body; and anyway, sometimes it was important to treat yourself to things that you couldn't afford.

The front door opened again, but the footsteps didn't stop at the first floor. They continued upwards, then paused on the second-floor landing. There was the sound of knocking on the bedroom door next to Clara's, followed by a thump and several soft thuds. A voice rose in shrill exclamation. The footsteps proceeded less steadily up to the next level.

Clara removed four dryish mugs from the stacked and balanced pile of washing-up on the draining-board, prompting a minor avalanche of cutlery to tumble on to the floor, clanging, tinkling, jingling and pinging.

'Shame you can't eat mice,' Si observed, as several of the alarmed creatures stampeded over his ancient trainer.

He hadn't noticed Clara's only female lodger, Geraldine Crowe, standing in the doorway. Geraldine was holding a self-help manual entitled *I Am Me and You Are You.* She wore a long Laura Ashley, circa '72, with a wide sash and a flounce around the bottom. A thick auburn fringe all but covered her unusual eyes, which at present were filled with an expression of horror.

'Geraldine. Coffee,' Clara said, sharpish.

Geraldine ignored the offer.

'Please withdraw your recent comment,' she said to Si. 'It distresses me beyond measure. Mice are most sensitive. You will have wreaked havoc on their psychologies.'

Si sank lower behind his comic.

'*With*drawn. Got any bread?'

'No. However, I was summoned to the kitchen for crisps and peanuts.'

'By voices?' Nevertheless, Si sounded a bit optimistic.

'Actually, no. By Kim. Who knocked on my door, only to get tangled in an unforeseen carrier bag, fall over and break a heel.'

'Not her gold slingbacks?' Clara poured a mug of the coffee liquid and put it down in front of Si. She lifted the old bicycle basket on to the table and rummaged through for superglue, tin tacks and a small hammer. Though really, Kim had lodged in the house long enough to know to be careful.

'I cannot tell.' Geraldine lowered herself into a chair.

'Crisps and peanuts?' said Si, dropping the comic. Then, 'So what was in the carrier?'

'I'm clearing out my room,' said Clara.

'What for?'

But at that moment Kim entered, cradling bags of crisps and peanuts to her breast with one hand; in the other holding a broken-heeled shoe. Followed closely by Muncher Barrow, his stubby old pipe smouldering in the corner of his mouth, the T-shirt stretched across his barrel chest spattered with raindrops and giving off a slight odour of washing-up water. From under the good tweed jacket over his arm – Clara found all of Muncher's clothes – he produced a bottle of red wine.

'Brazil,' he said in his husky voice.

'Where the nuts come from,' put in Kim, spilling the bags on to the table, and watching the hands dart out for them. 'Pull a cork for me someone, and save my nails.'

Clara rummaged in the bicycle basket again, her mouth full of roast-chicken-flavoureds. The corkscrew had lost most of its handle, but it worked if you got a grip with a tea towel. She poured the wine into the mugs she hadn't yet used for coffee and into a couple of jamjars – all the glasses were dirty – then passed them round.

Kim accepted a jamjar, placed the shoe on the table next to the superglue, and seated herself beside Geraldine, letting her floral peignoir slither open with automatic professionalism, to reveal a lavish portion of long and gorgeous leg.

'Rain rain go away/And let the boys come out to play,' she chanted. Her trade, too, had evidently been hit by the weather. The drag club justified the girls' salary by the tips they got and by paying them commission if they sold a bottle of fizz. To Si, she said, 'Eat nicely, dearie.' To Clara, 'Spring cleaning, are we?'

'Clearing out.' Clara took a breath. 'I'm getting a new lodger.'

'Stone me!' Muncher unhooked his pipe from its nook.

'But, sweetheart, how can you?' Running perplexed fingers (painted Almost Blush) through short, honey-blond hair.

'This must not be contemplated!'

'What for?'

'Because I'm skint. I mean, skinter than usual.'

Clara looked from face to face.

Geraldine had gone into one of her quivers. Her striking eyes were teary with emotion. 'Your penury is my fault,' she proclaimed, in a wobbly manner. 'But I shall remedy the situation. I take complete responsibility.'

'So all's well that ends well,' said Muncher,. for a quiet life. He replaced his pipe, put a match to it and sucked, making strange popping noises.

'You can't and you won't, Geraldine,' said Clara.

'If I hadn't gone to Calalu, none of this would have happened.'

'It was a project,' said Clara.

Which indeed had been the case. Long entranced with the religion of that cheerful island, Geraldine had used money inherited from a godmother to fly to Calalu, in the West Indies, in order to see it in action. She returned a Cargo Cult Spiritual Consultant and resigned from her part-time job in the candle shop. She scattered cards across the bulletin boards of the astrology outlets, wholefood cafés and holistic surgeries of Neal's Yard and Neal Street, advertising her new-found supernatural services.

The work wasn't steady. Partly due to there being some pretty hefty competition on the spiritual front in that area of

London. Partly because – in addition to a belief in reincarnation for all living things, and a whole lot of other benign notions nobody could much take issue with – one of the central tenets of the Cargo Cult of Calalu Island was that sooner or later something good from the gods would wash up on your beach, or fall out of the sky on to your vegetable plot, and all would be well with you thereafter. Given the nature of its ocean currents, major crops and air traffic control system, this article of faith received considerably more positive reinforcement on Calalu Island than in Covent Garden. And in spite of most of the Cult's precepts having a definite appeal, Clara had never yet encountered any luck that didn't need a fair degree of coaxing.

'Y'know what, Clara?' Si had shielded himself behind his comic again.

'What?'

'Whoevercums'll've seen Bethany on telly.'

It was a point. Clara had done so herself. The day before Bethany showed up in Lisle Street, and on and off since, she had featured on Clara's dotted screen with its coat-hanger aerial, variously described as 'extremist', 'rebel', 'political activist' and 'known dissident'.

Actually, the total sum of Bethany Smile's political dissent had been to sing socialistic calypsos in public places, opposing the new Calaluan government, which was not socialistically inclined.

Another toss of the coin and Bethany might well have been a freedom fighter – or at least encourager – in the eyes of the British media. Unfortunately, however, this was Calalu's first election. (Nobody had really felt the need of one before. There probably wouldn't have been one now but for international insistence.) Rather overlooking the fact that the handful of Calaluans who did vote hadn't exactly been spoilt for choice, the British Prime Minister had gone on record, stating his solidarity with Calalu's democratically elected government as soon as it came to power.

All of which malarky explained why the immigration authorities were out to get Bethany Smile.

Shortly after the new Calaluan government took office, Bethany had got wind of a warrant out for her arrest, whereupon she'd hastily booked a package hol to London and the Beautiful Home Counties. On arrival in England, she'd been let into Heathrow without a murmur.

There was a smug international outcry following this mistake; the Continental Heads of Government in particular questioning what level of control the British Prime Minister and Foreign Secretary had of the 'grossly inefficient' authorities 'supposedly under their jurisdiction'.

As a result both men hastily went on record, vehemently maintaining that they wouldn't rest until Bethany Smile had been caught and returned to her native land. Face-saving time all round, and oodles of damage limitation: if their snoops and satellites were doing their jobs half-right, the two politicians would know full well that Bethany Smile wouldn't harm a fly. Image was evidently all, however. As long as it disposed of their embarrassment, PM and Foreign Sec were clearly quite happy to dump Bethany back on the tender mercies of a regime determined to spoil the fun.

Geraldine Crowe had made friends with Bethany when she was visiting Calalu Island. Really, she'd made friends with most of the island's population: apparently it was that sort of place. As sure as eggs, when she saw Bethany's mild face on the six o'clock news, topped with a wonderful coil of multicoloured turban, Clara knew it was only a matter of time until she arrived.

For six months Bethany had been here now, and all of them loved her like they loved sunshine and fresh bread, warm towels and fried chicken. The women of Calalu Island were famed for their fabulous skills at batik. Bethany passed her time in the attic making intricate patterns in wax on silk, linen and muslin, which she dyed the shades of sunsets and birds of paradise, shallow seas and reef creatures. Bethany hung her designs on the washing-line

Clara put up for her. Anyone who wanted to iron had to do so in the attic; Bethany had commandeered it because it was needed for the batiking. When there were any around, Bethany fried plantains on the calor-gas ring she used for melting her wax. She also sang, and listened to the World Service.

The attic was reached by a very steep staircase, with doors at bottom and top: sufficient insulation for Bethany to continue most of her activities. Food would have to be taken up to her – which wouldn't necessarily be a disadvantage.

'We'll have to check the coast is clear when Bethany comes downstairs, but she doesn't a lot,' said Clara, alive to the fact that her utter skintness had registered, and the discussion had in a way moved on to practicalities.

'Get a geezer as has a daytime occupation,' said Muncher.

'Or a woman,' said Clara. Though speed *was* of the essence: the credit cards lay prone and helpless, scattered across the table.

'In the evenings we could say we operate a curfew,' said Geraldine.

Kim delicately brushed some crumbs off her lap with the tips of her Almost Blush. 'We couldn't do that, they would think we were just too, too odd. Besides – take it from one who knows – the day-to-day cover-up isn't really a problem. The real headache is how to get Bethany out of the building at the same time as concealing her from the new lodger if, heaven forbid, we should ever need to.'

Exactly! Now that the lodger was agreed to in principle Clara's mind started off at a gallop, ransacking the ground plan of the house for possibilities.

'We could lower 'er out by a rope,' said Si.

'Block and tackle'd be what you'd want,' said Muncher.

Geraldine said, 'Might not people notice?'

'She could go out the skylight and over the rooftops,' Si suggested. 'Like a cat-burglar.'

'Dearie, she weighs seventeen stone if she weighs a pound.'

'Shame there ain't no fire escape,' said Muncher.

'Got it!' said Clara. 'But we'll need a dry run to check it'll work. I'll get ads up round the place tomorrow.' She paused. '*Person wanted for nice room with lots of storage. Quiet household. Central London. Near tube.*'

'*First come, first served,*' added Muncher. 'Makes 'em hurry up about it.'

'*First come, first served,*' echoed Clara.

She hoped it wouldn't be a man, though. Not one her own age, anyway.

CHAPTER THREE

Steps to Self-Actualization

Mark Upshaw was hot and irritable by the time he got off at Leicester Square. Although he'd decided he really must use the Tube, he was nevertheless dismayed by the crush of humanity, which made it impossible to sit down and difficult to find floor space for his four suitcases. It felt as if every stretched foot, each wide-open newspaper and razor-edged briefcase had been put in place owing to a general desire that Mark Upshaw should be elsewhere.

Since it was June the weather had lately turned from cool and wet to boiling and sultry. Even in T-shirt and jeans – a disorientatingly unfamiliar garb for daytime, or indeed any time except the most casual of country weekends – Mark could feel himself becoming sweaty. As the crammed train lurched and hurtled in an uncontrolled manner through the dark tunnels, the resentful expression which this sensation inspired unwittingly attracted several appreciative glances. Mark Upshaw was tall and dark, with large, black eyes and a swarthy, imposing, muscular body. Though he didn't know it, the newly acquired two-day stubble and embittered demeanour only served to enhance his good looks.

If Mark had been given the job of designing the London Underground system, he would have worked it so that the side on which one alighted was completely uniform and predictable. At Leicester Square, needless to say, he found his way blocked by several of the most solid individuals he had ever seen in his life.

When eventually he had apologized his way to the open doorway, a woman with a pushchair made a sudden dash at it also, obliging Mark to permit her to alight in front of him, and to assist her in getting the pushchair safely on to the platform. This involved various manoeuvres with the suitcases, which were met with considerably more ill-will than Mark would have thought was merited by someone who was helping a lady. The last of his suitcases wasn't yet off the train when the doors started up their wild yodel, forcing him to snatch it from between their twin blades with all his strength.

Mark Upshaw would also have indicated the direction of exits more clearly. Then people wouldn't walk right to one end of the platform before discovering that it was the other end they wanted.

The escalators weren't functioning, owing to some form of construction work. Instead of ascending without effort, Mark had to climb up countless static metal stairs, knowing that each unavoidable bump was likely to scuff his luggage, which was made of Italian leather and had been purchased at vast expense the last time he was in Florence. There weren't even any advertisements to relieve the monotony. These had been replaced by offensively chummy explanations as to what was going on, and assurances that all this mess and bother was no more than a temporary nuisance, there to guarantee that in the fullness of time life would be very much better for everyone: a good thing, in fact, if you looked at it in the right frame of mind, and didn't insist on being negative. Mark was reminded of the opening lines of *Paradise Lost*, which he had done at the Queen's School, Pitsbury: the renowned and expensive educational institution which had provided him with his clipped but impeccable manners, and a rigid and unimaginative code of conduct.

Ground level was a clanging, buzzing palaver of turnstiles and ticket machines; its floor a mosaic of flattened chewing-gum and cigarette ends. The space you put your suitcases through was approximately half the width of the average suitcase, and a quarter the width of a sumptuous Italian one. While battling with this, Mark fed his ticket into the slot in front of the turnstile, only to be ordered to seek assistance. That came unbidden, however, in the form of an insolent hand, which grabbed his ticket from him and contorted it in the way that the machine deemed acceptable. Comments might have been made to accompany this action, had the man not caught sight of the look on Mark's face, taken in his physique, and thought better of it.

The final exit spat him out at the end of Little Newport Street, beneath a hazy sky which had turned the sunlight a jaundiced shade of yellow. Mark put his cases down on the filthy pavement – the fingers of both hands had frozen into hooks – and surveyed the scene with a grim, masochistic satisfaction.

He'd skirted these streets on occasion, of course. Some of the restaurants on the other side of Shaftesbury Avenue he knew rather well. But until two days ago he had never actually walked in Chinatown.

A noisome piscatorial stench, reminiscent of rotting seaweed, hung on the scummy air, along with an aroma of monosodium glutamate and raw cabbages. Rubbish was piled everywhere. Battered pigeons drank from rust-coloured vestiges of the sopping time before the heat wave, which lingered in thin lines along the edges of the pavements.

Mark clawed up his luggage for the last lap.

A Chinese travel agent's radiated homesickness and alienation, as did the cheapjack noodle bar and the many, confused foreign faces. Everyone seemed to be lost, drunk, down-and-out, or speaking into a mobile telephone. (Was there a law that all media types must wear black and white and sport ponytails?) A pub on the corner called the White Bear was blasting out appalling music at such a volume that it seemed not so much sound as an invisible wall of jagged matter. Mark wondered whether this could be legal.

Lisle Street was filled with delivery lorries, parked so close to the buildings as to completely deny access to the pavement in most places. Restaurants displayed troughs of offal and strung-up slabs of greasy meats. (The only place in London to eat acceptable – and actually authentic – oriental cuisine was Kensington.) Any remaining bit of walkway which might otherwise have been available to pedestrians was covered in the overflow from ethnic supermarkets – snagging crates of fruit and vegetables, precarious pails of sugarcane, unsteady mounds of watermelons. The open door of a cramped shop whose sign boasted French Food & Wine revealed it in fact to be selling sweets, cigarettes, tobacco, washing-powder, scourers, mops and lurid feather dusters, crammed on to undulating shelves whose stock couldn't have changed since the 1950s.

It was opposite this depressing establishment, in a building above one of the street's unappealing restaurants, that Mark had come to live.

For a moment the wretchedness of the situation overwhelmed him. He took a step backward farther into the road, and was rudely hooted at by a motorbike whose speeding logo indicated it was carrying rushes from Wardour Street. Perhaps because he'd been born to leisure, Mark despised dash and hurry. He tilted his head and looked up at the ramshackle piece of architecture that was to be his place of residence.

One, two, three storeys above street level it rose – a glimpsed smear of skylight in the roof must belong to the attic. All of the building's angles were irregular: warped, grime-encrusted sills; dusty, lopsided curtains; bowed, crack-mottled window frames. The front door was painted black but wind blown dirt had dyed it sepia. Beyond and beneath the wear and tear there appeared to lurk a grand nineteenth-century façade: patterned brickwork in different colours, the odd decorative flourish; obscured, however, owing to a patent lack of investment.

At which thought a series of images pushed their way into Mark's head and, unwelcome though they were, caused his expression suddenly to soften. In place of this grubby outlook he saw honeysuckle-framed views of the gentle fields of Surrey and Sussex; majestic Scottish hillsides; crystal-clear swimming-pools. His eyes surveyed London from high above the South Bank: a Michelin-starred landscape of museums and theatres. Spare bedrooms: those places where friends could be put up for indeterminate periods.

Surely somebody . . . ? The idea butterflied across Mark's consciousness. His expression spontaneously darkened.

But then, what an imposition a semi-permanent guest would be upon the harmony of his friends' households, and Mark himself would be loath to endure day-to-day contact with an individual who was down on his luck. Many were those, moreover, who had indicated an earnest desire to help Mark re-establish himself financially. Far better to focus his sights on those forthcoming social events which would give him the chance to discuss these matters with his acquaintances than mentally to upbraid them for not offering facilities which it would be unreasonable in him to expect. It was hardly their fault that a few hundred pounds bought very much less when it came to daily life than it did in restaurants, say. Probably it hadn't even occurred to them that a few hundred pounds now represented the sum total of Mark's resources, and pride would never permit him to bring this sombre fact to their attention.

Hitherto, Mark's life had given him little need to become adept at seeking consolation. It was with bitterness that he compelled himself to contemplate the solace of a clean room and fresh paintwork, in a building which was otherwise a pit. Sparse – though some – comfort could also be derived from his having noted that there had been no actual food left out among the kitchen's outrageous clutter, and that there weren't any telltale mousetraps.

The quietness of the house during his early morning interview with the landlady had led Mark to conclude that the other lodgers – of whom there were four, including the lady's uncle – had jobs which took them away from home during working hours, suggesting people of routine habits. Although she must be responsible for having permitted the building to suffer its inexcusable degree of neglect, the landlady herself had struck Mark as a respectable, if somewhat loudly dressed, individual. Arresting, though far from pretty. Around his own age of thirty-two. She had been rather distant – Mark wasn't a conceited man, but he was accustomed to women finding him pleasing – but maybe coolness was considered appropriate in a relationship of this nature. Or maybe it suggested a more widespread depreciation of Mark's charms: his appeal had recently diminished in another female quarter.

When all was said and done, however, neither his landlady nor his fellow lodgers were of the least importance to Mark Upshaw. At this precise moment he was very far from enamoured with human society. With the exception of those inclined to be useful to him, other people were something Mark wanted nothing to do with. His intention was to keep himself to himself and, if necessary, make it clear to others that where he was concerned they should act in a similar manner.

It was 4.30, precisely when he had said he would be arriving, and Mark had rather expected his landlady to be there to greet him.

Instead, seated at the kitchen table, spooning cornflakes into his mouth, and reading a comic propped up against a bag of sugar and the cereal packet, was a teenage boy. Mark was taken aback. Did his landlady have a son? If so, she certainly hadn't mentioned him during the course of their interview, and guessing the boy's age she would have to have been absurdly young when she gave birth to him. Perhaps he was a nephew or some other relative? A friend's child on a visit?

And why was he eating breakfast at teatime?

Rudely, the boy didn't stand up, or give any other sign that he was aware of the presence of an adult. He just kept on spooning the cereal between his lips, his eyes glued to the page in front of him.

The kitchen was less tidy than it had been two days earlier; something Mark wouldn't have imagined possible. Dirty crockery covered every surface, and the sink was occupied by a mound of washing soaking in a froth of bubbles. A box of soapflakes stood next to it on the draining board, along with a few washed glasses and a little pile of price tags – 35p, 70p, £1. The floor was a tangle of clothing. As was the sitting room, which Mark could see through the open doorway.

Dresses, on and off hangers. Scarves draped over the edges of lampshades. Items of jewellery dangling from unused picture hooks. Strewn blankets, pillows and sheets. The whole garishly reminiscent of a gypsy caravan or Bedouin tent. Mark's eye was caught by a glittery, upturned shoe and two long silk stockings apparently drying on the mantelpiece, a small patch of mould on one of the walls.

So this was what he would have to put up with, was it? Mark's face took on a set cast. He addressed the boy sternly.

'What's your name?'

'Si. What's yours?' From behind the comic.

'Mr Upshaw.'

'Mr *What* Upshaw?'

'Mr Mark Upshaw.' Striving to maintain a level tone in case this was his landlady's relative.

'Do people call you Maz?' Raising his head from the comic at last and looking straight at him. The teenager was of mixed race, with rather striking eyes and skin colour. Doubtless this brought the girls flocking, which would account for the cocky manners.

'No they don't. Ever,' Mark replied, looking back. 'How old are you?'

'Twenty-one.' (This was blatantly untrue.) Then, insolently, 'So how old are you?' Returning his gaze to the comic.

'I don't think that's any of your business.'

This was followed by a meaningful silence, during which Mark had the infuriating feeling that he had somehow been worsted.

'Is Miss Hood expected?' he asked.

'Who?'

'Miss Hood. Clara.'

'Nuh-uh.'

'I am the new lodger. Has she left me a note?'

'Nuh-uh.'

'Is anyone meant to see me into my room?'

'Yup.'

'Who?'

'Guess.'

'In that case' – now Mark really was having to rein in his temper – 'please carry two of these pieces of luggage to my bedroom, and I shall follow with the remainder.'

'Oh, all right.' Loudly pushing his chair back from the table, picking up the bag of sugar and the cereal packet, opening the refrigerator and mystifyingly shoving them inside. Mark caught a glimpse of perhaps a dozen sweet potatoes, and what appeared to be a purple cardigan.

Care was needed not to damage the suitcases further, but Si tom-tommed them up the stairs and let them fall, quivering, on to the landing, beside a large, walk-in cupboard opposite Mark's door and next to the bathroom.

'She said not to forget you've got this extra space.' Indicating the cupboard with a desultory gesture, and looking set to vanish.

But then, as if a thought had suddenly occurred to him, or he'd just remembered something, a complete change took place in the boy.

'Do you know what? I like you, Mark,' he said, turning so that they were facing one another. 'And I think you could like me too.'

Startled, Mark tried to make a gracious sort of sound, though he didn't give a damn for the boy's opinion, and the latter observation wasn't a remote possibility.

'I'm going upstairs to get changed,' Si continued. 'My room's on the next floor, and I'll always be available to you.'

'Good,' Mark managed. This had scarcely been borne out by Si's previous behaviour.

The boy smiled. 'I think so.' And he ran off up the stairs.

Relieved to be alone, craving the peace of his own room and a cooling shower or rather bath, Mark raised a hand to open the door, only to discover . . . nothing.

'That was quick.' Si was wearing just a pair of jeans. His hair was loose and he reeked of aftershave. 'I didn't expect you to want to come so soon.'

'It wasn't my intention to disturb you either, but I am without a knob.'

There was a long silence.

'I can't get into my room,' said Mark, since Si seemed to be failing to understand.

'Oh, that.' The shoulders drooped and something of the boy's earlier aspect seemed to return. 'Well, you can borrow mine, I s'pose, but you've got to let me have it back.'

'Have it back?'

'Yeah, else how'll I get in here later?'

Mark unpacked his suits and dinner wear, carefully placed them on hangers and put them in the wardrobe. Grey. Pin-striped. Charcoal. Each tailored for him specifically. He hung up his shirts as well. Blue. White. Slightly crumpled. He wondered if he would be able to avail himself of an iron. His ties he rolled neatly and put in one of the wardrobe drawers, with his underwear and eleven cotton handkerchiefs: having duly returned the doorknob, the twelfth was being used to wedge the bedroom door open. In another drawer he placed his second pair of jeans, two sweatshirts, two T-shirts and a jumper. He put a carriage clock on the bedside table, next to the lamp, then made up the bed with the sheets provided, which were shocking pink, though the pillowcases were orange. The invitations to the three events at which he and his friends would get the chance to discuss his financial future Mark positioned on the shelf above the blocked fireplace.

Once all four cases were empty, he carried them into the

corridor and stacked them in the cupboard next to the bathroom.

He returned to his room, undressed, and put on a black towelling robe. A flowered beach towel had also been left out for him. The bath was metal and inordinately deep. After running the taps for what felt like half an hour there was just enough tepid water to bathe in, beneath a bunting of damp towels, dripping skirts and blouses; surrounded by a clutter of cosmetics, perfumes, salts, cubes, oils, slivers of soap of various scents and colours, two stubs of candle and a dolphin-shaped sponge studded with joss-sticks.

In clean jeans and one of the T-shirts, Mark lay on the bed for a very long while. Not drawing the curtains, not putting the lamp on. His hair dried. The room grew cooler. The front door slammed. The building filled with a strong smell of bananas.

Thinking that his landlady might have come in at last, and was making a banana custard perhaps, for Si's supper, Mark descended to the kitchen.

Unless you counted the mice, it was quite empty. Unless you counted the mice, there was nothing on the stove or in the oven. He looked for clues in some of the cupboards, but found only mess and an ominously massive collection of candles, some decorative, some rather ecclesiastical-looking, doubtless indicative of a recurring problem with the building's electrics.

The light outside his bedroom window seemed to have changed during the few moments Mark had spent downstairs, as if London had suddenly been switched on and its diluted illuminations were floating in the air. This was the hour at which he used to set out for the evening with his ex-girlfriend, Fleur, until she discovered she needed 'more space' – in spite of the fact that she already had a fair amount of it at her disposal.

Such as the house in Little Venice. The cottage on the edge of the New Forest. The lodge, for instance. The villa. At a pinch, her parents' place, not far from Guildford. And lately, too, a proto dress shop, which was being stripped and gutted while Fleur made many trips to fashion shows in New York, Milan and Paris to view potential stock.

Mark always maintained it was the shop that had been responsible for the decline of their relationship.

It was an ironic coincidence that the enforced idleness of penury should have begun striking him just as Fleur was obliged to be so madly busy. As the stark details of Mark's situation became common knowledge, so had Fleur's purchasing decisions become ever more time-consuming. In the end, having a social life, setting up a business, *and* maintaining a relationship was just too much for her. 'Space' turned out to be something of a euphemism – as Mark should have guessed from the beginning: although it *was* true that Fleur did particularly like former-warehouse cafés with large tracts of emptiness between the tables, she was also pretty fond of a small champagne bar in Brewer Street, and had never objected to cramming herself into Riddle's Nightclub. One of her cars was an MG.

Which wasn't to imply that Mark blamed her. Women weren't designed to cope with life's difficulties, and a man shouldn't really expect them to.

Suppressing a sigh, Mark clicked on the lamp and spontaneously let out an undignified yelp. There was a person standing in the doorway. A female of most alarming appearance, who must have soundlessly pushed the door open while he was deep in thought, and was now spotlit against the dark corridor.

Although the woman looked in her mid-forties, she was wearing a girlish frock with lots of bows and frills to it. She had a thick fringe, which curled outwards at the sides. In her hand was a fat book, entitled *Seventy Steps to Self-Actualization.* Most disconcerting, however, were the woman's eyes. There was something not quite right about them, which was hard to pinpoint but equally hard to ignore. Reflex courtesy prevented too close a study, but Mark kept finding his gaze drawn back to them. Was one eye, or were they both, slightly off-centre? Were they constantly moving from side to side? Could it just be that the woman had a squint, or was the left eye artificial? Maybe her wild look wasn't physical at all, but merely the outer manifestation of severe inner derangement?

'My name is Geraldine Crowe,' the woman said. 'I startled you, I think.'

'Not at all.' Mark rose from the bed and walked to the door, coming to a standstill with a good arm's length between them.

'Have you read this book?' the woman asked, waving the volume at Mark, in such a way as to cause him to calculate the possibility of its inflicting concussion.

'No, I haven't.'

'You should. Clara and I think it's marvellous. Take it.'

Hastily, Mark did. The woman fell silent.

Downstairs, to Mark's relief, there was the sound of the front door being opened, then voices. It occurred to him that Geraldine Crowe was possibly here on his landlady's behalf, in order to summon him to sign legal papers relating to his position as lodger – something which Mark had assumed would in due course need to happen. But the silence only deepened, and Geraldine Crowe appeared to find it in no way discomfiting or awkward.

Eventually, unable to endure the situation any longer, Mark said, 'Why is there a smell of bananas?'

This proved an unwise question. Geraldine Crowe took a deep, deep breath, gave a little cry, clapped a trembling hand to her face, and uttered something which sounded like, 'Sassy! Sassy! Sassy!'

'Forgive me but I . . .'

The eyes had filled with tears, and were sort of pointed in Mark's direction.

'Sassy is trying to get in touch with Clara!'

'And Sassy is . . . ?'

'A dog. A most exceptional one. And still in this dimension.'

'There's a dog as well?' No mention had been made of it during the interview.

'It's deceased.'

'You are telling me there's a *dead dog* in the building?'

'A dog spirit, striving to make contact. I must inform Clara immediately. By the way, there will be a fire drill in thirty-five minutes. The assembly point after evacuation is the White Bear.'

CHAPTER FOUR

A Lovely Evening

At least a spirit dog wouldn't need feeding.

Of all the Cargo Cult's beliefs, the recycling of souls was the one that made most sense to Clara. It would have been such a waste otherwise – that good raw material entirely used up by a single owner – especially if unhappily or to no purpose. It was like those self-help books that she and Geraldine read, exchanged, and tried to pass on to others. Thanks to the writers' clever insights, Clara had learnt to swoop with the swallows and soar with the stars, upsize, downsize, accept herself, make make-up work for her, self-actualize, stop being a Sleeping Beauty, remember that *Female Is Two Letters More than Male,* etc., etc. The ideas stuck with you long after the book had floated downstream. It was in the nature of everything to grab every chance it could. Why should life be any different? Why not keep coming back indefinitely for more?

Sassy had been a starving stray, then a big, bouncy ginger dog, with thick rabbit ears at ten to three, short oily fur, a loopy grin and a pungent doggy smell. You'd have thought the lorry would have bounced her right into the next dimension, but maybe the surprise had got her confused. Sassy had never been very bright. It was no great wonder if she'd stuck around Soho rather than sniffing the trail to the next dimension where her soul would be turned around; nor that she was having trouble getting through to them either. When Sassy did manage to make contact, Geraldine said, Clara must give the dog precise instructions as to what to do next.

Clara glanced at the funny old kitchen clock, which gained a quarter-hour in every twenty-four. It was thirty-five minutes exactly since the time they'd fixed on for Geraldine to inform the lodger about the drill. Si was at work. The others were in their rooms and on stand-by. The plan was to get Bethany out first, hide her in the entrance to the Underground – Clara reckoned the Underground would be Bethany's best bet if officialdom ever actually showed – then smuggle her back in once Clara could safely assume that Upshaw was inside the White Bear. Clara just hoped that Geraldine would have calmed down enough not to forget that she was meant to play a diversionary role at this crucial second stage.

She picked up the two catering-size saucepan lids which were going to stand in for a siren and ran to the bottom of the stairs. 'Fire!' she bellowed at the top of her voice. 'Fire!' Banging the lids together like St Paul's, dropping them, hurtling up to the second floor landing and ducking into the lodger's cupboard. As soon as she was sure the coast was clear she'd go on to the attic and fetch Bethany.

So far so good. They'd feared the lodger might have filled his extra storage space with clutter, and there'd be no room for a person, but luckily there still was. So far so good, though only just. Barely had Clara pulled the door of the cupboard to when she heard Mark Upshaw's footsteps on the landing; he had probably been monitoring the clock in order to be ready at the precise moment. To Clara's great relief, she heard Geraldine's door open.

'You cannot come out here, I regret,' Geraldine said in her usual, declamatory tone.

There was a pause. Clara would have given her eye-teeth to be out there doing the job instead: a quick explanation, none of those portentous silences. But then Geraldine was so very much her own dear self. Hers was a voice designed to summon mysteries, as much a part of what she was as the frills and sashes. And although she wasn't usually very strong on instigating action in the first place, Geraldine was fairly okay at carrying it through.

Mark Upshaw said, 'And why not? Isn't the purpose of a fire drill to vacate a building as hastily as possible?' Cold, assured, and oh so correct. He could have been reading from a safety manual. Clara remembered the closely shaven cheeks, still with the slight darkness of a dark-haired man; the grey suit that had made her think of tailors. Upshaw was tall and broad and proud. He took up a lot of space, and appeared to think he deserved to.

'For the purposes of the drill, we are assuming that this section of the corridor is a wall of flame.'

'So I needn't go to the White Bear?'

'I fail to follow.'

'Just that I don't think in such an eventuality my chances would be terribly great.'

'Significant, however. We would be fighting the blaze from below.'

'Is this something to do with the regulations relating to lodgers?'

Yes, mouthed Clara, *yes, yes, yes.*

'Indeed it is.'

'Then can you tell me how often these events will have to take place?' Icily polite.

'I cannot. Nevertheless, you will be informed when we have succeeded in dowsing the inferno. Cower in your room until then, please.'

'I should prefer to read a book.' Upshaw's door closed abruptly. Clara heard Geraldine stride away in the direction of the kitchen.

Now was the moment to hare on up, grab Bethany and skedaddle, yet Clara's nose suddenly began to twitch, her body to experience the frisson she got wandering around big department stores, in the presence of designer dresses, jars of caviar and whopping bottles of perfume. The thrill that ran through her was the same as when she watched a holiday being booked, someone purchasing a bit of art, leaving a wedding list, ordering a hamper. Her thumping heart recalled the time she'd slipped into an auction at Sotheby's – a free show – and felt her temperature rise, her pulse quicken with every aching hundred.

Clara's eyes had dark-adapted. The other occupants of the cupboard were suitcases. She stretched out a hand and touched one. Its skin was soft and smooth, tanned she guessed, unmistakably foreign. What had sparked her attention proved to be the gentle aroma of leather. Or that was the subtext: in a wider sense, what Clara could smell was money. She took her hand away. For a passing instant she felt like a ragbag, a patchwork, a makeshift scarecrow of a woman, shoddily tacked together. To have anything that matched like these four perfect pieces of luggage!

To have anything that matched at all!

But what on earth were they doing in her house, in her cupboard? And what was a man who owned them doing in her bedroom? Couldn't these suitcases – and that tailored suit, come to think of it – find themselves a better crash than Clara Hood's, Lisle Street, Soho?

Clara breathed in sharply.

Unless, of course, Mark Upshaw had an ulterior motive for being there? Unless he was a government official, for instance, sent underground to flush out Bethany Smile? Now that would provide more than something of an explanation . . .

Silently, Clara pushed the cupboard door open. The edges of Upshaw's door were outlined in thin, golden light. As soon as she was sure he was off the premises for a while, Clara would have a thorough hunt through Mark Upshaw's things. She needed to suss out what he was up to.

* * *

If the White Bear was unprepossessing from the outside, this was as nothing compared with its interior.

While sitting in his room, listening to the assortment of footsteps fleeing the building in which he would be only too grateful to be left alone to metaphorically perish, Mark had convinced himself that a brief appearance on the establishment's threshold would suffice. His name would be ticked off on some Fire Services list and he would be at liberty to depart.

This was not what had transpired, however. In order to avoid causing unnecessary offence Mark had been obliged to accept the offer of a drink – a mineral water, he'd chosen; all save himself had had a laugh about that – and sit at a table with his fellow lodgers. They'd squeezed on to one in a cranny upstairs, next to the 'dunnies' – everything about the pub, from the staff to the piles of brochures and newspapers, the life-sized effigy of a rugby player, and what appeared to be a makeshift travel agent's had an Antipodean slant. It was, mercifully, quieter up there than at ground level, but there was still a giant screen depicting Australasians, presumably, doing white-water rafting, hanging from ropes over canyons, surveying the view from the tops of mountains and engaged in various other brash activities. There was no sound accompanying the images, and the colour quality was reminiscent of cheap icecream. The windows of the pub were open, but this neither cooled the room's scanty oxygen content, nor displaced the odour of Muncher Barrow's noxious pipe.

Mark had hoped that Geraldine Crowe was an aberration. She wasn't. A survey of his housemates brought to mind the paintings of Brueghel, or a particularly needy assemblage *en route* to Lourdes in the hope of a miracle.

Mr Barrow himself was a bulldog of a man, perhaps sixty, perhaps more. He had a crooked nose, a crooked face and one cauliflower ear. He was covered in short bristles. There was Geraldine Crowe, of course, and also an abnormally tall woman, who introduced herself as Kim, with dyed hair and admittedly a rather beautiful face, but overly made up and with a hyperbolical amount of leg on overt display.

The glasses were cleared away at last, by a Missing Link with a mermaid tattoo, who turned out to be a friend of the household. Mark rose to his feet.

' 'Nother round?' said Muncher Barrow.

'Thank you, but no.'

'Broke?' Kim spoke with a raspy purr, most unlike the crisp, scissory women's voices to which Mark was accustomed.

'I beg your pardon?' Mark's tone of voice attempted to convey how impertinent he considered the enquiry.

It failed. 'Skint?' the woman continued. 'Distressed? Pinched? Straitened? Hard up? Strapped for cash?'

They were all laughing again now, including the Neanderthal, who'd returned with a filthy cloth, and was flicking ash on to laps and spreading the sticky marks across the surface of the table. On the screen someone was looking up at a million spearheaded stalactites from the bottom of a flooded underground cavern.

'Know why there's so many names for it?' put in Muncher. 'Coz there's such a lot of it about.'

'Oh, come on, I'll buy.' Kim produced from her handbag a little heart-shaped purse. 'It's my day off and I feel like celebrating, and you're not to leave before Clara gets here. But do me a favour and have something stronger, would you? Paying for water is like paying for wee-wee.'

Clearly, Mark was trapped until Clara Hood arrived with the Fire Services list. Again, he took his seat.

'Thank you for your offer, but I am no longer thirsty.' Imbuing his voice with a warning to proceed no further, though he could have murdered a large whisky and soda.

'Please yourself.'

'Lovely evening. Nice and warm,' remarked Muncher Barrow, when Kim returned with the drinks. He looked out of the window as if there were something to see out there other than the upstairs of the noodle bar and the sludge-coloured back of a cinema. 'This time of year, never gets dark really.'

'Never gets dark in London ever,' said a voice behind them. Mark leapt to his feet. While he had been following Muncher's gaze unawares, Clara Hood had come upon them. She seemed slightly startled that he had risen but nevertheless continued: 'If you want to make a wish, you have to make it on the flights out of Heathrow.'

'I saw the comet from the depths of Kensington Gardens,' said Geraldine Crowe.

'There's the Planetarium,' said Muncher.

Clara Hood wasn't carrying a clipboard, or even a piece of paper. She manifested no inclination to tick anything off on anything. She pulled up a stool and joined them at the table. Once she had done so, Mark had no choice other than to sit also.

'Vod ton?' asked Kim.

'I'd prefer some rent.'

'That isn't going to quench your thirst – any more than a mineral water.' This evoked another raucous explosion of laughter.

'Marky-boy here's an absteemer,' Muncher Barrow explained for Clara's benefit.

'Is he?' Not so much as glancing in his direction. It was a pity about the jaw, it completely marred any hope she might have of being attractive.

'Actually, not. I just happen to prefer to drink in the company of people I know and like.'

There was a silence.

Then, 'I sympathize,' said Geraldine at last.

Mark felt grateful and shabby, and angry with both emotions. He resented the lot of them for their overbearing chumminess. It had forced him to look bad. It had driven home to him how much more difficult to appear likable and pleasant it was going to be in the future. He also resented Clara Hood's haughty attitude towards him. He was accustomed to commanding interest and respect, to his company being courted. Did she have no idea what kind of a person he was?

Life had thrown in Mark's direction plenty of women, but none of great complexity. Now, as he turned to contemplate Clara Hood – gobbling peanuts, jabbering with Kim; the conversation having gone on without him – he was surprised to find that he was wrong in believing that he'd pinpointed her stance and could henceforth either challenge or dismiss it. Clara had twisted and flipped, and slipped from his grasp while he wasn't looking. Cool, distant, haughty, unprepossessing, but other things also. Though she didn't bat an eye at him, Mark had a vague sense that he was being monitored; a strange intuition that Clara was slightly afraid of him possibly. This was even more infuriating. Ask any lady in the upper echelons of British society if Mark Upshaw was boorish and insensible to the feelings of others, and they would protest: on the contrary, he was charming, a perfect gentleman whom no woman could fear.

To show just how bloody nice he was, to let them know that he could be every bit as pleasant as the next man, Mark decided to engage in some talk with these people at his table. Social intercourse was something he was good at, and they could damn well learn that about him.

He waited for a pause, then asked, 'Why isn't Si here? Didn't he take part in the fire drill?'

The question, however, seemed to upset.

Geraldine said 'Oh!' and scooped her hand to her lips, as if she had only just recalled to mind the fact of Si's existence. Was it perhaps she, Mark wondered, who was Si's mother?

'Like I say,' said Muncher Barrow, 'lovely evening.'

'He's a casualty,' said Clara Hood. Her eyes did a quick circuit, briefly flicking across Mark's face at long last.

'Unfortunately he couldn't make it,' said Kim. 'Ow!' Glaring at Clara as if she'd been kicked, though Clara's little lavender silk stilettos were demurely crossed for all to see.

'We thought it would be more real if somebody didn't escape,' Clara continued.

'A degree of verisimilitude that did not extend to the probability of our having a drink afterwards?' An attempt at wit which, as Mark should have foreseen, went down like a ton of bricks. Blank expressions. A confused silence. There really was no point in bothering further, but Mark was determined that they should appreciate him before he avoided them hereafter. 'There seemed to be a strong smell of bananas in the house this evening,' he ventured.

'There's a lot of smells about,' said Muncher Barrow.

'It'll be one of the Chinese supermarkets,' said Clara Hood. 'They fry them up and puree them and make a cake with rice flour and vanilla.'

'And a cream and caramel topping,' added Kim. 'It's sinful.'

No, Mark was quite correct, Soho Chinese was far from authentic. Nevertheless, he was doing better. 'Another thing that has puzzled me,' he said, 'is – I couldn't help noticing – you have a large store of candles. Can I expect a lot of power cuts in the building?'

'Nah,' said Muncher Barrow. 'Oh, blow! Sorry, luv.' Looking at Clara.

'They're for decorating the house,' said Clara. 'At the weekend. We're having a party.'

'That's right,' put in Muncher. 'My birthday.'

'Maybe we'll buy one of those banana cakes for it,' said Kim.

'Home-made is better,' said Clara. 'You could make us one from that own special recipe you've got.'

'A party?' Mark had taken the room here in order to escape other people, not to listen to them celebrating on the level below him. 'Will there be many guests?'

'Nah,' said Muncher. 'Hundred. Hundred'n'fifty.'

CHAPTER FIVE

Knight's Bridge

There was a certain charity shop not far from Berwick Street which people left bin-bags of cast-offs outside, especially on wet Sundays. A few days before the heat wave started, Clara had reaped a particularly good harvest: a rug, a lampshade and the dress she now wore which a couple of stitches and a thorough wash had brought up good as new. It was made of quality, hospital-sheetish cotton and was white with a pattern of twin cherries with an oval leaf at the meeting of each pair of stalks, and a usefully full skirt. It seemed a shame to have to cover it over with anything, especially in view of the heat, but there you were: a very big man's shirt she'd laundered the maleness out of took the role of a jacket. It was cornflower blue. Clara had cut a bit out of the dress's hem to make ribbons, which she'd glued to a pair of ivory shoes in little rosettes. On her head she wore a frayed straw hat.

The trick to being where you weren't meant to be was looking like you belonged there. The spotless sky, the gleaming sun had turned Old Compton Street into how Clara imagined Rome or Paris. The exotic ruby glazes and velvety folds of chocolate on the buns in the window of the Patisserie Valerie, where she sometimes went mad when flush, looked well at home in London this afternoon. There was a dusky musk of coffee beans in the air. The stylish gossipers in the pavement cafés were drunk as honey bees on wine and summer, in a perfect mood to be forgetful.

Clara found a discarded French newspaper on a chair – more stylish than the British variety, she thought, with its small print and only one black-and-white picture on the front page. A woman returned from the toilets to an outside table; she and her companion had the compulsory small squabble over who was springing who, then they left cash, bill, a couple of freebie biccies, most of one glass of wine, enough coffee in the bottom of each cup to make nearly half one when combined, and the best part of a sort of custard thing. Clara smiled at the waiter and waved away the change when he brought it. She didn't always, but it was a small enough tip and times weren't too too bad at present. Besides, a resentful waiter was more inclined to get to thinking than watching to monitor who was eating what. While Clara sat there sipping and savouring, and looking French, perhaps, with the newspaper, someone walked out on a salad they'd eaten the leafy component of, leaving pretty much all the char-grilled chicken topping.

You got used to eating meals back to front. Clara had seen a programme on telly about hunter-gatherers, and though it didn't say so, she reckoned that they often had to do that also.

Normal women were something of a puzzle to Clara. Men – standard men – she only gave the head space needed to ensure they couldn't gatecrash into anywhere they shouldn't. But normal women she studied closely when in joints such as this, and through the glassy frontages of those crazy juice bars, where they perched on strangely shaped chairs at kidney-shaped tables with their bowls of rocket and exorbitant glasses of pulp. What Clara couldn't have achieved with a lemon-squeezer and some sort of musher! A killing would be there to be made if it hadn't all come down to setting. These women were more into that than the nosh, it appeared. Especially, they seemed to like scrubbed wood and turquoise decors, with stark names and holey-lettered logos; places with mega-rents but no real decorations. These women wore mostly black. They had razor fringes and no appetites. Was Clara Hood the only woman on the planet to dream of being in a room with row upon row of velvet dresses and every flavour of Häagen-Dazs?

She *would* make a cake for Muncher's birthday. A fridge cake, her speciality, because you could put whatever you got hold of into it and it always turned out splendiferous. As a start to that, Clara emptied the bics and a good lot of sugar lumps into one of the plastic bags she'd got with her – they were those tawny, misshapen lumps, the kind the normal women liked to look at. Old Compton Street on a sunny day was the best place for sugar that Clara could think of – so much of it available, and of such high quality.

The waiter shouted bye and thanks.

Direction: Hodge's Department Store, Knightsbridge, to purchase underwear for herself and Bethany before the landlord gobbled up all the new rent, and to procure goodies for tomorrow's party. But it was too lovely to hop a bus or burrow down the Underground. One day Clara would arrive at Hodge's in a taxi that wasn't driven by a friend of Muncher's, but on this glossy afternoon on foot would do nicely, and there wasn't any obligation to take the directest route. *Knightsbridge*: Clara's mind fiddled with the word as she passed the place in Brewer Street where Kim worked – languid and lustreless and not quite right till dusk, like sequins. *Knightsbridge, Knights' bridge, Knight's bridge.* She could imagine a band of horsemen or one only, in armour, crossing some lost causeway into a littler city, a cramped 'O', stuffed with etched buildings. If you knew where to look you could probably see bits of the bridge's brickwork from the Tube train. Strange, that an area could hang on to ancient glamour. Was that, too, something to do with reincarnation?

Just to check out what was what and to prolong the pleasure of having dosh on her, Clara carried on up past Golden Square, where all those whopping new restaurants were forever opening, and had a nosey at the place that did free tickets for telly and radio programmes. Muncher's birthday last year, they'd gone off to round Waterloo to see a recording, then bought four family-size chicken buckets for the price of two with coupons, and eaten them in front of the extinguished power station, near where they'd put back the Globe Theatre. They'd discussed how unimaginative it was to name a tower after a stock cube, and Muncher had got nostalgic about when the Waterloo arches weren't blocked up with wine bars.

Clara always avoided Carnaby Street, but Newburgh Street – only a step, a hop, skip and a jump away – was indisputably classy.

And as with the juice bars, that had much to do with restraint. No hubbub of articles on display in these windows; a few things only, shown off at their best. There was a jeweller's with two necklaces and a bracelet hooked on to a bleached bit of driftwood, as if they'd been washed up on shore, or sunk to the bottom of an ocean. Frail and simple, with thin clasps and little chips of precious stones; you'd have to be careful they didn't catch on the taps when you were washing dishes, or get tangled up in the tools when you mended things. Actually, it would be better to take them off on such occasions: they weren't designed to cope with any real degree of wear. But of course, the kind of woman who possessed them probably didn't indulge in that sort of activity anyway, though Clara found it hard to imagine not trying to fix what was broken.

The small boutique next to the jeweller's sold shoes, scarves and handbags, and then there was the one opposite the pub, on which the work was being done.

Clara had been watching its progress for a while now. Dresses, it was going to be, according to the builders who'd ripped the old insides out and replaced them with new everything. Clara had drunk a cup or two with the sparks as well, bought from the Coffee Café round the corner – at a premium – and stayed to watch him tack white lengths of cable and secure the unblemished fixtures to the walls, ready for the plasterers to come in and smooth everything over. He hadn't minded her having a gander. The shop was a big one with bags of retail space. It could take a lot of stock without looking full up. Those walls would absorb more than a few gallons of emulsion.

What colour scheme would Clara go for, if she had the play of it? Strawberry, perhaps, or terracotta, with woven wall hangings and a big glass mobile and pictures of trapeze artists. Or saffron and violet with Van Goghs and Gauguins. Scarlet and peppermint, palms in pots, an indigo parrot and gold-framed mirrors. Certainly not the insipidity she was looking at, and had naturally expected. The scrubbed-pine floor had been covered with sheeting. The walls were in the process of being painted pale crispbread. Some tubular dress rails on casters shrouded in plastic tarps, and ordered much too early – the blokes doing the painting would forever be having to move them – stood icily in a corner. Not many of them, given the size of the premises.

Oh, well. Liberty's was some consolation, with its tadpole paisleys. Mayfair (*May Fair!*). A detour into Green Park, where deckchairs had sprouted like mushrooms – though Clara had never quite believed in the mushroom's life cycle: it seemed too good to be true. Then at last, the revolving portals of Hodge's, the commissionaire with white gloves and a peaked cap, to whom Clara gave a confident smile before twirling into the emporium.

Downstairs to the Food Hall, and the familiar excitement, like she'd experienced in the cupboard, though this time tinged with that, also familiar, pounding apprehension. For this part of the proceedings Clara needed all her wits about her.

How she would have liked to have got some fresh stuff. There was fish and seafood from everywhere. Displayed against a backdrop of squeaky-green samphire were rosy mullets, cream and tangerine scallops, knobbly oysters, ugly monks, etc., etc. There were wine-red steaks and beeswax-skinned ducks; girolles the colour of egg yolks, eggs the colour of surfers.

But it was too risky. Fresh would have to be picked up at the market. Besides, the pre-packed stuff very definitely wasn't to be sniffed at. Bath Olivers for the fridge cake. All sorts of wonderful nibbles. Tins of spreads and pâtés. A bag of dried cranberries, which could go in the cake also. A jar of pumpkin purée. Some hand-made truffles, which would do as a present for Muncher. Creamy dips from the chilling cabinets – quite chilly enough against the skin to make it home without spoiling. Savoury biscuits with seeds on. Dried pasta. A floury *saucisson* in a string net. A jar of mayo. It was a terrible shame when she had to stop.

Clara took the lift up to Lingerie, for the pleasure of them having someone whose job it was to push the button for you. It stopped on the third floor, next to a doorway which opened on to a stairwell and a corridor leading to Luggage. 'Please pay for all your purchases before proceeding to other departments,' read a sign beside the exit. Clothes were a different matter. Every item had a flying-saucer-shaped security disc that didn't come off except with a special machine.

The underwear range was dazzling, right through from bullet-proof to clingfilm, and in every size from stick insect to Bethany Smile. Clara chose seven pairs of strictly functional – their price was a stinger, but that was probably due to the substantial fabric requirement. The next half-hour or so Clara devoted to assessing the merits of tight and shiny; thirties chorus line; landgirl cotton; lacy; athletic; all-in-one; courtesan; barely present. In the end she fixed upon a bikini-sized pair in cocoa silk edged with lace, some waist-highs with a drawstring in apricot muslin, and a burgundy thong, which she draped over her arm along with the functionals while she went on browsing.

Which was how she came to make her fatal error.

Mark heard the telephone ring but he didn't bother to go down and answer it. He had kept his friends vague as to his whereabouts, so it wouldn't be for him. Half an hour later there was a sound against his door, not so much a knock as the kind of dull thud you would have expected if someone had fallen against it while succumbing to a heart attack.

After the fire drill Mark had requested a proper doorknob. Later that same night he'd nearly jumped out of his skin when a spike was suddenly thrust through the hole where a knob should have been. This proved not to belong to a doorknob proper, but to a large screwdriver which it took much subsequent practice to become adept at manipulating. Mark didn't like to contemplate the consequences had he been leaning against the door when it was delivered.

Now, as he rose from the bed where he'd been lying all afternoon to see what the thud was about, he tried not to admit to himself that part of him was relieved to have a reason to put this newly acquired skill to use. Until the meetings with his friends could take place, Mark was spending most of his time staring at the ceiling and thinking about all the things that had gone wrong with his life. He was getting bored with it.

The thud had evidently been caused by a book entitled *Why Not Turn Your Dog's Hair into a Sweater?*

'Have you read this?' asked Geraldine Crowe. She seemed to be addressing a flickering empty space to the left of Mark's shoulder.

'I haven't.'

'We might have used the technique with Sassy, but Sassy's fur was short and of an unpleasing aroma. Would you like to borrow it?'

'I don't have a dog.'

'Do you frequent environments where they shed?'

Mark had a brief memory of autumn weekends in Scotland, long walks across the damp landscape with Labradors or setters before returning to log fires and whisky-laced fruitcakes. He had appreciated these things too little. 'Not at present.'

'Nevertheless, please take it anyway.' Forcing the volume into his hand. 'Though that isn't what I have come about. There is a message for you on the answerphone.'

Si was in the sitting-room reading a Batman comic, stretched out on what, beneath cushions, a daisy-patterned duvet, a crocheted bedspread and several piles of tea towels, was probably the sofa.

'I have a phone message to listen to,' Mark said.

'Swot?'

'I beg your pardon?'

'*So what?*'

'I would appreciate privacy.'

Geraldine Crowe said, 'Privacy is inessential.'

If she was Si's mother then the only family resemblance discernible was a uniform obtuseness. 'You may deem it so. However . . .'

'We have both heard the message already. It lacks power to surprise or startle.'

In their case, perhaps. Mark pushed the *Play* button not knowing who to expect, hoping for Fleur's trim cadences, but certainly not anticipating the voice of Clara Hood:

'Whoever of you hears this, I'm at Hodge's Department Store and they want to do me for shoplifting. I think they'll believe it's a mistake, though, if someone comes and vouches for my character. They've implied as much already, and they haven't called the coppers.'

Mark swung around. 'This message isn't for me at all.'

'It's for Whoever, which includes you, I'd say,' muttered Si from behind his comic.

'Why can't *you* go and vouch for Clara?' Mark asked Geraldine.

'It would be to no purpose. I cannot vouch, indeed I cannot. I would lack credibility.'

She had a point: Geraldine was wearing a blue-and-red frock with a laced bodice and built-in apron; it could have been the national costume of some humourless Scandinavian principality. Mark made a noise somewhere between a cough and a murmur, which he hoped would come over as both polite and non-committal, while his brain undertook a concise analysis of the situation. Kim would carry scarcely more conviction than Geraldine, Si was a minor, and Clara might as well have the Kray twins or Myra Hindley show up at Hodge's to assert her moral standing as someone with the looks of a Muncher Barrow. There *was* the option of doing nothing, of course . . .

But no there wasn't, not according to the Queen's School, Pitsbury, whose dictates concerning the championing of women (a nod in the direction of coeducation notwithstanding) were only marginally different during the dwindling years of the twentieth century from how they had been at the ebb of the nineteenth. The sharing of a roof, moreover, brought with it certain obligations, the consequences of ignoring which had been frequently and graphically illustrated by many an end-of-term Greek tragedy. In the light of his own recent experiences also, it wasn't hard for Mark to empathize with the shame and outrage that Clara Hood must be experiencing, confined in the office of some pipsqueak manager (minor public school at the very best; polytechnic turned university) undoubtedly without even a decent cup of coffee.

Mark was wearing jeans and a T-shirt. He was unshaven.

'Do you have an iron and an ironing-board?' he asked Geraldine.

'Why?' Geraldine's face took on a panicked expression.

'My shirts got crumpled during the move here. I need to iron one.'

'Must you?'

With great patience, 'Yes, I must. I also need to shave.'

'Then do it now. Please, shave now – first. The iron and its board will be forthcoming.'

'If they're heavy I am more than happy to fetch them myself, if you tell me where they are kept.'

Geraldine looked as if she were about to cry. 'They will be forthcoming,' she repeated.

While Mark was applying the shaving foam he was puzzled

to hear a faint scraping sound, which seemed to come from roof level. This was followed by a series of bumps and more scraping; another series of bumps, and then scraping outside the bathroom; a final volley of bumps and scrapes, then silence.

The ironing-board had been set up in the sitting-room. It was covered in a rainbow of variously sized dots which Mark initially mistook for a pattern but turned out to be random stains. There were similar stains on the iron. The shirt Mark had chosen was a pale blue one. He had never thought of ironing as an intimate act before, but it felt like that with Si watching. Mark would be glad when the school holidays were over.

'Is the ironing-board stored in the attic?' he asked, partially to distract Si's attention but also because this bizarre conclusion was the only one he could derive from the number of flights of stairs it had been brought down. There were two other rooms – Kim's and Muncher's – on Si's floor and a little door behind which, Clara had informed Mark when first he viewed the lodgings, was a wafty staircase that led to a treacherous area of disused roof space.

Si did not reply to the question directly. Instead, 'Y'know what, Mark?' he said, gazing at the blue shirt's tailored sleeve with rapt fascination. 'If you was to go up in the attic you'd probably break a floorboard like Muncher, 'cept you'd go right on down and then you'd be paralysed and have to be in a wheelchair you'd work by blowing into a mechanical computer on the end of a metal stick that looked like a mouth-organ.'

This was not the first time that Clara had been behind the scenes at a department store, so she was unsurprised to discover that Hodge's luscious interior was encased in a rind of drab administration. The route to the manager's office took her and the store detective past poky cubby-holes where disconsolate men and women dabbed at old-fashioned computers with all the vigour of the underpaid. Nobody's expression suggested they got much of a percentage reduction on the stock either. A staff canteen wept deep fat and gravy smells. Anaemia of the spirit was clearly the order of the day.

Which perhaps was why a desperately vigorous, heart-pumping defence had – potentially – come up trumps: probably the manager was more accustomed to people simply caving in and resignedly waiting to be shovelled off by the Bill. The fact that the case Clara put was actually (and oh so ironically) true could have helped also. Did the manager honestly think that if she'd been planning on half-inching the underwear she would have walked off towards Luggage with it draped over her arm? Wouldn't she have secreted it in her baggy shirt, for instance?

Reasonable doubt had resulted in the manager indicating that the intervention of a responsible member of the community on Clara's behalf might, just might, bring about a satisfactory outcome for all parties; though Clara was pretty sure that her idea of what constituted a responsible individual – and, for that matter, a community – could well differ quite a bit from the manager's. Did it take in the group of girls from down the drag club, say, who God knew had their work cut out to make sure things kept running smoothly? Muncher's old boxing mates, who he met up with at Cohen's in Great Windmill Street, and who for years had ensured that no one went home from a match too unhappy? Probably not. Meaning Clara's best bet was Geraldine, *if* she felt herself up to it. Meaning it wasn't in the bag yet.

When eventually the manager's stone-faced secretary announced the arrival of 'Miss Hood's guarantor', however, it wasn't Geraldine who walked in with the grubby store detective, or Kim or Muncher.

'Sit down, please,' said the manager, not looking up from the papers he'd been fiddle-faddling with all the while Clara had sat there waiting. 'I shall be with you shortly.'

But Mark Upshaw didn't sit. He just stood there, looking down at the floor, looking up again, the edge of his lip curling slightly. His eyes were darker than any Clara could remember having seen before; brimful of sarcasm. In his smooth, impeccable shirt, that suit, he seemed to embody a distant breed of perfection. Clara didn't trust the man, but at that precise instant she had no choice but to admire him. Surely the hunched little manager could not long remain impervious? Surely he must sense the sort of presence he was in and respond? Mark Upshaw's dignified silence rendered the attempt at dismissiveness not so much rude as flimsy and pathetic.

At length, 'I have no intention of attending your leisure any longer,' Mark Upshaw said. 'If you are unable to speak to me exactly now, I shall be obliged to pass on the decision as to the handling of Hodge's inexcusable error to Ms Hood's solicitor, who has already been appraised of the situation and is awaiting an update.'

A whole wonderfully implied structure of support. A safety net of connections and ominous consequences. Clara herself would have been proud of a bluff such as that.

The manager rose to his feet as slowly as he appeared to figure he could get away with, and opted for mutual concern as his angle.

'Allow me to introduce myself, and forgive my preoccupation. Mr Hill. I agree, this is most regrettable.'

'Mark Upshaw. And since you have admitted the fault, Ms Hood and myself shall be leaving.'

'Please, just a moment longer while we clear things up completely. A great deal of money is lost per year due to shoplifting. We are obliged to take every possible incident very seriously.'

'Your allegation being?'

'Our store detective here' – nodding in the man's direction – 'apprehended Ms Hood after she had left Lingerie with certain items for which she had not paid.' To the detective, 'Produce the evidence.'

Clara could have done without what happened next. Out of a Hodge's bag she hadn't noticed he was carrying the detective now produced and laid out upon the manager's desk Bethany's enormous functionals, the cocoa and lace, the muslins, and the minute burgundies, thong side up.

There was an awfully long pause while Mark Upshaw surveyed the array of undies, his eyes seeming to become larger, his gaze more intense.

At long last he cleared his throat, threw what might have been an aghast look at Clara, cleared his throat again and said, 'Ms Hood was in the street with these . . . um . . . items?'

'Not in the street, no. Ms Hood was halfway between Lingerie and Luggage. It is clearly indicated throughout the store that purchases must be paid for in the department from which they emanate before the customer proceeds to another. Her location therefore gave our detective cause to suspect an attempt to appropriate, though Ms Hood maintains that it was a case of absent-mindedness.'

Mark Upshaw had regained his composure. 'And what reason do you have to disbelieve her?' he asked coldly.

'People always protest their innocence.'

'Ms Hood is not *people*. She is a respectable lady who lives with her retired uncle, and who has already been afforded considerable trauma by this totally avoidable ordeal.'

At which point it was over bar the shouting. Having argued her innocence earlier, all that remained for Clara to do was exude respectability and upset, and by sheer force of will keep her palms unclammy for the no-hard-feelings handshakes, her forehead clear of any giveaway sweat. At the same time, pints of the stuff were running down her back, her breasts, stomach, thighs. What would they have done at home without her? In a daze, Clara paid for the underwear and was handed a receipt. What would have happened if Hodge's had insisted on searching inside her clothes? Thank God the stores were all so jittery about getting slapped with an assault action. Thank God she'd prevented them getting in the rozzers, who were well immune to any such fears. However would the lodgers have dealt with the landlord and looked out for Bethany Smile?

Exiting from the department store was like coming out of a cinema. Clara blinked as her eyes watered in the sunlight that didn't feel as if it should be there still. It was awkward to be standing on the pavement beside Mark Upshaw. She didn't like to be in the position of having to thank someone. Need she offer to buy him a coffee? A gesture of some kind was probably called for. Heaven forbid he'd want to walk home with her, discuss what had happened, deliver a little lecture.

'I hope you'll make it to Muncher's party tomorrow.' Clara could offer that much and it wasn't too personal.

'I doubt I will. Please do not feel any need to recompense me for vouching for your character. Vouching with negative recompense is something with which I am quite familiar.'

And at that Mark Upshaw turned his back on her and walked off in the direction of South Ken.

CHAPTER SIX

Living with Earthquakes

Preparations for the party appeared to start early: at 3.02 a.m. to be precise, when Mark was woken by the sound of giggles, puffing and farting noises on the landing.

His mouth was dry and sandpapery. He'd had quite a few whiskies in a nondescript pub off the Brompton Road after leaving Clara, before heading to Chelsea and blowing yet more money he couldn't afford on a meal at Chez Veronica, where he used to go with Fleur, along with several more aperitifs, a 1990 Gevrey-Chambertin and a concluding Calvados. The place seemed to have got more expensive. What with that and the taxi he'd taken to avoid any delay in getting to Hodge's, Mark had somehow managed to exceed his week's budget by half as much again. If the idea had not been so abhorrent, and if Mark had been able to bring himself to mingle with the other guests – he had a vague memory of being waved at by the mermaid-tattooed Neanderthal on his way back to the house – it would have made some sense to attend Muncher Barrow's party, purely for any food that might be on offer. Thank God his affairs would shortly be embarked in the direction of equilibrium. Tomorrow evening was the first of the events which would offer an opportunity for Mark's friends to outline the recovery measures that they would be willing to initiate on his behalf. A substantial number of them were likely to be present at the private viewing of a new special exhibition of the Art of Southern Asia at the British Museum. Mark had been invited to the viewing some while ago. He knew Sam Thorne, managing director of the British branch of Wassen, who were sponsoring the exhibition.

At this unearthly hour Mark was far from desirous of an encounter with his fellow lodgers; nevertheless, he was greatly in need of a drink of water. The opening of his door heralded a lot of shushing, even though it was they who were making all the rumpus.

'Muncher's asleep. It's a surprise for his birthday,' said Kim. She was standing on a rickety chair, clad in tight denim shorts and a sleeveless top, tying bunches of balloons to the flex that the light bulb hung from. Si was handing them up to her. His hair was loose and he wore nothing but a pair of jeans. 'Y'know what I gottim, Mark?' he said.

'I don't.'

Again, Si and Kim exploded into giggles. The fact that Kim was allowing the boy up this late suddenly suggested to Mark that *she* was the one in a position to issue a maternal bedtime dispensation. Were Si to fill out and get taller, he could see that their physiques would be somewhat similar.

'A plastic dog turd to fool his mates with.'

'Nice.'

Maybe Mark slept again that night. If so, it was only fitfully. The noises didn't cease. By 5.48 a.m. they were accompanied by cooking smells. Then, of course, came the seismic bombardment of metal barrels being delivered to the White Bear; the gritty churning of a dustcart; the great throbbing engines of delivery lorries parked directly under the window, causing the entire room to shake. Someone started digging the road with a pneumatic drill.

At 7.06 a.m. Muncher Barrow must have got up because there was the sound of singing and clapping and the blowing of hooters. After which there was much running of water and pulling of lavatory chains, followed by a cacophony of door-slamming. Mark assumed they must all have gone out for a celebratory breakfast, though where you could procure one at such an ungodly hour he couldn't begin to imagine. A van parked up outside and left its radio on full blast.

The melancholy which had assailed Mark just after the events at Hodge's became more intense. Neither whisky nor good food, faith in the loyalty of friends or numb inactivity seemed capable of budging it. At Hodge's Mark had worn the vestiges of past authority only: the awareness of that was what it came down to. Vestiges! The very word suggested ragged standards, the torn and desecrated relics of some lost war. Whatever swathe he might have cut in the manager's office, Mark himself had been horribly conscious that those assembled there were witnessing a remnant only of his former status.

Twelve years before his death, Mark's widowed father had agreed to stand as guarantor, to vouch for the integrity and business sense of a large insurance syndicate. In exchange for an additional so many per cent on his investments, Mark's father had guaranteed the syndicate to the tune of everything the family possessed – should its liabilities outstrip its assets.

Which they duly did.

It was a disaster that struck in slow motion; a dire situation that Mark eventually inherited in the late nineties: the product of a decade of legal wrangling – claims, counter-claims, declined compromises and refused deals. While Mark had been managing the estate, his father had been solely engaged in a desperate struggle to keep the family capital intact. Sometimes Mark could convince himself it was loyalty to his father's memory, rather than stubborn stupidity, which had led him in his turn to reject the final rescue package on offer and continue to pursue the case in the courts.

Two years later, Mark was bankrupt. Two years later he had fetched up here in Lisle Street at the Year Zero, consoled only by the knowledge that a healthy dose of capital would get him on his feet again.

It couldn't have been far away that they'd gone for breakfast – Mark's hungover body almost made him want to ask them where, his parched throat overriding his usual cavil at the thought of mugs and Formica. By 8.52 a.m. the din from the street was again being matched by the din inside the building: bangs; shouts; bursts of music; laughter. And this quite unexpectedly brought another small, unlooked-for consolation: at least at Hodge's Department Store Mark Upshaw had done the right thing. In spite of what he had said about negative recompense to Clara, at Hodge's, Mark realized, he had actually been vouching for something real.

Though she didn't sleep a wink all night, Clara still felt as if she was running late that entire day. Even time was something she never seemed to have enough of.

She kept going through the little hours just on adrenalin. She was wired up, fizzing, her throat was slightly sore and her eyes were dry and itchy. She had to wear her spotted-in-Cannes sunglasses for the birthday brekkie at Betty's, where she drank about a litre of black coffee, but couldn't cope with more than half a doorstep with a scrape of marge. Her hands shook a bit holding the coffee mug.

What must it feel like to live somewhere where there were earthquakes? Where all of a sudden half of Berwick Street could find itself eye to eye with Savile Row? Could you manage to keep your mind off something like that just by keeping busy?

When they got back to the house they had a thorough hunt for the rolling-pin but didn't find it, so Clara wrapped a shoe in a plastic bag and got Kim to bash the Bath Olivers, the two freebie biccies and the sugar lumps with it on the wooden chopping-board. She melted a small bar of dark chocolate in a pudding basin over a saucepan of simmering water; that was made to go further by adding one of the condensed milks from the batch of dented cans, and the pumpkin purée. The cranberries went in also, and half a stale sponge cake, which Clara showed Kim how to crumb once she'd done bashing. She cooked pasta for the pasta salad with mayonnaise and appropriated the board to slice the *saucisson.*

Strange, how at the moment dollops of truth kept falling into Clara's lap: some of the candles Mark Upshaw had asked about really were earmarked for Muncher's party. They hid a multitude of sins, candles. Put dozens of them round any place, however squalid, and folk would reckon they were in a fairy palace. Geraldine noticed a big patch of mould on the sitting-room wall not long after lunch, when they were discussing where best to put the big cathedral ones. Everybody came and had a look at it, but no one was sure whether it had appeared in the night or been growing there since the wet spell. Clara had to go across to French Food & Wine to borrow a stepladder, so they could cover it with an old sheet that Bethany had tested out a colour combination on, which had been going to be used as a tablecloth.

The stepladder was also useful for reaching high-up cupboards during the stashing blitz Clara had after that, in both sitting-room and kitchen. The fullest cupboards needed tying shut so things couldn't spew out of them on to the partyers.

Late afternoon, Muncher went down Cohen's for a pre-party celebration with his mates, taking his dog turd and the truffles. Kim left to put in an early sesh at the club, since she and as many of the other girls as they'd allow to were knocking off round tennish. Geraldine started a headache so Clara made her some ginger tea and insisted she lie down on her bed with *How to Discover If You're Mountain or Sea.* Si went out.

In the ensuing lull, Clara hid the cake in the fridge, away from the mice; found saucers for all the candles and dispersed them around the building; put out ashtrays; got bowls and plates ready for the dips, spreads and nibbles, and the green salad if there was one. She decided what to wear for the evening and left a clean shirt on Muncher's bed. Gave the lav a good sluicing with bleach, then had a quick bath so it would be free for the others, and did the taps with lemon-scented bathroom cleaner: a few good strong smells like that round about could trick guests into thinking you'd been scrubbing away for hours. The same strategy worked with wood. After she'd dried and put on an old pair of lavender leggings and a khaki crop-top, Clara stood in the middle of the sitting-room and jetted a couple of hefty squirts of furniture polish into the air in there. The spray particles glittered in the amber rays of sunlight.

There was still Bethany to take a special party tray up to, but that would have to wait. Mark Upshaw was in his room, which was a nuisance. Clara had heard him go down to the kitchen and then return to it while she was in the bath.

She probably should have acted more graciously towards the man, though, shouldn't she? A tad of being looked out for couldn't really have hurt her. Not when Clara knew full well she could look out for herself and others besides – keep the whole shebang ticking over.

The market! Pray nobody had got there before her.

Shaftesbury Ave was a clog of pre-theatre. There was a queue outside the restaurant block in Wardour Street, and the sister shop that cashed in on it, where people were buying up olive bread like there was no tomorrow. Geisha-type women, with very red lips and very pale faces, were ensconced in all those numerous black-and-white hairdresser's shops, getting trimmed and styled by dapper, balding men in black polos. Betty's was still going strong but the sausage shop was just closing. The Berwick Street lock-ups were grilled and gridded and battened. All that remained of the market were a few open vans stacked with wooden crates, the metal frames of stalls, and an empty barrow resting at an angle like a seesaw.

Clara did a quick scan of the ground. If there was something really worth having it was best grabbed first. Yes! An only slightly battered cauli, half concealed by a chip paper. In a flash it was in her carrier. There was the usual small crop of oranges and lemons, rolled to the edges of the kerb, like balls on a pool table. Also, four tomatoes. One, unfortunately, too split to be worth having. An upturned lettuce in the middle of the street had somehow neither got taken nor trodden on. Some shrivelled chillis, which had obviously just been emptied on to the pavement, would add a nice touch of spice to the pasta salad. And that was about the sum of it.

The market stuff always took quite a lot of washing, and even then Kim and Geraldine would never touch it, but Clara reckoned years of eating scavenged food was what accounted for her ace immune system: and who'd had to nurse who through flu and bronchitis last winter? Anyway, the cauli got parboiled, which must sterilize it, surely. Not a green salad exactly, but cauliflower, lettuce and tomato, dressed with a lick of oil and a good squeeze of lemon.

The shadows outside the kitchen window were cornflower blue, the sunlight had gone from amber to copper.

Between Si and Geraldine's turns, Clara managed to snatch another five minutes in the bathroom. Si was wearing his work clothes for the occasion, plus a Tintin T-shirt. He'd put on some of his aftershave.

The dress Clara had chosen was one of her favourites: a fifties cocktail frock made of heavy silk; cinched waist, sleeveless, tight around the hips and narrow at the hem. When she bought it, it had a long scorch mark down one side, a tear in the lining, and the zip was gone. Clara had replaced the zip, removed the lining altogether and dyed the silk puce. Once it was on she scraped her hair into a little knot on top and secured it with a black velvet ribbon. She hopped into a pair of high black strappies with spinning-top heels.

Geraldine was standing outside the bathroom with a towel and her bridesmaid's dress.

'How's the head?' Clara asked.

'Departed.'

Clara was on her second, no, third, fourth, fifth wind now. A different outfit, a new person. If she ever had to, she was sure she could run through identities as fast as some of Muncher's friends, who were shortly swarming around the kitchen. Bring all the booze you plan on drinking, it had specified on the invitation – though Muncher and Kim had come up with a few bottles of wine, and Clara had bought some beer and cider. In his clean shirt, Muncher distributed paper cups and his mates filled them with gin and whisky. French Food & Wine arrived also. Si switched on the sound system and there was a minute or two of feedback, then music.

The restaurant people were coming in relays. Someone handed Clara three metal containers full of egg-fried rice and barbecued spare ribs. Someone else handed her a joint. She took a couple of deep drags and held her breath till it exploded out of her. It was prime stuff: nought to ten in the same number of seconds. Very mellow, she emptied the ribs and rice into a bowl, got the cake and salads out of the fridge, then floatily decanted and put out the Hodge's items, dropping the tins and wrappers into the open bin, which was already overflowing. She accepted another drag of dope, assembled Bethany's tray and sent Si up with it, telling him to be careful to check that the coast was clear, and to bring it down to the kitchen when Bethany had finished.

The supermarket staff arrived, the projectionist from the cinema, and the fishmonger, with a special present for Muncher. Several girls who rented rooms. Quayle Jones and his band, between sets at Ronnie Scott's. Kim, in indigo chiffon, and her curvy friend from Puerto Rico, and the nice Swedish girl with the wonderful English. Everybody from the White Bear.

Clara didn't drink much, but she had two glasses of wine, more blow, and did a line of coke. Time concertinaed. It was midnight. It was 4.30. Clara was discussing the ins and outs of putting money on the ponies with an intense little bookie's runner. It was three o'clock. She was dancing with Quayle himself, who had gone and come back, and was saying he didn't feel as if he was seventy. It was two o'clock and they were singing 'Happy Birthday, dear Muncher'. It was 1.15, and Clara was lying on the sofa, eating goose-liver pâté and aubergine dip off a saucer. The candle flames were elongating and contracting, and she was remembering that Mark Upshaw could be a government official and had haughtily said he almost certainly wouldn't be coming. It was 1.45 and Clara was bopping to 'Maggie May', and she thought she glimpsed Mark Upshaw in the kitchen, but she was probably mistaken.

Before Mark lost all his money, people who just slumped on park benches or – according to documentaries – spent hours crammed in front of small television sets in tiny bedsits came across as dismally lacking in initiative. Were there not playgrounds, walks, museums and libraries at their disposal? The impecunious at least had the luxury of leisure hours, which they could – and, indeed, should – use for exercise and intellectual improvement.

Mark hadn't known that a lack of cash caused energy to seep away also. When there was no real reason to be in one place as opposed to another it was easier simply to stay put. Despite the noise, he fell into a heavy slumber shortly after they all returned from breakfast, not waking until late into the afternoon, when he went down to the kitchen to make tea.

Although it was indisputably an under-the-carpet job – Mark had learnt about true spick and span in the school corps – the house cleared of its mess did look rather nice, actually. Silent and sunlit, the sitting-room wore an air of pleasant expectancy, which cheered him as nothing had done for some while. He liked the pale candles, the new spaciousness of the surroundings. Perhaps he could maintain it? Perhaps he could keep things under control while his housemates were out?

Though what in God's name was the thinking behind the piece of material Clara had put on the wall to cover the expanding patch of mould? Dabs of orange, pink and purple on an old sheet emphatically did not constitute a wall hanging; or, more puzzlingly, appear to attempt to. The design, if you could call it such, was dispersed and random, more akin to the spatters on the ironing-board than any striving for composition, however inept. Anyone capable of combining that blue with that cherry pattern had sufficient artistry to make a better fist of it than this. Especially considering the trouble it would have taken to assemble the paints or dyes.

That it was Clara's work Mark did not doubt. It had not escaped his notice that she was the practical and emotional centre of the household. There was a vague atmosphere of cluelessness when she wasn't around, as if the others were always waiting for her to return and tell them what to do next. For a moment Mark was aware of the effort Clara must have to exert to hold things together – hadn't he done the same himself, only to fail? Never in his life had he felt so lonely as during those days he had spent endeavouring to prevent his assets from slipping away. Did Clara Hood feel lonely too, marooned among misfits in her battered hat, nobody there to vouch for her but a stranger whom she apparently both disliked and was intimidated by?

The kitchen also was tidy, though not clean; denuded, save for some empty bowls and plates on the table. Mark could almost feel every hinge, every lock, every knot on every cupboard door (he examined one to check it would hold) straining with its secret hoard of disorder. The thought made him smile. His own, personal storage space – the others appeared to pool everything – was almost bare of provisions, but there was a crumpet, two eggs and some butter. Mark made himself tea and a hot, buttered crumpet and took it back to his room.

The party began with a terrible screech, as from the very abyss of hell, followed by a great, relentless barrage of heavy metal that would have done credit to the White Bear.

As the evening progressed, Mark's fragile equanimity swiftly lessened, then vanished. In his experience, parties took place in rooms to which they were allocated. As a rule this meant ground floor only, *not* the level of house guests. From almost the outset, however, it was clear that no area of the building was to be barred to anyone. At one stage – repeated bumps against his wall having brought him out into the corridor – Mark was confronted by the unseemly sight of a couple copulating standing up, their ardour abated neither by his presence, nor by the sound of somebody vomiting in the bathroom. No sooner had they departed than rhythmic vibrations along the full length of Mark's skirting-board, laughter, loud voices and herbal odours suggested that a group of people was sitting out there, smoking marijuana and kicking along to the music.

Mark put his head around the side of the door. There was an elderly gentleman in a wide-brimmed black hat. There were two young women, all curves and cleavage. There was a little ferrety male drinking gin out of a half-bottle, and there was – inevitably, it felt – the Australian barman with the mermaid tattoo. A joint was zigzaggily waved in Mark's direction.

'Thank you, no.' Mark ostentatiously removed the screwdriver from the doorknob hole, went back inside and pulled the door shut with his little finger, thereby effectively locking himself in. He threw the screwdriver on to the floor, and flopped on to his bed.

It wasn't that he had any intense objections to drugs *per se*; it was rather that he *was* in favour of the law. Obedience to and respect for its dictates ensured the existence of a civilized and just society. So they had said at the Queen's School, Pitsbury, and so Mark still maintained. Which meant that informing the police must be seriously considered.

Balloons popped. There were whooping noises. There was a commotion in the street. Mark went to the window. A snake of people had spilled out of the party. Hands round each other's waists, they were weaving in and out of the traffic, jumping over the ditch of sewage and drainage pipes exposed by the pneumatic drill. Step, step, kick. Step, step, kick. Every pause for any kind of obstacle or blockage crushed them tight together: a Chinese lantern of stockings and boas, sequins and leather. A cussed taxi was hooting, but they were ignoring it. A tall black man in a trilby lifted a gleaming trombone to the sky: *Oh when the saints, come marching in / When the saints come marching in* . . . 'Get out the fucking way!' yelled the taxi-driver.

Mark realized he was hungry. In fact, he was starving. He'd had nothing but the crumpet all day, and it was 1.25 in the morning.

The door wide open, Mermaid Tattoo was availing himself of the lavatory. A very thin girl in a nylon skirt was hunched on the stairs leaning over a mirror, a five-pound note shoved up one nostril. The sitting-room was jam-packed, a rugby scrum, a crush of sweating, smelling bodies; the air, a coalpit. The kitchen was similar, awash with the rancid tang of red wine. Mark took a rapid step backward to avoid treading on a dog turd, before remembering, and found himself staring into the face of a platinum blonde, with enormous tangerine lips, who said 'Ha-llo, gorgeous' in a breathy northern European accent. There was a small sea bass in the sink.

An orang-utan arm reached up and clamped itself around Mark's shoulders. 'Gladyer made it.' Muncher Barrow's breath stank of both gin and whisky. 'Whatsyer poison?'

'I'm not drinking. I came down for something to eat.'

'Well, there's plenty here.' Muncher indicated the table. 'Everything money can't buy.' He had a good laugh at that before being dragged off by a man with a greyhound on a piece of rope.

The food was somewhat mutilated and disparate, but surprisingly sophisticated. Mark looked back towards the draining board, in search of a plate. His eyes fell on the bin, the contents of which had overflowed on to the floor. Empty tins. Empty cartons. Empty bags. *Hodge's Alsace Goose Liver Pâté, Hodge's Hand-baked Bath Oliver Biscuits, Hodge's Italian Free-Range Egg Pasta, Hodge's Aubergine Dip with Virgin Olive Oil.*

'Maggie May' came on the sound system.

Clara didn't have any bags from Hodge's Food Hall with her when Mark went to Knightsbridge to vouch for her character. Was it possible that she had returned to Hodge's some time thereafter to make all these purchases?

An outstanding flash of colour caught the corner of Mark's eye. Clara Hood was in the sitting-room, dancing: a gyrating blur of wild pink on thin, twirling heels.

No, it wasn't.

Mark Upshaw didn't help himself to any of the Hodge's food; of course he did not. It would have been like eating one's own pet rabbit. He fled to his room and secured it against the prevailing anarchy.

Yesterday morning he had been merely a bankrupt. Today, he was a bankrupt and a felon.

Clara Hood's message on the answerphone resounded in his ears, louder than anything the party could produce: she had never at any point asserted her innocence; on the contrary, what Clara had said was that she thought she could get away with it. No moral scruples there! No ethical qualms of any kind. Such a contrast, such a heinous contrast to Fleur's overall . . . niceness. A woman such as Fleur would never go round filching tins from Hodge's Department Store, and neither would anyone else Mark had ever even considered to have the potential to be an acquaintance. He was overwhelmed by a sense of betrayal, so profound he could actually taste its bitterness. Against the insurance syndicate, which had made guarantees that it couldn't keep. Against Clara Hood, its mirror image. Both had cynically used Mark Upshaw as their personal credit card. Was there nothing in this bloody country, in this whole bloody world, that you could trust?

Tomorrow he would go straight to the nearest police station and tell them that he lived in a house where drugs were blatantly consumed, and whose landlady he had unwittingly helped to get away with robbery.

None of which reflected very favourably on Mark's intelligence. Nor was he quite certain the police would afford the situation the time required for it to be accurately understood. On the contrary, perhaps they would assume he had come in to give himself up to the charge of aiding and abetting, the alliterativeness of which made it sound pretty bloody serious. Grim though his current lifestyle was, it was still marginally preferable to what might be imposed on him in prison.

He was up to his neck in it. Implicated.

Mark didn't feel capable of confronting the horrors an attempt on the bathroom might reveal, so he didn't bother to wash or brush his teeth, just stripped to his underpants, got into bed and dowsed the lamp.

The darkness was soothing, and Mark Upshaw was a fair person. Soon, a cool strand of rationality began to quench his overheated emotions. Clara Hood's message hadn't asked for Mark specifically, so he couldn't justly claim that she had used him. He remembered her funny, crooked face, not quite looking at him when she asked him to the party. The abuse of hospitality: that notion returning, gentler and more complex than the legalities it was washing up against.

But Mark was asleep now, and whatever about him might be being eroded had retreated to the caverns of the subconscious. If any errant fragment of id whispered, as soft as a Swedish drag-queen, *Hodge's can afford it,* that was deep in the unexplored channels of his mind. Nearer the surface, however, were women's knickers; always sleek, slippery, satiny and expensive in Mark's experience; he had learned how to slide them down the female body, stopping at certain places. Beneath that prickly exterior and warning-off look, Clara Hood wore lace next to her body, did she? Satin and muslin and the thinnest of thongs; a warm nest of tightly clenched sensuality.

Mark shot wide awake. It was light outside. The party was over. What was the explanation for the seven other pairs, though? Those enormous drawers, unimaginably bigger than any Mark had ever seen in his life?

CHAPTER SEVEN

Shiva as a Dancer

Somebody was hammering on the front door. No one answered.

The house was bathed in early morning sunlight. People and objects remained where they'd fallen, gilded. Mark picked his solitary way over slumbering bodies; cups; articles of clothing; a fiery blossom of napkins; a puzzling tray on which were a plate, an empty wineglass, a chocolate-smeared bowl and a banana skin. Had somebody assembled themselves a little hoard of food to carry away and eat in secret?

Clara was asleep on the sofa, curled up into herself. Si hadn't made it upstairs. He was spread-eagled on the floor, arms splayed, mouth open. Clara was wrapped in a pale blue web of shawl, not quite long enough to cover her feet; one foot still wore a shoe, the other was bare. A black velvet ribbon had come loose and trailed across her hair. It hadn't previously occurred to Mark that Clara didn't have a room of her own.

The hammering on the door continued. Mark went down and opened it. He was confronted by a burly man in a thin fawn raincoat. The man's hands were stuck into his pockets. Beneath the raincoat Mark could see the greyish collar of a nylon shirt and a shiny green tie. The man had razor cuts on his face and greased-back blond hair. A guest arrived late for the party, perhaps? Though none of the guests had inspired quite the instinctive revulsion Mark now experienced.

'Let me in, please.'

The man showed every intention of going round Mark and up the stairs without greeting or explanation. Mark leant on one side of the door frame and reached a hand out to touch the other, thereby creating a posture that could just have been relaxed.

'There's people sleeping up there. Suppose you tell me what you want first?'

Their eyes met. The man's were liquid and pale. Mark watched him consider the possibility of managing to enter the building if Mark decided he shouldn't.

'I want to know how many people reside in this property,' he replied at length.

'Why?'

'That isn't your business.'

'In which case it's hardly my business to supply you with information.'

There was a pause. The man looked riled but inclined to call it a day. 'You could come to regret not being co-operative,' he said.

Mark gave a slow smile. 'I can live with that risk.'

Once he'd closed the door and returned to his bedroom, however, it suddenly struck Mark with crystal clarity precisely who it was he had just encountered and why. The tenancy agreement Mark had expected had not been forthcoming. Clara hadn't ever produced a shred of paperwork in need of his signature. Nothing had been put into writing. Clara Hood was illegally subletting the rooms in this building. The man, though sleazy, was a landlord, with every right to be disgruntled.

A bankrupt, a felon, an illegal lodger: merely by existing Mark seemed to be accumulating a criminal record. Probably it was too late to ask for justice; he should just fall on his knees and beg for mercy. Mark briefly considered a call to Keele, Warren & Masters, before realizing he could no longer afford the cost of their time. Maybe he should run after the landlord and tell him all? Maybe it was his duty to shop Clara Hood – even to someone so intrinsically distasteful?

But as Mark torturedly debated these moral ambiguities, unexpectedly there came into his head the image of his health club in Covent Garden, where he used to go to work up a sweat, do laps in the pool, have a sauna or a massage. The air there was warm and moist and smelled of massage oil and chlorine. The club was decorated with banks of fleshy-leaved palms; you could play squash, have a Jacuzzi, stretch out on a sunlounger. And although he hadn't had the heart to visit it in recent months, Mark's membership still hadn't quite expired.

The thought somehow served to distract attention away from moral conundra, and to underline the patently obvious fact that it was vital for Mark to cease his self-inflicted ethical pummelling. At the end of the day, whatever happened in Lisle Street was as nothing. Instead of agonizing another second, he should go to Covent Garden and have a work-out and a body-rub: get himself into shape physically and mentally for this evening's private viewing at the British Museum.

After all, from tonight onwards Mark's life would start to return to normal.

Mostly she catnapped, but very occasionally Clara had long and furious sleeps during which she was dead to the world. She always awoke from them crammed with a new store of energy, ready to tackle anything.

Mark Upshaw had been around the house for too much time now without a single one of them knowing the first thing about him. Each of the lodgers had their opinion, needless to say: Geraldine found the man 'refined'; he was 'all right really', said Si and Muncher; Kim described him as 'prissy but a hunk'. What Clara wanted though, was a bit of hard knowledge. Mark's standoffishness, followed by his absence from the party, had put her back on red alert and given her brain a protective prod in an investigative direction.

What did the man do up there in his room for most of every

day, with no one to talk to? Geraldine maintained he was reading *Seventy Steps to Self-Actualization* and *Why Not Turn Your Dog's Hair into a Sweater*? But the leather luggage and tailored suit left Clara unconvinced things were that simple. There was more to it, she was certain. What, for instance, was the 'negative recompense' Mark had mentioned outside Hodge's? Did he perhaps mean that he was on the lookout for Bethany Smile, but making no progress? For all Clara knew, he could be on a mobile every day, relaying hunches back to the Yard. Information was well overdue.

The house was a sea of stale booze, a racket of groans, moans and snores, plus a bit of laughter. There was a whole lot of aspirin-taking going on, tea-making, toast-spreading, frying of bacon.

Clara knocked on Mark's door softly. If he appeared she would say she'd come to check that the party hadn't disturbed him. There was no reply. Clara turned the screwdriver. If Mark came back, the excuse would be that she was opening everyone's windows to give the house a post-party airing. Clara entered the room and closed the door behind her.

She had expected it to be meticulous and it was, even more so than she would have predicted. It could have been an institutional dormitory, liable to unannounced inspections. The bed looked as if it had been made then ironed; every fold was sharp and geometric. There wasn't a speck of dust on any surface. A pair of black leather shoes, precisely aligned next to the wardrobe, had been polished to mirror standard. A gleaming clock discreetly marked the seconds with wafer-thin ticks.

What Clara was unprepared for, however, was the cool aura of masculinity the room contained. The window was open, actually; the air smelled fresh and clean and distinctly male: a mingling of soap, talcum powder, shaving-foam and the indefinable and characteristically unique aroma of a man's body. Almost, Clara turned tail. This she hadn't bargained for. This was too close for comfort. It was only an atmosphere of calm accompanying the maleness which enabled Clara to master her instincts and concentrate on the task in hand: to plump for fight rather than flight.

Drawers were the best places to find out about a person. That was where they usually hid the most telling things concerning their identity. First Clara opened the wardrobe to have a look through Mark Upshaw's and felt her eyes almost pop out of her head.

Sea colours – English sea: leaden skies, bleached light and rock. Suits and shirts of shadowy neutrality, yet so incomparably exquisite, so obviously Mark Upshaw's alone and meant for no other, that they were completely distinctive. The outfit Mark wore to Hodge's turned out to have been no one-off. Though Clara had noted its artistry on his body, she hadn't been aware of the gorgeousness of everything that had gone into it. Now she reached out and ran her fingers down a hand-stitched lapel, marvelling at the buttonhole. She pulled the jacket open to reveal a hand-stitched lining of Jacquard satin. Mark's shirts were of Irish linen and silk. There was an ivory evening one, smooth as cream, a mass of tiny, perfect pleats. Everything was lined and immaculately finished, each varying texture delicious: Clara rested her palms against pure new wool, held a cuff to her cheek, traced its stitchery. No detail had been neglected, not even those that were hidden away and might never be noticed.

Dazzled, only half conscious of what she was searching for any more, Clara pulled open one of the drawers: coiled ties, silk again. Clara knew how to fasten a proper bow tie too – one of Muncher's friends from the ring had taught her. Next to them, crisp squares of handkerchief, etc. Clara blushed. Suddenly she felt intrusive. The blood in her cheeks slapped her back into an awareness of what she was at, however. The foraging accelerated. No film stubs, diary, receipts, address book, passport or payslips. Diddly-squat in fact that told Clara anything. Ditto in the next drawer, which only contained jeans, sweats, Ts and a dark grey cashmere sweater. All in all, a suspiciously thorough lack of giveaways, as if Mark Upshaw had made a calculated decision to be anonymous.

But then, when Clara resecured the wardrobe and turned her attention back to the room, she spied three cards clear as day on the shelf over the fireplace. She couldn't think why she hadn't spotted them sooner.

The cards proved to be invitations, each of them attempting stylish.

The first was for an upcoming *Queen's School Alumni Dinner, to be held in the Private Dining-Room of Rumbles, Maiden Lane. Black tie. RSVP.* Scrolled lettering, of course. Clara knew Rumbles, or at least the back end: Muncher worked there occasionally. Its pitch was being the second-oldest restaurant in London, and acting like it. Still, good luck to them if they could get people to part with up to a ton a head for stew and mash followed by rice pud. Clara made a mental note of the invitation's date so she could tell Muncher – they might well need an extra washer-up that night.

An Opening. Fleur's, Newburgh Street. Designer Dresses. The place whose progress Clara had followed, right through from gutting stage to electrics, plaster and crispbread-coloured paint!

The invitation was appropriately anaemic. Holey typeface, sepia on buff: doubtless meant to reflect the finishing touches still to be done on the crispbread – the opening wasn't for a while yet. Clara turned the invitation over; there was no personal note.

The final invite was pure corporate PR. Yellow on black. *A NEW SPECIAL EXHIBITION OF THE ART OF SOUTHERN ASIA @ THE BRITISH MUSEUM. Sam Thorne, Managing Director of Wassen (UK) PLC, invites you & guests to a private viewing. Please give your name at the Montague Place Entrance.*

At 5.30 this evening.

Clara's heart jumped. They loved art, her and Geraldine. Often they made use of the hour or so's free admission to the V & A just before it closed. Kim went with them sometimes, to look at the costumes. Clara and Geraldine did the National too; and it wasn't that long a walk along the Embankment and Millbank to the Tate – though it could be a pretty parky one in winter, with the wind blowing off the river.

Special exhibitions, on the other hand, were something they could run to less than never.

Most of the population of southern Asia was very much like Geraldine, so Clara had read in a book from the library. A tad less optimistic than the followers of the Cargo Cult, perhaps, but similarly committed to a belief in reincarnation, which was expressed in their sculptures, scrolls and whatnots. Geraldine would simply love to go to that exhibition; Mark Upshaw couldn't conceivably take any interest in the bits and bobs of religious movements. Beyond a shred of doubt, the invitation was just going to get wasted.

There was only one problem: they'd need a man to pretend to be Mark Upshaw. Si was too young and Muncher couldn't do posh to save his life – the PR personnel would smell a rat in an instant; that was what they were there for. But if Clara could just this once persuade . . .

What a treat! What a wonderful surprise for Geraldine. They could doll themselves up, and nip into a Boots *en route* for a few puffs of tester.

Clara glanced at Mark's clock. It wasn't that late, and the suits had inspired her, their linings in particular. She would get out the sewing-machine and find some pattern paper, then run up to the attic and cadge Bethany's latest batik. Bethany always loved to give them away, and this was a stunner. It used the colour combinations she'd tested on the sheet they'd made into a wall hanging – sunset streaks of rose, salmon and fuchsia – and set them against the palest lavender. With that design underneath and something plain on top of it – she had a purple offcut which would be just the ticket – Clara would design a dress like she'd never made before, the radiant interior exposed at crucial places to reveal its hidden beauty.

'I'm afraid you've already been ticked.' The girl pointed a finger at Mark's name and its accompanying box.

Mark studied the clipboard. 'There has been a mistake.'

' 'Fraid not. Oh dear, this is rather embarrassing.' She didn't sound embarrassed, though. There was a meaningful pause. Clearly, Mark was expected to reassess who he was, apologize and slink away.

'I repeat: somebody has made an error.'

With a firm smile, 'This isn't the kind of thing we get wrong, Mr . . . ?'

'Upshaw.'

'Well, anyway.' The girl's eyes flicked to the people behind him.

Once, everything had been easy. Now each round had to be fought, every point hammered home: nothing, but nothing, could be taken for granted.

'Fetch the managing director, please.'

Irritation swept across the girl's pretty features. She pursed her lips, the way Fleur did on the rare occasions she was crossed. 'The managing director?'

'Thorne. Sam Thorne.'

'I don't really think . . .'

'Evidently not. Because if you did, you'd figure that Sam Thorne might not be overly delighted if your public relations outfit refused admission to someone he shared rooms with at Oxford.'

Though when Thorne was finally hauled out – shaking hands, nodding various groups forward, in a systems override that caused a PR flurry – he didn't give the impression that Mark failing to be there would greatly have marred his evening.

To the girl, 'It's okay.' To Mark, 'How's things?' A handshake and a nod; at the same time, turning back into the museum.

'Good. Things are good.' Mark followed Thorne up the wide stairs, but Thorne was busy speaking to an assistant. Mark fell back. If you were running the entire show, as Thorne was, you wouldn't have the same availability as someone who was just there as a guest.

There was another PR person at the top of the stairs to funnel people in the right direction: 'Carry on through Room 33. The exhibition is in 33b.'

Oriental Collections.

Room 33 was naturally lit but the lighting in 33b had been dimmed. Spotlights hung from the ceiling, directed at the glass cases and the hospitality area. There was a board near the entrance, which gave information about Wassen PLC and about the exhibits, but no one was pausing to read it. All activity was focused upon the centre of the room, where flutes of champagne, glasses of mineral water and trays of sushi were being offered around. One didn't come to this sort of event in order to study the artefacts.

'You all right, Mark?' It was Pods Morris, corpulent as ever; puppy fat, they'd called it at prepschool. The sight of him standing there, evidently slightly drunk already, was immeasurably cheering. Pods had always said he and Mark should 'do something together', even before Mark's misfortunes.

Mark grinned and shrugged. 'In a way . . .'

'Well, whatever way. Doesn't matter.' And Pods wandered off to talk to someone else.

Mark accepted a glass of champagne.

Rickie MacIntyre said hallo. The weather was wonderful up in Scotland at the moment. Mark should have paid them a visit . . . he *should* pay them a visit: Rickie would be in touch as soon as he'd had a proper chance to check out plans with Kirstie – who was over there with Miriam Collet and looked in dire need of rescuing. Cavendish Collet was strung out after two days on the East Coast then three days in LA and would catch Mark later. They should do lunch but, look, Cavendish didn't have his diary on him. Better call his secretary.

A few of the women Mark knew seemed disposed to flirt with him, but turned brittle when he showed himself disinclined.

The gallery was full of heat and murmurs. A thin tincture of wine mingled with the stark aroma of antiquity.

Fewer of Mark's acquaintances were present than he had anticipated; or perhaps he was acquainted with fewer people than he had hitherto imagined. His own social group apparently exhausted, Mark kept finding himself on the edges of groups of the half-known, smiling at nothing, hoping a comment would gather him in, and reflecting that he used to be a man to whom strangers introduced themselves.

Gradually, however, this miserably errant and wretchedly isolated position did at least begin to afford a unique perspective on the event. Mark observed the way in which a word dropped by one party would be picked up by another and spark a completely new conversation. He became conscious of under-currents. In particular, there was something or some*body* who most of those present had perceived, but were studying aslant, because it would be unsophisticated to look directly.

Strange that Mark himself had so far failed to locate whatever it was that was inspiring such general interest.

He moved away from the central cluster, and found a standpoint from which to view the room in its entirety. The spotlights emphasized the guests' chic charcoals and gave a silver sheen to the greys. The exhibition cases were bathed in clean, white light, whose residue spilled on to the floor in rectangles.

Mark gave a start. For a moment he thought his eyes must have deceived him. In one of these rectangles was Clara Hood. Illuminated, as if upon a stage. Her hair a soft blur. The contours of her face outlined and highlighted. The hollows of her collar bones in shadow. Her arms gleaming against a backdrop of darkness. Thin, damsony silk scooped low beneath Clara's breasts, exposing a flush of pink against a background of lilac. At the centre of her belly the strands of silk met, then parted again to slide down her hips – revealing streaks and smudges of orangey rose – and finally came together in a rush of amethyst just above her ankles. Her shoes were high and glittery and sharply pointed.

Beside Clara was Geraldine Crowe, and a tall and rather good-looking man whom Mark had never seen before. As Mark watched, Clara raised her hand and pointed at the calm, almond eyes of an androgynous stone Buddha, then lowered it and excitedly patted the man's arm in order to draw his attention to something else.

'Jolly nice frock,' breathed a voice in Mark's ear. It was Pods again. 'The girls are all agog to know who designed it. Not an unattractive lass either, though a bit on the quirky side.'

'No, not unattractive,' Mark repeated automatically. But even as the words escaped his lips he knew that they didn't reflect the truth, for Clara had spontaneously transformed herself beneath his gaze and he felt that only now was he seeing her accurately. Clara Hood wasn't quirky at all, she was beautiful. The crooked jaw didn't mar her features; on the contrary, it was what lifted them above the commonplace and provided the slight strangeness that clinched it. Clara Hood was beautiful. How had Mark managed to remain so long unaware of this glaringly obvious fact?

A simple explanation hastened to present itself. Embroiled as he had been with Clara's moral shortcomings, Mark had not been in a position to assess her dispassionately – as Pods could, say; or perhaps that male companion of hers, who might remain blithely oblivious of Clara's undoubtedly slippery nature, until it was much too late to do anything about it.

Suddenly, Clara appeared to register Mark's attention. In another instant she'd picked him out. An assortment of indecipherable expressions sped across her face before it settled into a smile, accompanied by a little wave which skewered Mark's emotions after all the evening's prior coolness. Clara quickly turned away and said something to Geraldine and the man, who both glanced at him, then wandered off, leaving Clara alone beside the glass case.

'You know her, do you?' Clara seemed to be something Pods *was* disposed to discuss.

'I do.' Abruptly, Mark strode over to where Clara was standing before Pods could enquire further or request an introduction.

She smelled of citrus and spices, like a punch or a Christmas pudding. Mark could almost imagine the perfume fizzing as it came into contact with her skin.

'Clara' – he gave a courtly nod – 'what are you doing here?'

'Looking at the exhibits, of course. What else?'

Networking, consolidating contacts, keeping up with the gossip, being seen to be seen: none of these seemed to have crossed Clara's mind. Mark was touched. 'What else indeed?' He hoped he'd managed to keep the irony out of his voice. It was at his own expense; the solemn artefacts had totally escaped his notice – except for the Buddha. 'Are you somebody's guest?'

'Yes.' Clearly, Clara was unwilling to be drawn on the subject of her male companion and Mark had no choice but to respect that and keep his curiosity in check.

'Geraldine Crowe is with you too, I see.'

Clara nodded. 'She wants to take in everything while she's got the chance, that's why she went.'

There was a silence.

'Geraldine likes the art of southern Asia?'

'And she believes in reincarnation, like they do – for people as well as for dogs.'

'And you, do you believe in it too?' Mark fixed his eyes on Clara's.

It worked. Clara blushed, but responded to that by lifting her chin and briskly raking a hand through her hair. 'I'd give the supernatural the benefit of the doubt, but I still think it's worth shaking the branch as well.' With which she moved away to another, smaller, case holding only one exhibit.

Mark followed her. In the case, encircled by an intricately decorated gold hoop which he was holding like a skipping-rope, leaning backwards and with one leg raised in the air – precariously but perfectly balanced – was a long-nosed, earringed figure, with ornate hair and a mischievous expression.

'This one's part of the museum's permanent collection,' Clara said. 'It's "Shiva as a Dancer", ushering one time cycle out and the next one in. A bit like jump-starting an old motor.'

CHAPTER EIGHT

Upon Westminster Bridge

Clara did not like this. She didn't like it one little bit.

Although she was still slightly groggy from the free champagne, she'd rolled a big joint of Nepalese red and stood smoking it in front of the kitchen window in an attempt to damp down. She was wearing comfort clothes: a nylon petty under a candlewick dressing-gown, and some South American slipper-socks. It was around four o'clock. The house was quiet – everyone had crashed early owing to the party – and even the street had a slightly abandoned air, what with the drains all dug up and most things closed. The starlings and the dossers would be kipping round in Leicester Square. London was taking its brief zizz, but Clara Hood's mind was caught in the rush hour, with the evening's events stuck nose to tail in her head.

Oh yes, she'd gone down well all right – quite overwhelmingly so in fact – especially given the chic of the assembled company. At first Clara had felt like a parrot among pigeons, but then she'd noticed a yearning look – the kind you felt in your cheekbones when you saw something you wanted but couldn't have; usually it was accompanied by a road-bump flop of the stomach. Few things could cause that look. One of them was dresses. And the same envious expression had recurred again and again throughout the evening. For once, Clara Hood was the object of desire.

Seeing Mark Upshaw there had been a shock. Momentarily, Clara had reckoned this looked like trouble, but then read Mark's unsuspecting features and knew they were still in the clear. She'd never met a real man who was interested in art, but Mark seemed eager enough to accompany her from case to case, asking questions and making comments. Partly, Clara was heading him away from Geraldine – just in case she panicked and blurted – and from the exit so Kim could make her escape. Luckily, Mark hadn't recognized Kim, but if he had, he might have got to wondering what she was doing out of drag and guess how they'd got in. Mark Upshaw could be pretty insightful – what he said about the exhibits told Clara that. He seemed to have an abundance of cogitation to draw upon too, not to mention a ton of reading. Such a grave person, however. Clara would very much like to see him laugh.

The floor needed a good scrub. It was sticky underfoot with spills from the party. The dope hadn't dowsed her thoughts a jot. Maybe she should set to with the Vim and exhaust herself into calm?

But Clara remained motionless at the window. Who the hell was he? Who the hell was Mark Upshaw?

She shivered and pulled the dressing-gown tight, cradling it around her. Another big mistake, most probably. A potential betrayer. A danger. And yet . . . he'd smelled of soap and chlorine, as if he had been swimming and washed his hair after. Although he never let his seriousness slip, at times there was a smile in his voice.

Re-in-carnate: make into flesh again, make back into a body. Would one want that? Would one want that really, having found somewhere pleasant and out of reach? Clara's mind might still be a-bubble but this Nepalese was strong stuff – spiked even, possibly – she was thoroughly gone. All the shadows had lost their angles. The great amphitheatre of Leicester Square was suffusing the upper atmosphere with lovely mother-of-pearl. There was a beautiful veil of newspapers on the sodium-lit pavements, lifting and falling in a little wind that had sprung up. Clara sat down at the table, covered her head with a tea towel and put her ear to the wood. It was at times such as this that the city's pulse became audible. Like you could hear the sea in a shell, London's traffic, trains and footsteps, its subways, domes and towers, thudded inside every object. The sound was life.

Clara threw off the tea towel, startled. Tonight there was a smell too. The *smell* of life. Doggy life. It was the smell of Sassy the dog. Sassy's spirit had returned to Lisle Street and was here, now, in the kitchen with Clara, smelling as Sassy always had of salty, doggy oils, sweetly rotting meat and gutters. Geraldine had been right after all. Probably Clara had unwittingly chinked a dish or rattled the tin-opener and that had been enough to alert Sassy's spirit to the way in.

Clara straightened up.

'Hallo, Sassy-dog,' she said softly. 'Hallo, the girl.'

Immediately, she sensed the thudding front paws and jack-knifing backside as Sassy went into her joyful, rocking-horse bounds, an ecstatic tail beating into the air yet more pongy tang.

'You shouldn't really be here, you know.'

Sassy's tail seemed to slow for an instant, just as it always did when those words were said to her. In her mind's eye, Clara could see Sassy's loopy face, grinningly resigned to being turfed off a bed or prevented from drinking out of the toilet.

'No, really, Sassy. Geraldine – you remember Geraldine?' The pounding tail indicated Sassy did. 'Geraldine says I'm to tell you what you must do, and that isn't stay here, I'm afraid.'

Still the grin. As Geraldine had anticipated, Sassy didn't understand, which meant that Clara was going to have to take the dog back to her final resting place and explain in detail. Sassy's final resting place was the River Thames under Westminster Bridge. Unless you went right out – and they'd wanted Sassy in a place they'd often visit – there was nowhere except the parks to bury a dog in London; and as Muncher had observed, people might get suspicious if they spotted you, in the middle of the night, in St James's with picks and shovels and something in a sack. So they'd borrowed the minibus and thrown poor Sassy off the bridge – which had been suspicious too, but quick enough for no one to notice.

Clara shed her dressing-gown and put on a coaty thing that was lying scrunched in a corner. It would completely hide the petty, so there was no need to faff around looking for anything else to wear. She jammed her purse and keys in a pocket, replaced the slipper-socks with a pair of wedgies, and whistled up Sassy, who seemed to have become a touch more obedient since her demise, for her stench obligingly followed Clara down the stairs and out into the slightly breezy street, over the open ditch with its sewers and drains, and into the Square, where it started to dissipate. Normally this would simply have meant Sassy had wandered off, but Clara was pretty sure the dog was beside her still, and the fading smell only indicated that Sassy was finally cottoning on to her spirit status.

The odour had disappeared altogether by the time Clara got to the Charing Cross Road, but she kept going. She wanted to see the river anyway.

The darkness was lifting. In Trafalgar Square the fountains smouldered whitely. The very earliest folk started to be about. By the time Clara got to buttoned-up old Whitehall the sky was cornflower, edged with saffron; there were a few pale-faced night staff on the streets and one or two yawning coppers finishing their shifts.

From Westminster Bridge you could see right across the city – all browns, blues and greys. The river was a coffee sludge, overlaid with a glinting honeycomb of light. As Clara watched, the sun appeared. Suddenly, the buildings were outlined in scarlet and the water was a swirling mass of flame. She slipped the coat off her shoulders to experience the sun's first rays against her flesh.

'Time to move on, girl,' she said, and stopped feeling stoned at that precise instant, but refreshed and ravishingly hungry instead. She let the coat fall further to expose her naked back. There was heat in the air already; it was going to be a roasting day. Sassy's apparition had taken on a hazy, unreal aspect. There were many kinds of waking dreams; perhaps this had just been one of them. Certainly, Clara knew that the dog had gone and was never coming back.

Nevertheless, 'Time to move on,' she repeated. 'Time to get going.'

The trouble with not having any cash worth speaking of was that a bit more didn't make much difference. Mark Upshaw's rent had rendered things less dire, but not a whole lot less. The same could be said of anything piecemeal. Shelf-stacking, checkout, charring: there were plenty of jobs you could slave away at – on half the minimum wage if you were lucky – but they'd never pull you clear of the wreckage. In fact they'd pull you under. Which was why Clara wouldn't do them; she couldn't risk being too dead on her feet to care, should the big one ever present itself. That happened. She'd seen it.

So although galvanized, here Clara was: sat in Betty's at 6 a.m. approx, without the wherewithal for more than a milky coffee, into which she'd emptied two tablespoons of energizing shug – not that that would fool the tum for more than an hour when what it wanted was breakfast.

After leaving the bridge, Clara had taken a detour in order to see how Fleur's was coming on. The builders had whited over the windows now, so you couldn't see the interior any more, but a sign-painter had been on the job. The name of the place had been done in longhand, to look as if Fleur – if there was a Fleur – had scribbled it up there herself and filled in the outlines with a favourite nuance of beige. The address was in the usual Emmenthal script.

Less salubrious Berwick Street was busier at dawn than Newburgh, whose opening hours must reflect when its target punters had sufficiently slept off their clubbing to be ready to shop. Opposite the caff, over the other side of the street, a van pulled up and gave a couple of loud revs of its engine before switching off. The metal grid of a lock-up rose in response – someone illicitly nighting in commercial premises, perhaps. Or perhaps not. Though pop opinion would have it everything shady happened at night, a good deal – many good deals – took place at dawn, when loading and unloading attracted less attention, and the fuzz were less liable to be bored.

Their business. Clara lowered her eyes to her coffee. (Strange, how fast the level went down when you were trying to nurse it.) Offsetting would be the aim of Fleur's colour scheme. Grey, brown and black were too serviceable ever to go out – they alternated as woman-about-town's school uniform, and should make up Fleur's staples if she had any sense – but London, Paris and Milan were ablaze for the coming season. Probably, Fleur thought her autumn ranges would cut more of a dash against a background of neutrals – though too much of a good thing had never seemed cause for concern to Clara. Come to think of it, maybe Clara's up-to-the-minute colourfulness was why so many people had wanted an eyeful of her in the museum? Maybe they'd thought she was just a jump ahead of the pack.

Clara looked across the street again. The back of the van was open now. Hot, hot, hot – no doubt about it. Berwick Street had a rag-trade aspect, but these were no rags – though who'd expect a copper to pick out silk from shoddy if you stashed them together?

'Like I say: market stuff, Constable. Here. Petticoat. Brixton. Bell.'

'Yeah, well, general check. Okay. This lot looks kosher to me.'

Though so would a bacon sandwich. Even from this distance Clara could see the thickness and weave of the stuff being unloaded. Colours of such subtlety could only be custom-made and hand-dyed. *En route* from a London fashion house to an overseas one, she guessed – word on the street had it that the shenanigans of the fashion biz would make your average debt-collector's hair stand on end.

What Bethany Smile could do with material of that quality! What Clara herself could!

Clara took a swing from her mug. Her body had gone cold; her mind started racing.

These blokes would only be go-betweens, there to muddy the trail. By tonight this load of schmutter would have vanished into thin air. Tomorrow they'd be handling some completely different clobber – soft toys, watches, car alarms. Bulk carrying would be their usual game. Lots of items of little value. Hard slog. Biggish risks. The kind of working conditions that made you open to the idea of the odd thing going missing, if the cash was right and ready.

The café's blue fog of cigarette smoke had become a trillion swirling particles. Pin-prick sensations pulled at Clara's arms and legs. A good idea and a lump sum: that was all you needed to get yourself off the financial hook for ever. Start-up capital, the banks called the money component, and it was the sticking point always. Clara could have screamed with frustration. Good ideas she'd never lacked, but you needed money to make money; just like you needed money to save any. Small use the economy size being better value if you didn't have the extra to buy it with. Small use a wonderful plan if you didn't have the dosh to put it into practice.

Clara racked her brain for answers. Nothing of value in her possession, of course. Not a single solid object worth turning into liquid. But what about the rest of the household? Clara held her breath. A solution began to come to her. The technical term for it was a sleeping partner. The only way in which their case would be different from the norm was that this particular partner would be faster asleep than was customary. Clothes would be too noticeable, and anyway it was moot whether Clara could borrow those without waking him. Suitcases, on the other hand . . . What was the use of a suitcase unless you were headed somewhere?

CHAPTER NINE

A Giant Rat

Mark found himself deriving comfort from the noises of the house. Although the quietest it had been up till now, the building was still far from silent; nor was it surrounded by silence either. But the sounds of the city, combined with the creak of floorboards, clanks and groans from the plumbing, and the usual opening and shutting of doors, felt oddly friendly; almost like a person lying asleep beside him.

Having said that, however, there was something curious about the noises also. Mark was convinced that some of them emanated from the supposedly disused attic. In his more fantastical moods he even wondered if there was somebody up there, before scotching the idea with more rational explanations such as giant rats, felines, a bat colony, or alighting wildfowl. In any event, nuisances that were nothing in the light of the vastly disturbing fact that this evening's event at the British Museum had changed Mark's situation not one iota.

Given the icy terror in which the thought immersed him – the imponderability of a supposedly temporary blip metamorphosing into inescapable fate – it was mad that Mark's mind could fix on anything else. But fix it did. On Clara Hood, and how obviously well she knew the British Museum. Her totally unaffected love of art. The things she'd noticed and drawn to his attention. Somehow, Mark had almost forgotten that he loved art also. Although one did, it was so much a given; like your entry in *Who's Who,* not something you considered really. Of course, that last time in Florence, Fleur and he had duly looked and admired, but there was no accompanying passion; the process had the quality of something to be gone through before shopping. In contrast, last night Mark had recalled the way in which beauty and humanity could momentarily loosen one from the horrors of now.

Who was the male, though? The fellow without the good grace to linger for a handshake, the pretty-boy chap Mark had not seen around before. It was hardly surprising that Clara had a boyfriend, but what sort of a man was he? Was theirs a fly-by-night relationship or one of long standing?

Gnawed by anxiety and all these actually rather inconsequential questions, Mark eventually fell into a restless slumber. At one point his fevered dreams conjured up an irregular tom-tomming against the staircase walls, which he mistook for a couple having intercourse. Later they started up again, forcing Mark into wakefulness, turning out not to be lovers at all but somebody urgently knocking on the door of one of the rooms on the floor above.

Mark looked at his clock. It was 8.30. He got out of bed, pulled on a pair of jeans and a T-shirt and went on to the landing.

'Kim! Kim! Wake up. I need you.'

The voice was Clara's and there was a desperate edge to it. Mark made his way upstairs to see if he could be of any help. Just as he reached the top Kim's door flew open and Kim appeared looking rather odd; her face was sort of grubby and she somehow seemed more knobbly than usual. Despite her high wedges Clara looked small in comparison, in frayed denim shorts and a sleeveless top. Neither woman had noticed Mark's presence.

'Clara, my beauty sleep!'

'Kim, listen. I've got some heavy rolls of material in the minibus.'

'The minibus? What time is it?'

'Too late, I know, I know. But anyway, I need help unloading them and they're ho . . .'

The end of the word, whatever it was going to be, was stifled by a clump of Kim's painted fingers.

'Mr Upshaw. How rugged you look when tousled.'

Clara twirled round. She was still as beautiful as the night before. Mark ran a hand through his hair. He felt his cheeks redden. He probably did look tousled. 'Good morning. I'm afraid I overheard you. Can I be of assistance? I'm happy to do any heavy lifting.'

Clara said, 'Thanks, no.'

Kim sang, 'What *time* is it, Clara?'

Clara said, 'Half eight and it's hot already.'

Kim said, 'I'm sure Mark won't notice a bit of heat – should we *accept* his generous offer – whereas stuck in his room it could become more noticeable.'

Mark was rather affronted by Clara's doubts about his physical stamina. 'Really, I assure you,' he said in a more distant tone, 'the temperature is no trouble to me.'

There was a pause.

'All right,' Clara said at last, more to Kim than to Mark, it seemed. Then, less ungraciously, 'I mean . . . thank you. I . . .' Tailing off and for some reason avoiding Mark's eyes.

'Give me half a mo to get dolled up,' said Kim. 'Apparently our carriage awaits.'

While Mark was detousling and Kim having her shave and primp Clara sat outside in the minibus, which was on a double-yellow. A needless precautionary measure – this sort of vehicle was most unlikely to be towed, clamped or slapped with a ticket – but it meant Clara could pull off the second Kim and Mark were in. The only other occasion that had been this tight for time minibus-wise was when she and Muncher had run out of petrol, after an all-night sesh with some friends of Muncher's in the Fisher Arms down Thornton Heath.

It was a nuisance having Mark come along. Clara concentrated on her irritation hard, in order to squash the other feelings inspired by Mark's offer. Kim was right – being willing to involve him looked oodles less suspicious than coming over all cagey then leaving him alone to think. On the other hand, bearing in mind where the material was going to be stored for the time being, it suddenly and worryingly occurred to Clara that maybe, just maybe, Mark hadn't realized Kim was a gender-bender. If that was the case, once he did suss it, how would he react?

The questions opened unexpected floodgates. Spontaneously, Mark Upshaw ceased to be simply a rugged anonymity beneath which was pencilled: *Man. Threat?* Clara saw she could no longer dismiss him as someone who just popped up every so often, in charming mood or terse. Instead, she was forced to confront the fact of a disturbingly complex human being, with opinions and suppositions; a past Clara knew nothing about; a future which might lead him . . . wherever. Away from Lisle Street probably.

Not squashing hard enough. Two more realizations shouldered their way to the forefront of Clara's thoughts. One was that Mark Upshaw had been kind to her. The other was that a future leading somewhere would surely involve suitcases.

Folk squandered guilt as much as they did everything else, but Clara reckoned she had good reason to feel guilty. Assumptions based on all but diddly-squat had allowed her to break an important moral precept: You do not borrow something off someone without asking, *unless you are sure of their particular circumstances* – like the proprietor of Hodge's, for instance, who probably wouldn't notice the diff if you swiped a couple of his Rollers.

At some point those cases had been carefully chosen and purchased. Half an hour earlier, Clara had borrowed them from their cupboard and pawned them. They were currently sitting in a pawnshop.

She'd prayed the shop would be open as she'd zoomed over there. Fifty-fifty it would. Certain kinds of commodity dealer, certain varieties of premises, never really had an out-of-hours. CLOSED only meant there might be nobody about except the Rottweiler. Often, as in this case, such businesses operated from narrow back streets. Clara had a job squeezing the minibus between the alley's grubby walls.

The pawnshop's exterior was a whole lot more upbeat than its setting, however. Very clean windows in which were displayed, on blue velveteen-lined shelving, a Japanese pot you could have hidden Bethany Smile in, a clock with cherubs, a hi-fi, a hearing-aid, several walking-sticks with silver and ivory handles, and a pair of tan riding-boots. It had been a deliberate move, freshening up the place's image; designed to appeal to the classier individual such establishments could hope to be attracting nowadays. Clara had heard all about it from Muncher, who played poker with one of the partners.

She was buzzed in by a chalk-on-a-blackboard Pin-stripe, who seemed unsurprised by such early custom.

The Old Man wore a black kimono over a vest and pyjama trousers. On his feet were a pair of carpet slippers. There was a thick gold ring with an embedded diamond on his little finger. He was seated at a reproduction Victorian desk, surrounded by a mass of still-redeemable objects; others were stacked on the shelves behind him, along with numerous cardboard boxes of various sizes and several half-full decanters. The Old Man had a magnifying-glass in one hand and a fob in the other. He put them down.

'Barrow's niece, isn't it?' To the Pin-stripe, 'Told him this ticker wasn't a runner. Bloke doesn't know he's born some days.' To Clara again, 'Those cases Italian?'

'I reckon.'

'Scuffed.' The phone rang. 'Two thous what I said and . . . Seven-fifty? Okay. Done. Bring it over.'

'Designer label.'

'Let's see them open. Want a coffee?' To Pin-stripe, 'We got coffee?'

Pin-stripe. 'Nah.'

'You see, you see, there's a trouble with suitcases.'

'That being what?'

'Demand.' A shrug, accompanied by stigmata hand gesture.

With a smile, 'Perhaps I'd be better off hanging on to them, then?'

'You know what, Barrow's niece, you are awful pretty.' To Pin-stripe, 'Isn't this one pretty lady? And because you're such a pretty lady and I'm feeling very, very generous, I'll offer . . .'

'And I'll keep these to put my bikini in.'

The phone rang. While he spoke, the Old Man wrote a slightly revised sum on his notepad and turned it to face Clara. Clara picked up a pencil, wrote a higher one and swivelled the pad towards him again. Without a pause in his dialogue with the blower, the Old Man gave an atom of a nod in the direction of the Pin-stripe. Five minutes later Clara was walking out with a wad of cash, a receipt and a Terms and Conditions – mainly to do with getting back said item or items.

Which she would.

Now, waiting on her double-yellow, Clara looked into the rear-view mirror, and in spite of discomfiture and guilt her spirits soared again as she contemplated those beautiful rolls of material.

Like all the dosh she'd ever known, no sooner had that bundle of notes been in her hand than somebody else was trousering it. As she'd watched the blokes loading the material into the bus – keeping a careful tally on quantity – Clara had been well aware that the little money left was going to need skilful stretching if she and Bethany were going to set themselves up in the fashion biz.

Though that said, it did seem as if things were finally coming together. The splash Clara's dress had made at the museum had immediately been followed by an opportunity to put it into manufacture. She'd struck the deal she'd expected to at the pawnshop. The minibus had been available for transporting – an especial bit of luck that, sometimes it was off on a Duke of Edinburgh. Even the fact that Clara had access to the bus at all was fortuitous: the result of Si's looking to extend his custom, and enjoy free tea and biccies to boot.

The duplicate key which Si had got cut for her was on Clara's key-ring, along with all her others. Clara was assiduous about siphoning more juice into the petrol tank whenever she used a noticeable amount of it.

'CHRISTIAN MISSION TO SOHO'S YOUTH?'

'It's borrowed,' said Clara.

Mark was astounded. 'You are involved in a Christian mission?'

'Move along,' said Kim from behind, giving Mark a prod in an area sufficiently intimate to cause him to leap into the front seat. Kim followed. The rest of the minibus was crammed with material, so there was no choice but to sit between the two women. Before Mark could get his safety belt fastened Clara jammed her foot on the accelerator. Briefly, Mark's body touched hers. He was aware of a racing pulse, a high level of anticipatory tension. The minibus rounded a bend rather like in a police drama, then came to a shuddering standstill a millimetre from the bumper of a taxi waiting to cross Shaftesbury Avenue.

'Not me. Si,' said Clara.

'Si is committed to Christianity?' Nothing in the boy's conduct had ever suggested it.

This time it was Kim who answered. 'I wouldn't exactly say Si's committed, but he is very good friends with some of the younger ministers.'

Even that seemed highly unlikely. The minibus shot into the path of a car, a motorbike and an oncoming van. Clara was a breathtakingly accurate driver, with an almost physical instinct for the vehicle's width and braking power, not to mention the agility of pedestrians and the reaction times of other drivers. Unexpectedly, Mark found himself rather enjoying the ride. Clara's urgency and sense of purpose were infectious. So much of Mark's recent life had been devoted to trying to prevent things from happening that it was an age since he had actually been involved in *doing* anything.

Though the precise nature of what he was doing now was something of a mystery. In Brewer Street the minibus ground to a halt, outside an establishment entitled 'Gurlz' Nightclub. For an instant Mark thought Clara was going to consult an *A to Z*. But, 'Here we are,' she pronounced, aiming a challenging look in Mark's direction. And with no more explanation than that she jumped out, ran round the back and flung the rear of the vehicle open.

'My place of employment,' added Kim, slithering on to the pavement and unlocking the club's front door with a key she'd produced from her handbag. 'Coo-ee,' she called into the building's interior, then went to join Clara at the back of the bus, hefted the largest roll of material on to her left shoulder and marched inside.

'Let me do it,' said Mark to Clara, who in the light of Kim's ease of manoeuvre was finding it surprisingly hard even to lift one of the rolls. He spoke curtly, for the look she had shot him rankled. Did Clara really think he was so naïve as to be shocked by a place such as this, for God's sake? He was a man of the world: whatever sleaze he was about to be confronted with was scarcely going to throw him.

Mark pulled the roll of material on to his back and nearly keeled over. Either he'd grossly underestimated their relative loads or Kim must be a woman of quite disproportionate strength.

There was a black curtain, with a table and chair in front of it, just inside the nightclub's doorway. Small gaps at either end of the curtain provided an entrance. The building smelled faintly of cigarette smoke. Several of the blacked-out windows had been opened to let the place air. Sunbeams fell on to the carpet, which was patterned with big white stars. There was a duster and an aerosol spray on the semicircle of bar, along which were ranged half a dozen tall stools with plastic tops. A vacuum cleaner stood in one of the corners. A stage, elevated about eighteen inches above the floor, was empty save for a microphone stand, two loudspeakers and a backdrop of silver streamers.

'Through there,' said Kim, on her way out again already, pointing to an open door. Mark entered and found himself in an empty dressing-room. He dumped his roll where Kim had placed hers, next to a long rack of spangled dresses and feather boas, then straightened up and looked around. Blond, auburn, chestnut and black wigs hung from hooks on the walls: short, curly, straight, waist-length; all elaborately styled. There were two small dressing-tables, littered with lipsticks, face powders, rouges, eyeshadows, tubs of cold cream, false eyelashes, tubes of glue, pairs of tweezers and electric razors. The mirrors were surrounded with light bulbs.

It took another quarter of an hour to get all the material unloaded; Kim shifting considerably more of it than Mark did.

'I'm off,' said Clara the minute they were done.

'Yes, exit,' said Kim. She hooked an unwelcome arm under Mark's elbow as he made to follow. 'But you, my sweet, *you* are going to come and meet some of the girls from the night shift.'

'Really, there's no need. I would hate to disturb them,' said Mark, simultaneously attempting to extricate himself both physically and socially.

Either proved equally impossible. Clara vanished in a flash. Kim crooned, 'Don't be a silly,' and proceeded to propel Mark around the side of the bar into a small, sunlit kitchen with an old gas cooker, a smeared sink unit, a sofa, two armchairs, and a low table covered in magazines. On the floor, a fat black-and-white cat was eating tuna fish from a flowered saucer. The girls were making drop-scones.

'Ladies.'

There were appreciative murmurs and a brief pause in the cooking; then a curvy, Spanish-looking one returned to ladling batter into a frying-pan, while her platinum-tressed – and puzzlingly familiar – colleague flipped the scones over with a pallet knife. A thickly mascaraed third was buttering.

Kim fussed around. 'Earl Grey?'

For a second Mark thought he was being offered a complimentary choice from an exotic sexual menu.

'Er . . . Earl Grey. Yes. Thank you.'

The girls giggled.

'And I'm sure you could do with something to eat after all that humping. Plain? Or there's apricot, strawberry, marmalade, maple syrup or lemon curd.'

'Marmalade would be lovely.'

More easy-going giggles. It wasn't unkind, but Mark had the distinct impression a joke was being had at his expense. He avoided engaging in conversation and instead watched Kim's large hand spread lavish dollops of marmalade on to a plateful of gleaming drop-scones.

It was a very large hand for a woman, considered closely. Very large indeed, with wide fingers – stubby beneath their long, manicured nails. And Kim had been so powerful, too, when it came to heavy lifting . . . Aghast, Mark's eyes moved to Kim's face. Her cheeks had lost their early morning grubbiness. Dumbfounded, he scanned the other girls, noting muscles that were just a little too defined, shoulders a fraction too broad, a certain infinitesimal bluntness to the features.

He turned back to Kim. 'You're men,' he blurted, before he could prevent himself.

The marmalade knife stopped moving. The other three ceased their lazy gossip and curiously watched to see what would happen.

Kim's eyes rose to meet Mark's. 'Clara was none too sure you'd . . . And lo and behold, it turns out she was clever as always. What a waste of pennies it would have been to save for the operation! Not men, though, dearie. Neither fish nor fowl, some would say, but "Ladies" will do very nicely.' She handed Mark the scones and a steaming mug of tea. He accepted them automatically. 'Milk and sugar?'

There was a silence.

'Just milk, please,' said Mark. 'But I hope very much you are joining me?' Then, to the others, 'This all looks delicious. I greatly appreciate your kind hospitality.'

The Spanish-looking one burst into happy tears, which was not the least embarrassing thing that had happened so far that day. Mark could not recall ever having experienced so many awkward moments before breakfast; nor having ever felt quite such a confounded idiot. (Even unsound investments had respectable precedent.) Ruefully biting into a drop-scone, it occurred to him how very much what one saw depended upon what one expected to see; how easily one could be seduced into considering normal what others considered normal, however bizarre. For instance, sitting in this sunny kitchen with a group of transvestites and a black-and-white cat felt like no more than a mild and agreeable experience.

It would have been pleasant – and perhaps wise – to have stopped there, but now it occurred to Mark that he had also accepted as normal the early morning depositing of a quantity of material in a drag club, when God knew there seemed to be room for all and sundry at the house in Lisle Street.

'Lemon curd and apricot,' said Kim, joining Mark on the sofa. 'Shift your bum along a little.'

'Do you get much trouble from the . . . um . . . police here?'

'Why?' asked Kim lightly.

'The management give them cash and they no bother us,' said the Spanish-looking one, neatly providing Mark with as much as he cared to know about the origins of the material he, Mark Upshaw, had just been involved in the unloading of. Had Clara Hood not the slightest . . .

'What did you think of that lovely stone Buddha?' asked Kim.

'That lovely stone Buddha?' Mark's thoughts precipitately screeched off in a wildly new direction.

'Oh. I mean, Clara told me about it.'

So it wasn't a man she'd been with at the museum!

Mark looked at Kim. He felt like laughing. 'It was *you. You* were Clara's male companion. I assumed she had a boyfriend.'

There was a pause. After which, 'Yes, ducks. Me again,' said Kim. 'Clara doesn't have boyfriends.'

CHAPTER TEN

Scattering Glitter

Clara's emotions had been in a liquidizer lately. Buying treats made the world feel safer and more normal.

Once the business was ticking over, Si could go to catering college and become a chef on television. Muncher needn't do any washing-up jobs – not at Rumbles nor anywhere else either. They'd rent a Spiritual Consultancy Office for Geraldine round Neal's Yard, with mobiles and crystals and dark blue curtains. Kim would start her own drag club, employing the girls at decent rates. They'd get Bethany Smile out of London to someplace no one would ever think of looking for her. And Mark Upshaw could pack his reclaimed suitcases, find another lodging and give Clara back her old room. In the meantime, however, there was comfort in individual slices of gateau with twirls of choc; a half of rum and a tetra of pineapple; glutinous rice snowballs from a bun shop in Gerrard Street; and sweet potatoes for Bethany, who liked them baked with marshmallows.

One gown did not a collection make. Clara was going to have to work flat out if everything was to be ready on time. Which was dandy with her. She'd much rather be perched out of harm's way doing a running stitch than have to sit in the kitchen listening – yet again – to Kim making a palaver about how pleased Mark Upshaw had been to discover Clara hadn't *really* had a man with her at the British Museum; for which – if it was true – there were a million and one perfectly plausible explanations. Better consider instead how lucky it was Mark's thoughts hadn't trolled on to by what means Clara had got invited to the museum in the first place – particularly in the light of her latest plan.

There was to be a grand launch for Clara and Bethany's dress label.

Clara had come up with the idea after reading an article in *Ms London*. The subject of the article was Fleur, who turned out to be a real person and not just the name of a shop. There was a paragraph about the Newburgh Street premises and when they would be open to the public, but no mention of the opening bash that Mark had been invited to. Presumably that was going to be a private affair – trade, press, credit cards and intimates only. Fleur was photographed modelling some of her designer range. She was petite and pretty, with regular features and sculpted blond hair – the kind that didn't insist on curling under at one end and up at the other, in spite of gel, spray and rollers. Maybe Mark was among Fleur's intimates. Probably Fleur's hair always curled in the right direction, even first thing.

Anyway, the article got Clara properly focused.

The Dump South of the River was always willing to keep an eye out for specifics if you told them you were looking. Clara rang and asked them to tip her the wink should any dress rails on casters come in, but to be sure to talk to her only and not leave any messages.

She didn't care how delightful he'd purportedly been at the drag club, secrecy was still paramount. Kim could bring small quantities of the schmutter back from Gurlz, as and when, but Mark had seen the material already and would wonder how it was getting dyed and patterned – and perhaps, by whom. That potentially disastrous channel of interest just couldn't be opened. Nor must Mark be in a position to wonder why Clara was sketching and cutting; why she, Kim and Geraldine were beavering away with needles and cotton: what the *outlet* was for their activity.

How to Make a Multinational, and the ton of other library books on setting up in business, all said you should start small. Clara could do that, no prob.

The attic became a clandestine workshop.

The days of the cheap old cast-iron sewing-machines had come and gone, unfortunately. It used to be you could net them for a song, but people had learnt to appreciate their gold leaf and mother-of-pearl inlays and the natty mechanics. Nobody wanted an ugly fifties industrial electric, however. Clara found a couple in a junk shop and talked the price down for taking the pair, which meant that delivery was almost free. She checked out every skip she came across where they were doing a shop, pub or restaurant refit, then did a late-night pick-up in the minibus with Si and Muncher, trawling in two doors and enough timber to transform them into table-tops.

In order to optimize Bethany Smile's efficiency, dyeing buckets were necessary in increased quantity. Obtaining these was easy enough – people left them lying around at the bottom of ladders, under sinks, in the cleaning cupboard of the hall where the Christian Mission offered its helping hand to Soho's youth. (The hall also provided some extra chairs Clara needed, from among those the youth sat on while they got things off their chests.) The problems where buckets were concerned clocked on later, when it came to the tricky task of lugging full ones upstairs and in due course down again, unnoticed.

There must be no slips. Too much was hanging in the balance.

Clonks and footsteps. Sawdust and muffled hammering. Library books on financial enterprise and business start-up schemes. The odd finding of hidden stores of sweet potatoes, which may or may not have been related.

Mark suspected Clara was up to something purposeful and definite. He was also pretty sure it was going on in the attic, which cast doubt upon his earlier wildlife theory. Clearly, the area at the top of the house had been in at least spasmodic use for as long as he'd been living in Lisle Street. Opportunities to investigate further failed to arise, however; Mark never seemed to find himself alone in the building.

Curiosity apart, he didn't object to that. In his present very keyed-up and apprehensive state, the animation of the household was one of only two things that kept him buoyant.

A bank statement had arrived. Mark's eyes travelled across the room to where he'd put it, on the shelf above the fireplace, unopened. By late tomorrow it should, if things were handled right, have lost its sting. The Queen's School dinner at Rumbles was due to take place the following evening. Mark's oldest and most influential acquaintances would be present. Already, he'd chosen a dinner suit and the shirt to wear with it. Both were suspended from the front of his wardrobe. Mark glanced at them. There was a kind of courage that could be derived from clothing.

His gaze moved idly on, then halted abruptly, transfixed by a totally unexpected sight. For a wild instant he became quite light-headed. A flood of crimson liquid was seeping under his door, making a chilling patch on the carpet. Almost immediately, there was a loud knock. The screwdriver turned in the doorknob hole. Mark braced himself for something unspeakable. The door opened to reveal a startlingly sanguine Geraldine Crowe.

'Did I stain your carpet?' she enquired.

'Yes,' said Mark, adding hastily, 'But I don't mind.'

'So you won't tell Clara?'

'*And* it's all over this,' complained Kim's voice, in a tone mercifully suggestive only of nuisance.

'I won't tell Clara.' Mark endeavoured to sound as reassuring as possible. Geraldine vanished back into the corridor. Mark rose to his feet and cautiously followed. On the landing was an upturned bucket, and an ivory shroud of cloth which he remembered having unloaded at the drag club.

'Hallo, gorgeous,' said Kim.

'Hallo,' said Mark. 'Is this . . . dye?'

'It wasn't deliberate, I promise,' said Geraldine, her eyes pinballing.

'I'm sure it wasn't.'

'And you're positive the stain's presence doesn't bother you?'

'Um . . .' Mark hesitated, uncertain whether or not to contradict his earlier statement.

'We could put a Welcome mat over it and it would be invisible from the landing.'

'Of course a big red puddle on his carpet bothers him,' Kim answered on Mark's behalf. 'And besides, Clara would have a mat up in a trice to see what was under it.' She turned to Mark, her hands shooing him towards the stairs. 'There is the biggest box of Frosties money can buy on the kitchen table, courtesy of *moi,* and there's a nice cold tin of evap in the fridge. Put the kettle on, have some cereal, and I'll join you for a cuppa as soon as all is spick and span.'

'I'm quite happy to deal with it myself.' Mark's heartbeat had slowed a little. Even in her absence, Clara and her affairs were uniquely capable of shooting across his consciousness and throwing his mind into turmoil.

Geraldine suddenly became teary. 'Don't . . . Please. Do not increase our chagrin.'

Mark judged it best to do as Kim suggested.

Si was in the kitchen, spooning Frosties into his mouth, his eyes glued to a comic.

' 'Lo, Maz.'

'Good afternoon, Simon.'

Mark lit the gas and filled the kettle. He found a bowl, washed it, and did indeed help himself to some cereal and evaporated milk.

He ate in silence, thinking and puzzling.

Geraldine Crowe was convinced she'd be in trouble if Clara discovered that Mark knew about the spilled bucket. The question Mark longed to have answered was why Clara felt a need to be so furtive around him – to hide things that there was no reason not to reveal.

True, the acquisition of the fabric was perhaps dubious, but dyeing it thereafter – possibly with some commercial end in view – didn't strike Mark as meriting a veil of secrecy. Other considerations aside, his own personal level of involvement made it improbable that he'd go to the police with a story about the passing on of stolen goods. Particularly not one based on circumstantial evidence emanating from an establishment under the constabulary's protection.

'Is Clara doing something with material?' Mark asked Si eventually, riled at how shut out her secrecy made him feel.

There was a pause.

'Y'know what, Maz?' said Si from behind his comic.

'I don't.'

'When it gets cold, if you stand over the grilles where the Tube trains go under, there's warm air comes up and heats yer.'

'Geraldine's finishing,' said Kim, gliding in. 'Tea or coffee?'

'Tea, please.' So even Si was in on it. Mark was baffled. What precise factor rendered him alone untrustworthy?

'Tea it is. Strong enough to trot a mouse on, I think, after our trauma.' To Si, 'Mouth shut whilst eating, my sweet.'

'No point. Last spoonful.'

'Well, file the idea away for future reference.'

Si sloped off. Kim put two saucerless teacups down on the table.

What a strange and unlikely entourage to surround oneself with, Mark reflected.

'Kim,' he blurted suddenly, 'why doesn't Clara have boyfriends? Is she . . . ?' He hesitated.

Kim raised a pencilled eyebrow. 'Gay? I think not. A man . . . ?'

Mark cut in, affronted. 'Although I have recently come across as unobservant, the condition was temporary. I am well aware that Clara Hood's contours do not belong to a man.'

'Ooh, mercy me!' Kim gave an exaggerated flutter of her fingers. 'No need to go all of a smoulder, duckie – though I must say it suits you. To finish answering your question, the fact is I'm clueless. But for *your* future reference, you might bear in mind that just because Clara's contours *don't* belong to a man, that doesn't imply they couldn't.'

It was Saturday night, the time when people went out together.

The plan had been to work right through, but as the evening drew closer every thread had decided to snarl, each piece of cloth veered off like it possessed a mind of its own. Eventually Clara threw in the towel, put on her jade calico and the tap-dancer's shoes with the emerald buttons, and kept Muncher company on his walk to work. They parted at the back entrance.

It was hot. Already the restaurant's gargantuan kitchen was huffing and puffing. Clara headed into Covent Garden, which was doing its Barcelona. Every outdoor table was crammed with people glugging wine and wolfing crostini. A circle had gathered around a juggler with a nice line of patter. Others watched from a pub balcony. In an open-air café at basement level a chamber orchestra was scraping away like crazy. Late sunlight polished the cobbles and the sky didn't have a cloud in it.

Bad weather for taxis. Tonight most of London would be strolling, and they'd be rattling around just longing for a fare. If you were going anywhere fancy and wanted to arrive there cool, you'd only have to raise a hand and a cab would be at your heel.

In spite of her glad rags and the surrounding razzle-dazzle, Clara was seized by an untypical despondency. What she should do was stop her meandering, go into Sheila's and make the most of the happy hour there. She could sit in one of the funny plastic chairs, or up at the bar and watch the fellas fixing margarita cocktails. It wasn't automatically the case that the best parties were the ones you weren't invited to.

Clara didn't make a beeline for the bar's matey interior,

however. Instead, she sunk on to a bit of low pavement where lots of young foreigners were crouched also, eating baked potatoes off polystyrene platters.

That was when she spotted him, striding along, very preoccupied, apparently oblivious of the stir he was creating. In his dinner suit, silk shirt and bow tie, Mark Upshaw looked like one of those champagne ads that put exquisitely dressed couples in improbable places – sipping their fizz in a chippy; or on a park bench, serenaded by a smiling busker. The slogan something like, *Why not?*

Clara scrambled to her feet. Yanking the glances though he was *now*, she could imagine Mark looking even better at the end of the evening. Relaxed. Mellow. Tie loose, shirt button undone at the neck, the first traces of a stubble.

'Clara?'

Clara jumped. She hadn't expected him to catch her gawping, but now Mark was walking towards her, a pleased expression on his face. From his previous demeanour, Clara guessed he was wound up for some reason and relieved to have found a distraction. She was distinctly aware of the mass of eyes on the two of them; and you didn't need to speak French or Italian to know what the foreign girls were saying. Perhaps folk thought they were a pair of street performers who'd suddenly go into a slow waltz around the arcades and through the Jubilee Market; past windows full of handbags and ethnic dresses, among stalls selling jewellery, tie-dyed dungarees and multicoloured sweaters. Clara was wearing dancing shoes, after all.

'Are you busy?' Mark asked. 'I'm on my way to a dinner, and not wanting to be late I've made myself early. If you've no other commitments, would you like to come and have a drink with me? There, perhaps?' Indicating an airy, goats-cheese-with-everything wine bar.

Clara hesitated. Half of her wanted to say yes. Half didn't.

'If you've other plans, however . . .'

The knowledge that Mark sensed her ambivalence was what

convinced Clara it was okay to agree. It put them on a suitably distant footing. Or so she thought until she was seated opposite him at a small table with a lit candle on it.

Mark summoned a waitress.

'What would you like to drink?'

'I'll have a glass of Chardonnay.'

'A Chardonnay, please, and a large whisky and soda.'

Unless one studied the revolving ceiling fan or ogled the other customers, there was nowhere to look but at the table or each other. Mainly, Clara looked at the table, but that didn't mean she wasn't aware that Mark's eyes were fixed upon her. It was the first time they had been in a straightforward situation together; Clara felt lost without any immediate subterfuge to hide behind.

The drinks arrived. Mark downed half of his then leant forward, resting his elbows on the table. Clara stole a peek at him. Their eyes met. The expression on Mark's face suggested his mind was working on a lot of things simultaneously. Clara knew the sensation. Almost, she wished she could confide in him.

'Clara,' he said, 'I think I owe you an apology.'

'An apology?' Clara was stunned. She would have liked to have ducked Mark's gaze but her body was petrified.

'At times I have been brusque and discourteous,' Mark continued. 'For that you must forgive me.'

Clara was silent. She intuited that this was a kind of sweeping of the board; an overall desire to get things on kilter – probably not unrelated to whatever he was so uptight about this evening. But it did also seem genuinely personal. As Clara stared at his handsome features, Mark smiled. 'I hope and believe it was not indicative of any chronic character defect,' he added. For an instant Clara became angry, but then she perceived that the smile had a degree of self-mockery in it.

'I don't judge people,' she said quickly.

Mark took another swallow of his whisky. His tone changed.

'Yes you do. You'd be inhuman not to. You judge them, Clara, and sometimes you find them wanting.'

The baldness of the statement threw her. 'There's only so much benefit of the doubt one can afford to give,' Clara said. 'I ration it.'

'So I see.' Mark looked at his watch, drained his glass and signalled to the waitress for the bill.

'We'll go Dutch,' said Clara.

'No we won't. I invited you, remember?'

Mark got out his wallet, looking far from dissatisfied with what had passed between them. Although Clara had done her best to short-change him, somehow he knew that he'd got to her.

Rumbles was an establishment where men went to discuss things with other men, and to which boys were taken by their fathers at crucial junctures. Few of the Queen's School female alumni ever elected to attend the annual dinner.

As Mark was conducted past the carriage lamps, gold-framed mirrors and waistcoated diners occupying the main area, to the private room where the dinner was due to take place, he found himself surreptitiously brushing the sleeves of his jacket, as if Clara had scattered glitter upon them. Never before had the restaurant's atmosphere seemed quite so stiflingly oppressive. One could imagine the air being delivered daily, and running out shortly after the last customer had departed. How different from the wine bar with Clara, feral and beautiful in her Rain Forest greens; lemon light falling upon her face from that one stark flame. For a moment there, he'd had her cornered. For a moment, Mark had penetrated her guard; compelled her to look at him closely; made her open up to him a little.

'What are you so damn happy about?' It was Pods, clutching a kir royale.

'How are you, Pods?' They shook hands. Mark's mood shifted. Not a word from Pods. Not a word from anybody since the museum. The big guns were here. He must get his act together. He must stop feeling dissociated from the occasion.

'Good. Bloody good, actually. Seen the seating-plan? You're between Oswald and Charlie.'

'Oswald and Charlie?' Mark's spirits rallied. Oswald was somebody he really hadn't expected to be seeing. As chief executive of an international bank he was frequently abroad.

Charlie was Home Secretary.

'Well, I suppose it's because you were Head of House,' said Pods, as if an explanation other than Mark and Charlie's long acquaintanceship were now needed. They had first met during Mark's first year at the Queen's School when, as an eminent Old Boy, Charlie had been invited back to give a talk. Since then, there had been various pleasant social encounters. Mark opened his mouth to say as much, but at that instant Pods gave him a nudge. 'Looks like we're on.'

People were making their way from the reception area to the long tables. In the huddle before everyone was seated, Mark spotted and spoke to several of his acquaintance, but there was only time for the briefest of exchanges. And no mention of catching up with one another later.

The first course was a choice of either potted shrimps or chicken liver pâté. Charlie was absorbed in conversation with the person on his right, an Anglican bishop.

'How's business, Oswald?' Mark asked.

'Fine. How's Fleur?'

'Fleur and I are no longer a couple.'

'Oh. What a pity. But then . . . she is about to make something of a splash, I hear.'

'A splash?'

'That boutique of hers I keep reading about in the Sundays. It can't fail to be a success with so much run-up publicity. Though that was a foregone conclusion – Fleur knows simply everyone, doesn't she? Such a good idea to make use of it. She'd certainly have had *my* bank's ear if she'd needed any help in raising the capital.'

'Speaking of which, Oswald . . .'

'Is this course finished with, sir?'

'Yes, thank you.'

There was a menu in front of each place setting. 'Are you opting for the sole or for the turbot?' asked Oswald, then started talking to the judge on his left.

The fish was followed by roast wigeon, game pie or toad-in-the-hole. The meat was followed by angels or devils on horseback. The savoury was followed by treacle duff or banana custard.

'Don't you find it pleasing to see a plain old, honest-to-God, English banana?' said Oswald, turning back to Mark eventually.

'As opposed to what?' There was only so long one could feign interest in taxidermy, floral arrangements and skulls with antlers. After such a lengthy consignment to silence, Mark found it hard to keep his tone civil. He'd also failed to get a word in with Charlie. As soon as he was finished with the bishop, the Home Secretary had been called upon to debate immigration with a general seated opposite.

'Oh, star fruit, passion fruit, all that exotica,' replied Oswald.

Abruptly, Mark thought of the house in Lisle Street and its caches of sweet potatoes; which, now he came to consider it, he had never *seen* Clara or any of the other lodgers actually eating – though presumably someone must? Mark thought of that inexplicable tray of food with the banana skin on that he'd seen after the party. He was starting to get a nasty feeling in the pit of his stomach.

'Your Stilton, sir.'

'. . . come here, *to this country* . . .' said the general.

'I quite appreciate your concern,' replied the Home Secretary. '*Legal* immigrants, however, those who have a *right* to . . .'

Although she herself inclined to the simple, Fleur had always been interested in fabrics and the techniques involved in their production and embellishment. She'd flown to the Far East to watch the women weaving. In Africa and elsewhere, the batik method of dyeing material involved melting wax and using it to create designs such as those on the dress Clara wore to the British Museum. The wax was subsequently ironed out, which required use of an iron and an ironing-board. Mark thought of the weird, festive wall-hanging which Clara had put up for the party, with spatters so like those on the Lisle Street ironing-board, the location of which Geraldine Crowe had attempted to conceal from him. He thought of the noises coming from the roof level of the building.

'Pray rise for the loyal toast.'

Seven enormous pairs of knickers! Much too big for Clara, or any of the lodgers that Mark had actually *met*. Why hide somebody though?

'Coffee, brandy and Turkish Delight are served in the reception area, sirs, when you are ready to leave the table.'

Unsteadily, Mark stood. Automatically, his legs propelled him towards where a waiter was pouring the Cognacs. The large, batik-making, sweet potato and banana-eating individual was some kind of illegal immigrant. Harbouring an illegal alien, setting up in business with a proscribed person (it was now clear that Clara and this individual were in cahoots): now Mark was implicated in crimes he couldn't even think of names for. Who in charge of law and order would ever begin to believe that he hadn't known there was an unauthorized immigrant in the attic?

'Mark Upshaw, I am so sorry I haven't had a chance to talk to you sooner.'

Mark jumped. The Home Secretary was holding out his hand with a cordial expression on his face. In this man's gift were numerous, prestigious, well-recompensed positions. Whatever Mark had just realized, it was vital that he regain his composure. As he accepted the handshake, however, Mark became aware that he had lost Charlie's attention. The sound level of the room had diminished. Diplomats, jurists, bankers, educators, military men, politicians, clerics and industrialists were staring at him askance. There was a strong smell of dishwater, sweat, pipe tobacco and tea towels.

'Marky-boy! I knew you was going to be here.' Muncher Barrow clamped a damp arm around Mark's shoulders. ' 'Scuse me butting in,' he said loudly to the Home Secretary. 'The boss didn't want to let me out front, but I explained as how Marky and me are housemates down Lisle Street and he'd never forgive me if he heard I'd been washing up here and hadn't come and said hallo to him.' Muncher gave a hoarse laugh. 'You wouldn't now, Marky-boy, would yer?'

'No,' Mark replied, 'I wouldn't.'

There was no reason not to be friendly, since nothing worse could result. This was his social death-blow. All hope had vanished.

CHAPTER ELEVEN

The Wildest Risk Ever

Clara lay on the sofa propped up on two pillows and a giant scatter cushion. She'd changed into denim pedal-pushers and an army-surplus T-shirt. A lilac-and-white bandanna was wound around her head. The television was on with the sound down – someone had borrowed the coat-hanger aerial but Clara had managed to create a substitute by dismantling an old lampshade. She was sketching a ball-gown, monitoring the late-night news, drinking black coffee and having the odd spoonful of vanilla Häagen-Dazs from a pint tub. As the ice cream melted on her tongue, as she encountered its aromatic sweetness on her lips, Clara was aware that a similar sweetness had crashed in on her life.

The intimacy of the conversation in the wine bar had sent her reeling. Unaccustomed to being in any way transparent, she was floored by how wickedly well Mark Upshaw read her. Particularly in relation to himself. Mark realized Clara was dubious about him, yet he was confident enough to invite her to revise her opinion. He wanted them to know one another better. He saw that there was a part of Clara that found the idea seductive. He was convinced that if she let him in, she might well find plenty to like.

Clara put down the spoon and took a sip of coffee. After the ice cream it was an invigorating rush of bitterness. Could she really throw off her second nature, though? Much of her didn't want to muddy the waters any longer, but knowledge was currency. Trust was the wildest risk ever.

The ball-gown was full and puffy, like they should be if it wasn't the elegant sheath sort. It would be dyed vanilla and strawberry and pistachio. Pale spring colours: young sun, early blossom, new grass. Clara crammed another big spoonful of Häagen-Dazs into her mouth. With Mark safely tucked away elsewhere it was easy to seesaw between rational and rash. Once they were together again, however, she couldn't imagine finding it that easy to act in a calculated manner – not after what had passed between them this evening.

Clara felt suddenly exhausted. She shoved the remains of the ice cream in the fridge (where it would gradually melt but still be good on cereal), extinguished the telly and switched off lights. It was too hot to need a blanket, but she covered herself with a net curtain and was out for the count within seconds.

Some while later her eyes flew open. Her body seethed adrenalin. Every muscle was alert. There was an alien presence in Clara's building: her internal alarm system had registered it and torn her from deep sleep to utter wakefulness. She heard the sound of heavy footsteps, a large frame brush against a wall, steady itself, then proceed with a measured tread, up through the interior of Clara's house in the direction of the attic.

By the time Mark arrived back at Lisle Street he had only a hazy memory of leaving Rumbles. He could dimly recall introducing Muncher Barrow to the Home Secretary, knocking back a brandy followed by another; but then the picture jumped and he was sitting on a bench in Covent Garden, his tie undone, the night steamy and joyful around him.

Mark wasn't about to kid himself with alternative explanations. Clara Hood had entered his room for some reason. While there, she'd spotted the invitations on the shelf above the fireplace. That was how Muncher had known Mark would be at Rumbles. That was the reason for the embarrassing scene at the British Museum: Kim out of drag had stolen Mark's name and usurped his place on the guest list; the very audacity of the plot betrayed the identity of its perpetrator. Clara's underhandedness, her wanton disregard for Mark's privacy – his projects – was breathtaking. Small wonder he had failed to find a backer at the museum after such an inauspicious and humiliating beginning. And now . . . Confidence was the key; it was the watchword. If you could maintain the right people's confidence, nothing more was needed. If Muncher hadn't made his appearance Mark would most probably be due to see Charlie tomorrow morning, in order to discuss a range of possible appointments. Reveal that your fine feathers were a façade, however – let slip that you shared a house with a man who washed up for a living – and, quite understandably, no one was going to have any faith in you.

For this, responsibility lay at the door of Clara Hood. Clara Hood had wrecked Mark's chances. If he'd thought he was ruined before, he'd been mistaken. Ruin was when hope departed. You could make do with anything if you still had the hope that things might get better.

Was there a single drinking establishment in London not run by Australians? Mark sat at the bar. The place was alive with boisterous good humour, machismo and sex. Everyone was legless on slushy cocktails. A couple of girls tried to chat him up. Mark drank large whiskies, steadily, bitterly, but without losing control. He'd been beguiled by a woman; he had no intention of besotting himself on alcohol. A toothache emotion needed dulling, though.

Why stop at Muncher Barrow? Why not introduce Kim and the gurlz to the Home Secretary? Oh, and Geraldine Crowe in one of her frocks?

Beyond Covent Garden the crowds were less mellow and more jostling. They had their own momentum, swerving around tottering drunks and the limbs of bodies lying in doorways, flooding into the gaps between cherry-red brake lights, draining down the chasms of the Underground.

Mark let himself be carried along Shaftesbury Avenue to Piccadilly Circus which, as ever, was packed and disconsolate. Accordions of neon expanded and contracted. A stall hiked British gewgaws. There was a smell of mince-sodden fat from a burger restaurant. A late-night chemist was doing a brisk trade in reinforced condoms. Hundreds of tourists consulted guides and stared at Eros disbelievingly, filling Mark with a sudden, urgent desire to escape the sight of their disappointed faces. He plunged into the subway. Nothing was going to drag him back to Lisle Street. He'd head up to Soho Square and sit with the addicts, admiring the pseudo-Tudor cottage; he could brave the gamut of beggars at the nearby cashpoint and ascertain the state of his balance.

The subway twirled Mark three times around its disorientating hoop before depositing him near the narrow entrance to Glasshouse Street, where he promptly became clogged in the congestion. Elsewhere, the centrifuge of the Circus was hurtling humanity onwards. Here, the pavement was thronged with men; pausing, sizing up, negotiating deals. Mark's mood plummeted yet further. He attempted to retreat but was hemmed in on all sides. This was the Meat Rack, the rent-boy Stock Exchange. Leaning against the metal railings put there to stop pedestrians crossing the road at the wrong places were a dozen or so weary and bored-looking male prostitutes; exploiting the fair weather and rendering it virtually impossible for Mark to make any progress until all those in front of him had assessed the wares. The smell of aftershave was overpowering.

Very gradually, by dint of strength and politeness, Mark managed to elbow his way out of the thick of things. The effort brought on a compelling need for more large whiskies. A drink outside pub hours would mean a club entry fee. It was ironic luck that he'd withdrawn what was probably the last significant sum available from his bank account, in anticipation of going on somewhere after the restaurant. Mark paused, glanced back at the Circus, trying to decide his best direction.

Good God!

But then, of *course.*

Si's young face was caught in the amber of a traffic light; his dark hair gleamed in the cold illumination from the chemist's window. He didn't notice Mark looking at him.

In Riddle's Nightclub various women in clinging things and crusty gold bracelets attempted to get Mark on to the dance-floor, which was a maelstrom of smoke, lasers and jiving bodies. The whiskies came with straws, and paper coasters which stuck to the bottoms of the glasses.

Outside again some time later, the crowds were starting to thin. The dinner-jacketed bouncers yawned as they said good-night to him. There was a hush on the streets that seemed, not a peaceable lull, but the dumbstruck after-image of commotion. London had pulled back a century while Mark was topping up his alcohol level. He passed gold-and-crimson emporia with large gilded windows, through which were visible the bulky, lifeless forms of turned-off slot machines. Squat peep-shows huddled together down shadowy alleys. In a barber's shop, empty chairs stared into empty mirrors. There were still cramped and narrow places. Sometimes Mark felt as if walls would simply merge and entomb him. A dog woke and went berserk in a yard containing nothing imaginably worth protecting. In these back streets the dirt was old-fashioned. Grime, rags and rotting food rather than the creations of petrochemicals. There was a pawn-shop, three gold spheres hanging from a sign above a polished frontage.

Mark looked in. Here was the debris of sinking situations such as his; the detritus of lives going down below the horizon. Some of the objects were obviously family heirlooms, dropped from the generational relay-race of material possessions: an enormous Chinese vase, a Victorian clock, carved walking-sticks. Others appeared to be the small spoils of death: hearing-aids, a false leg, paste-and-glass brooches. Back shelves held cardboard boxes and packing material, more vases, a pair of riding-boots, some suitcases.

Mark recoiled.

The surge of anger was sudden and immediate but there was nothing hot about it. This rage was a burning, dry-ice glaciation, which froze dead in its tracks any trace of forgiveness that might still have clung to Mark's thoughts of Clara. Freely, Mark had rendered what assistance he could to the woman. First from a sense of obligation, latterly from a genuine desire for her friendship. Apparently this had meant nothing to Clara Hood, except that Mark Upshaw was a fool whose aid could be accepted even as she was occupied in pawning his belongings – presumably in order to set herself up in business.

Business. Yes, that was what it was about, wasn't it? Raw commerce, where emotions meant nothing unless they could be used as manipulable commodities; where all that mattered was striking the best deals.

And Mark had the wherewithal to do that, hadn't he?

An idea was beginning to crystallize.

The house in Lisle Street was dark. Mark didn't put any lights on, though nothing short of physical violence would prevent him from entering the attic. Climbing the stairs with little visibility, however, accentuated his underlying drunkenness. At one point he had to steady himself. He continued more carefully on up to the second, then the third floor. He was just reaching out a hand to open the door to the attic staircase when he was pounced on from behind and locked in a powerful half nelson.

The familiar smell of his body. The tension of the muscles. He knew better than to struggle but was poised – she could feel it – for a technical response. Like herself, he'd been trained in the movements. She could feel him making adjustments, assessing the strength of the opposition, marrying flesh to flesh in readiness for a sudden show of force, which she wouldn't be strong enough to withstand. If it had been a stranger, Clara would have taken countermeasures by now, while she still had the benefit of surprise. But it was Mark; she had known that as soon as they touched. However could she have imagined it was anyone else? She could feel the contours of his frame moving against her own, as they matched one another, breath for breath. Here was sweet familiarity, coupled with an animal newness. They were Mark and Clara, but they were also bodies in the dark. She felt the precise moment when he knew who she was. His muscles slowly untensed.

'There's no point trying to stop me going into the attic, Clara,' Mark said. 'I'm wise to what's happening now, and I'm willing to act upon it unless you and I can come to a bargain.'

There was a stunned silence. For an instant Clara's brain wouldn't register what she had heard, then she completely lost her grip on him and staggered a couple of steps backward before she was able to right herself.

Mark turned. 'So let's go down to the kitchen, open a bottle of something and do a bit of negotiating.'

His voice was thick with alcohol but controlled and steady. Clara recognized its coiled anger. Adrenalin stampeded across her torso. Was there nobody else in the building? Where was Muncher?

'There's only rum,' she said, in a voice as level as Mark's own; desiccated of feeling, all trace of a tremor wrung out of it, quite dry of tears also.

'Rum will do just fine.'

In the kitchen Clara poured Mark a glass from the half-bottle she'd bought to have with the pineapple juice, endeavouring to keep her hands from shaking. She sat opposite him, dizzy with disappointment and self-reproach. She should never have let her guard down. It was a wretchedly culpable error of judgment. She knew so much better than to indulge in trust. She shouldn't have needed any reminders. The best she could do now was be brazen, ascertain exactly how much the man had sussed and try to limit its usefulness to him. Surely, surely, it wouldn't include the presence of Bethany Smile. Clara could provide herself as a decoy. There was more to this situation than her own smashed emotions.

Mark didn't speak. He was waiting for her to take the initiative.

'I don't know what you mean about something going on,' Clara said eventually.

Mark glanced across the table at her. His eyes returned to his glass. 'Please don't take me for a fool, Clara,' he murmured. 'You know exactly what I'm talking about, so you might as well save time and admit it.'

'You'll have to be more specific.'

'Well . . .' Mark raised his hands and started to tick points off on his fingers with exaggerated gestures. 'You've been in my room for starters . . .'

'I was airing it.'

'Were you also airing the British Museum?'

There was a pause.

Clara said, 'Is that all?'

'No, I don't think so, but let me see . . . Ah, yes. There's the drugs on the premises, the shoplifting from Hodge's, and of course the illegal subletting – I had the honour of meeting your landlord.'

'I hope you noted that he's a squalid bastard.'

'That *was* my impression. But here I think one of us is rather more in a position to cast stones than the other. I am referring to the little matter of the appropriation of my suitcases, which came to my attention this evening, while browsing in a pawnshop window.'

'I'd have redeemed them.'

'That was after I spotted Si in Piccadilly. Taking rent from that boy amounts to living off the immoral earnings of a minor –

though I suspect the moral side of things doesn't greatly concern you.'

'So I should save my soul by sending him back on to the streets, is that what you're saying?'

'The child is a prostitute, for God's sake.'

'Who every night returns somewhere where they'd notice if he didn't.'

'Consigned to the tender care of a clip-joint transvestite, who exercises her calling under the auspices of a corrupt police force. Which, I can nevertheless see, *does* have its advantages when it comes to the storage of stolen goods, transported in a van that's presumably borrowed without permission.'

There was a silence.

Mark said, 'And then there's the illegal immigrant in the attic.'

Clara froze. There was a fist in her throat, a tightly bunched clump of emotion. 'You know about Bethany?' she whispered.

Mark's jaw dropped. 'Tell me you aren't referring to Bethany *Smile*,' he gasped, 'Tell me *this* Bethany isn't the Calaluan dissident I've read about in the newspapers.' Then, after a wry pause, 'But on reflection, why would we be hiding just any old illegal immigrant when we could have a notorious political extremist who's wanted on two continents? No run-of-the-mill, the-grass-is-greener immigrant for us. We get Bethany Smile, who questions are asked about in the Houses of Parliament.'

'And you're implicated.' Clara's voice wouldn't do what she wanted. This was her final trump, yet somehow she knew it wasn't going to swing things.

Sure enough, Mark nodded. Her last-ditch tack had been anticipated. She was cornered. There'd be no escaping whatever bargain it was he had in mind.

'True. Unfortunately, though, I frankly don't give a damn. You see, Clara, I'm a man who's lost everything he ever possessed. I had plans to remedy that but they didn't work out. As I said earlier, I'm not afraid to act. We can go down together or we can come to an agreement.'

A padlock thonked shut in Clara's head. It was several minutes before she was able to speak. 'So you're threatening to turn in Bethany Smile unless I comply with your wishes?' Her eyes met Mark's. He was handsome still. Unwavering, she held his gaze. Let him see how much she despised him.

Mark looked down at the table. 'Put it this way. If you consent to making me a partner in the business you're apparently setting up – which can serve as a minute recompense for my failed projects – I will divulge nothing about this household to anyone. I won't aid or abet the concealment of the immigrant, but I will keep it a secret.'

'I have your word on this?' In a voice crackling with sarcasm. Your word as a straight, law-abiding, heterosexual gentleman, hurling judgments left, right and centre, and striking unwelcome deals.

'I think that might be better than putting anything down on paper.'

Clara rose to her feet. Muncher's eggcup sometimes doubled as a shot-glass. She fished it out of the washing-up water, gave it a rinse and a wipe, poured herself a thimble of rum and Mark a refill.

'I've heard your stipulations. You can hear mine now.' She would cut her losses by every means possible, salvage what she could from the horrible set-up.

'You aren't in a position to make any.'

'But I intend to. One only – and you needn't worry, it's in your own interests.' Clara knocked back her drink. It burnt. She watched to see how Mark would respond.

Mark downed some of his rum also. He shrugged. 'I'm listening.'

'If we're going to be partners I want a proper investment from you.'

Mark raised his eyebrows. 'I'd just sort of assumed the cash from my suitcases already made me a major stakeholder in your enterprise. Besides which, I'm broke and no one will give me any money.'

'People don't. But I'm not talking dosh, I'm talking work.'

There was a pause.

'That makes sense. Looks like we're in agreement.' Mark made to reach a hand out.

Clara said, 'Bethany's involved in the business too. You'd better come and meet her. First, though, we'll discuss what you can start by doing.'

Emotionally, Mark had ransacked her hopes, but that little episode was slammed up for good and all. If there was no avoiding a professional involvement, however, Clara would have her revenge by putting Mark through the mangle. Hard labour. Mark Upshaw would learn to wish he'd never tangled with Clara Hood.

CHAPTER TWELVE

Precious Little

'Rise and shine. This is the night shift knocking off. I've been told *all*, and you're due downstairs in twenty minutes. Here's some tea, though Clara said not to bother.' Kim crashed the mug on to the bedside table and clattered out of the room, slamming the door behind her.

It was a clean hangover. No frayed edges. Rather, a preternatural brightness to everything, as if someone had driven a shiny metal stake through his head. Mark rolled over. The ache in his arms and back carried echoes of the aftermath of school Officer Training Corps exercises. The carriage clock said eight o'clock.

Mark pulled himself into a sitting position, reached for the mug and took a swallow. In the gap between the curtains was a lot of early morning sunlight. He'd slept perhaps as much as three hours, and that evidently would have to do. He was absolutely determined to stand by what he'd undertaken and perform the task Clara had set him – albeit without mentioning that it needed to start at this time of day. Old, tried and tested survival tactics could be called upon. He would dowse his body in icy water, vigorously towel it dry, have a close shave, then show up, damp and tingling and punctual, just as when he used to make it to a tutorial after a night on the town. Just as when he and his companions were able merely to laugh at the ghostly images of the night's behaviour.

Uneasy recollections of the previous evening slithered into Mark's brain. Replaying those shifting moods, powerful emotions and unaccustomedly sardonic turns of phrase made him feel like a stranger to himself. It was virtually impossible to synthesize the Mark Upshaw he'd known hitherto with the cool and meticulous deal-maker he had temporarily become. Drink and despair, and maybe other things besides, had somehow rendered natural a more lax ethical system. Which was possibly why – at this tilting moment, as what he had done and said came unsympathetically back – Mark's nice cluster of damning information flatly refused to gazelle him to the moral high ground. He was dumped instead with the questionable justifications of a man on the desperate lookout for something to give existence purpose. A hasty withdrawal, of course, would extricate him from this muddied realm, and maybe quench the blowtorch of Clara's undoubted scorn; but Mark was all out of choices. No alternative except to prove himself by doing as he was bid, and accompany Muncher on the quest to pick up dress rails from some unspecified urban location.

Mark took another grateful gulp of tea. He was at a loss to assess the extent to which he was forgivable. Lifted stones were supposed to have unpleasant, slimy things beneath them: surely it wasn't unreasonable to operate from that assumption? Was it his mistake if they were mottled with lichen and sheltered budding flowers?

When, at some hazy point in the small hours, Mark and Clara had mounted the attic stairs in order for Mark to make the acquaintance of Bethany Smile, the picture he'd had in his mind – television news notwithstanding – was of a scrawny, machine-gunned guerrilla in the bloody pursuit of supremacy for her own particular faction. But Bethany Smile had turned out to be a cumulonimbus of a woman, quite up to whatever tonnage of knicker anyone might present her with. Her brown skin glistered with a blue, mother-of-pearl sheen. She was listening to the World Service and dunking material into a bucket of indigo with an old broom-handle.

Not at all what he had expected. Mark had stared, dumbfounded, at the hints of leisurely dawns and unhurried twilights that permeated Bethany's lovely batiks, glimpsing as he did so, out of the corner of his eye, the treacherous, dotted ironing-board. He had listened in stunned silence while Bethany told him that on Calalu Island good things were always imminently expected. However improbable it might seem now, one day the regime that had taken affront at Bethany's calypsos would be ousted, and she would be able to return to her vegetable plot, her jerk pork and her palm trees. Until then, Clara Hood was harbouring and protecting her. Should the authorities ever knock on the door, Clara would set up a pretend fire alarm.

How could he ever have imagined that all his threats would lead to such a gentle encounter?

Now, in the unyielding morning light, Mark blinked in an endeavour to erase the memory. His eyes, he discovered, were surrounded by barbed wire; he'd finished his tea and was still thirsty. He threw back the bedcovers and hauled his feet onto the floor, but the change of focus only served to usher in more contentious subject matter. Hanging from the wardrobe, as neatly as if Mark had placed them there stone-cold sober, were his dinner jacket, trousers, shirt and bow tie: flat and empty.

Given the right circumstances, his friends would have delivered, a sullen voice inside him insisted.

He saw them, piling out of shiny taxicabs – legs and heels and cuff links and watches. A tap turned on somewhere in the building sent the plumbing into its customary spasms. A faint soya-sauce scent hung on the air. The traffic sounds were purposeful; different from the pleasure-seeking squeals of the cocktail hour.

Never, another voice countered. They were people who stopped at the point where things ceased to be easy, and that was where Mark lived now.

Inconceivable, to imagine Fleur kitting out an attic: upending doors and making them into tables; gathering together impromptu tools; amassing chairs and buckets; cleaning up ugly old sewing-machines – doubtless constructed for the services of nylon – and hurling silver paths across swathes of silk. The floor of Bethany's workshop had glittered with pins. Newspaper patterns and sketches with jottings on were scattered everywhere. Newly dyed fabric dripped on a washing-line. On a calor gas ring, a resinous pot of honey-coloured wax bubbled above a lavender flame. Dresses hung all about, in various stages of completion. As the great big world murmured on the radio, Mark had registered rows of tiny, beadlike buttons and tumbling layers of ground-brushing skirts.

Clara hadn't just set her project in motion, she was making it happen with rudimentary implements and unmatching table legs, an unwieldy assemblage of the rejected and unwanted. A saucepan-lid cacophony of feelings had clanged in Mark's head. For an instant he'd imagined Bethany must hear it also and would shortly put the escape plan she'd had described into action, fleeing away from an imaginary wall of flame. There was something almost unbearable about such inventiveness. Nobody else dealt with life for Clara, Mark realized. There weren't any assistants to field and filter. The other members of the household must require a mighty effort to prevent them from becoming liabilities, and even then they were unstoppable sometimes.

The recollection of these thoughts raised Mark to his feet. As he dressed he wondered whether his sudden inclusion in Clara's business would provoke any response from those involved in it from the outset. Kim didn't seem ill disposed, Bethany wasn't. Muncher must be okay about this trip they were doing together. Si and Geraldine? Ultimately they'd all troop behind Clara, because she was their best hope of not getting lost. Pride prevented Mark from making an obvious comparison, but he was glad that his sodden brain had instinctively carried through sleep the knowledge that self-respect alone demanded he should be useful. If he could genuinely contribute by running errands,

Mark would do that, however irksome. Clara didn't need and certainly didn't want him at any kind of organizational level.

Mark had anticipated confusion, but there too he'd been mistaken. The attic's frenzy of activity was nevertheless methodical. Tacked to the walls were time plans and schedules, lists detailing the order that things should be done in. All leading up to one fixed date, one focal occasion.

THE GRAND LAUNCH: Clara was vague, and Mark wasn't in any state to shuffle notions as to what she might imagine grandeur and launching entailed. Press and flowers and PR, lavish amounts of wine and things encased in filo, in Mark's experience. But there wasn't the money to buy anything like that. This morning, with his head clearer, Mark decided a grand launch could be simple hyperbole: the day the first strategically placed small ads were due to appear, perhaps. Or maybe Clara had arranged to suborn the upstairs of the White Bear, serve sausages on sticks and sell a few dresses.

Whatever Clara had planned, Mark would assist her. Because of the terrible, poignant way she could magic up possibilities and make success look coercible. Because she despised him now, and the thought of that was intolerable.

If Mark Upshaw thought he was just in for a quick hop in the Christian minibus to some chichi shop-fitter's, then he could prepare to be disillusioned. To Muncher the Dump was a sort of Mecca; a trip there a treat that wasn't to be rushed through. As soon as Clara had got the squeak about the arrival of five dress rails as specified, Muncher had arranged to borrow his van off Len Semerraro. Not a salubrious motor – sliding door held shut with electric cable, polythene side window, cauliflower bumper – but available at a stretch for an understanding. Diversity of vehicle in and of itself had much to be said for it, and this way Muncher didn't have to feel hurried. Mark Upshaw's participation, of course, was totally unnecessary – the blokes from the

Dump were always on hand to do loading, and Muncher was hardly going to get lost South of the River – but an outing like this would give Mark a good dose of what he'd got into.

While Mark was asleep Clara had briefed an incoming Kim about the new business set-up, woken Muncher and briefed him also, washed her hair, bathed and put clean clothes on. There seemed a need for formality. She wore a short-sleeved brown cotton top and a not very full cream cotton skirt; over them, though, a green plastic apron with yellow daisies because she was frying. The fine weather had meant a lucrative stint for Si; he'd arrived home only a short while earlier and Clara had felt like fixing him something. Italian sausage and fried bread sizzled in the pan; they made the same kind of noise as was going on in Clara's head. There seemed a need for formality, like when people regretted the night before over breakfast: the laying on of *pleases* and *after yous,* until all else except the sad truth and the knowledge that there were rings under your eyes was eradicated.

This would be Mark's tack too, Clara guessed, unless he was planning on putting his stuff in carriers and making an exit. Would the gods be kind enough to chuck Clara such good fortune? She cracked two eggs into the fiercely bubbling fat and glanced at the clock that was out by five minutes. Si was reading an old *Funday Times* and drinking strawberry Nesquik. Clara plated up and lowered the food behind the newspaper. 'Wicked!' Si grabbed a fork and started eating. If Mark had meant what he said, he'd be appearing shortly.

Sometimes Clara wished she wasn't so perceptive, so in tune with the bruised world and each mouse under her floorboards. Mark Upshaw had made it abundantly clear he possessed no sympathy either for who Clara was or for what she was at. He'd demanded enough already, without his motivations claiming her curiosity too. Ask Clara to predict Mark's reactions to his initial shufti at the dressmaking project and, judging by his conduct since figuring the full picture, she'd have bet her bottom dollar on disdain and condescension. It had been startling to realize he was impressed, bothered – moved even.

Thrown again. Tumbling through explanations. Trying to see things Mark's way, though why should she want to? Clara had shone a torch around her cobbled-together operation and found precious little to be overwhelmed by. Only square pegs forced into round holes by dint of serious hammering. Only a jigsaw with a great many pieces missing. Here and there the odd honest-to-goodness nugget – Bethany's artistry; that top-notch material – but beyond those just the whole grinding palaver of making do.

Clara extinguished the gas with a loud pop, plonked the pan in the sink and snaked it with Fairy. She whisked off her apron and hung it on a cupboard door. So what if Mark Upshaw had been touched for some reason? Flashes of all-rightness were treacherously misleading – the kindergarten of hard knocks had taught her that. Distance alone kept you safe from damage. Cool, grey distance, and plenty of it. Outlying places, where when they came looking they'd always just miss you – not so much as another glimpse ever. Marginal set-ups, where although you were needed, no other mortal being was vital to your survival.

' 'Lo, Maz.'

'Good morning, Si.'

Mark Upshaw was paler than usual. His eyes were slightly bloodshot. His hair was newly washed and he smelled of soap. It was twenty minutes exactly since Clara had sent Kim to wake him. As Clara turned back from the clock she saw Mark's hand fall to his side, as if he'd ruffled Si's hair or patted the boy's shoulder.

'Muncher isn't down yet and the van hasn't arrived.' Clara waited for complaints.

'That doesn't matter. Is there any tea going?'

'If you make some.'

Mark nodded. 'I'll do that. Would you like one?'

'No thank you.'

'Si?'

'Got a Nesquik.'

There was a sound like ack-ack coming from the Charing Cross Road direction and getting nearer. Muncher appeared in the kitchen in his summer-day-out garb, pipe billowing. 'That there'll be Len. He said the auto's timing's a bit wafty.'

Clara looked at Mark Upshaw, who was looking out of the window. Lisle Street was filling up with exhaust fumes. There would be black smoke too. And generously aftershaved Len Semerraro, puffing away at a roll-up squeezed tight between thumb and forefinger, surrounded by swinging dices, dangling rosaries and a stick-on pic of St Christopher, patron saint of brake linings.

'I'm ready when you are,' said Mark to Muncher.

The city looked as if it were made of metal, its outlines sharp against a hot grey sky. Behind a heavy black grid of railway bridge, trains slowly glided or idled at signals. The van crawled along in a traffic jam with no discernible conclusion; countless commuters, *en route* to airless offices.

Whenever Mark's door lurched against the knot in the cable there was a giddy view of tarmac. The fact it was to all intents and purposes windowless did nothing to remove the stomach-turning stench of mingled toxins. Where exactly they were going remained an unknown. Even had Mark felt up to asking for details, talk was out of the question above the noise of the engine; though from the movement of Muncher's lips Mark could see that he was whistling.

At weary length the river receded. The queue of cars elongated into stop-and-start bursts of movement and braking. Mark watched the people waiting for buses in front of high-rises with basketball courts surrounded by bulging wire fences. A community centre. A crèche. A benefit office and a small drop-in charity with coloured posters in its window. Sandwich shops, flower stalls, newsagents advertising lottery tickets.

They ducked under a series of grubby flyovers; bounced along a fast bit daubed with kamikaze graffiti; stood stuck for a quarter-hour at a seven-pronged roundabout, gazing out on a football stadium, a cluster of radio masts, an abacus of power station, and a long flat playing field terminating in an area of scrub. Muncher swung off a run of main road and Mark got an eyeful of crucifix. They stopped outside a bookmaker's on a short parade that also boasted an understocked greengrocer's, a pet supplies shop and a closed Indian takeaway that did fish and chips as well.

'Won't be a mo. Quick flutter.'

For forty-five minutes or thereabouts Mark contemplated the china cart-horses and Siamese cats in the windows of the bungalows that bounded the shops. The bungalows stretched to the horizon in either direction, protected from the traffic by crash barriers.

'Here,' said Muncher, emerging eventually. He handed Mark a very full polystyrene cup, jammed the key into the ignition, and they were off with a bang and a jump that deposited a third of the tea on to Mark's lap. Fortunately it was not hot, being so extremely milky.

One of the furry orange dice managed to catch Mark's other eye when they took a second apparent detour, through an industrial estate, halting in the carpark of a murky café opposite a large computer warehouse. 'Back in a sec,' said Muncher; this time indeed emerging speedily, with a bulging carrier which he handed to Mark before pulling off smartly. The bag was full of pipe tobacco. 'Cut-price. Geezer owns the caff gets it in from the Continent,' Muncher explained during a diminution of the sound level when they stalled at an intersection.

Depots. Factories. Warehouses. Works. They chugged down a dusty road round the back of a sewage treatment plant, screened from view by a wall of brambles and strange purple weeds. The vista spontaneously opened to a wide and far-reaching panorama. The clamour of the engine ceased and was replaced by a windswept silence.

'Good God!' exclaimed Mark. Acre upon acre of rubbish, detritus. Scattered across it – solitary or in groups – men, women and children scavenging.

'Amazing, innit?' said Muncher.

'I can hardly believe this is happening in England.'

'Well, folk have got better at enjoying themselves, I reckon. You think it looks like fun now, you should see it at Christmas – everybody wrapped up warm and choosing presents; all the kiddies. There's usually a fire going in an old oil-drum, and a bottle of gin doing the rounds. Often there's even a chestnut fella. That bloke's always here.' Indicating a grimy catering van. 'We'll have some nosh once I've looked about a bit. Meantime, p'raps you could go and chase up Clara's order. Them in there'll know where to find it.' Muncher pointed in the direction of a big corrugated-iron building. 'Tell them I'll settle for the lot after I've had my rummage.'

On the building's forecourt a row of rusty ovens were being loaded on to the back of a lorry and secured with ropes. Across the Dump the waste gleamed in the sunlight: bin-liner blacks, recording-tape browns; a dazzling flash of silver from a gleaner's broken shopping-trolley, the irregular Morse of smashed glass.

Stunned by this unimagined fringe of commerce, Mark located the dress rails and put them on board. Their casters skipped on the uneven ground, sending out sprays of loose gravel and pebbles. The muscles in Mark's arms and back were stiffer than when he'd just woken.

'Whatchyer think?' said Muncher, reappearing. 'I'd never be forgiven if I didn't scout a gift or two. This here's for Si.' A torn Spiderman T-shirt. 'Geraldine's partial to her volumes.' A slightly singed book entitled *How to Get the Most out of Your Houseplants*. 'Kim.' A pair of blue sunglasses. 'And Clara.' A long skirt, perhaps South American, frayed at the hemline, its decorative embroidery worn and snarled. 'Now then,' Muncher continued. 'What'll you have?'

'Have?'

'On me. There's burgers and dogs, sarnies if you like 'em, and we'll ask about the Lunchtime Specials.'

The Lunchtime Specials were Spam fritters and beans or meat pie and beans. Mark didn't know whether he was hungry or not, but he ordered the Spam fritters because he sensed Muncher would be disappointed if he opted for anything lighter. The tea came in enormous china mugs. The men carried their drinks over to a stained plastic table and sat down to await the food.

As he lowered himself into his chair, Mark gave an involuntary groan.

'Pulled something carrying?' asked Muncher.

'I don't think so.' Mark hesitated. There was no reason not to be frank. Presumably Muncher knew the story anyway. 'Actually, it was Clara. Last night she caught me in a half nelson.'

'Yeah.' Muncher chuckled. 'I taught her how to do that. I taught her all I know about fighting – including fisticuffs.'

There was a pause while the Spam arrived and they started eating.

'You were a boxer?' asked Mark after a while.

'Welterweight. Later, a sponge-man. Saw 'em all. Knew most of 'em. Watched Turpin beat Sugar Ray in '51 – just a nipper then, but I managed to wangle a ticket. 'Course, the greatest of the lot was Our Henry. Never really beaten, whatever anybody said at the time. Not by Bugner in '71. Not by Clay when they stopped it in the fifth.

'Yeah,' Muncher went on reflectively, 'Clara needed to know how to defend herself with that violent husband of hers.'

A silence.

Mark said, 'Clara had a violent marriage?'

Muncher glanced at him. 'Don't like the thought of that, do you?'

'But . . . I mean, why . . . ?'

'. . . didn't I do more to sort it?' Muncher sighed. 'I was on the road a lot, hadn't got a place of my own, strapped for cash. Followed the Game and lived out of bed and breakfasts. She was sixteen and always full of hope, and the boy came from a background you didn't tangle with – though that's not to say I shouldn't have.'

'But her parents?'

'Oh, Clara's dad was gone years back. My sister, her mother, was one of those women as is born exhausted. When the girl did run there was nowhere much to run to. For a spell – while the law was dawdling with its restraints and divorce doodahs – she had to put in a big vanish.'

'Where was she?'

Muncher shook his head. 'Lots of places probably.'

'Then?'

'Lisle Street.' Muncher returned to his fritters.

A gust of breeze twirled tornadoes of grit, sent napkins flying. The rubbish tugged at its moorings. Crumpled newspaper cartwheeled across the ground; flat sheets of it heaved and floundered.

Mark couldn't move. Couldn't eat any more. Couldn't swallow. All he could do was feel.

He grabbed him by the throat, that long-ago boy. He got him up against a wall, trembling and sweating. He scared the shit out of him, the bastard. Swore that if ever again he so much as even . . .

The breeze subsided. Things fluttered and fell.

Mark's rage came to a gasping standstill. He blinked, dizzy for an instant. Then memory rushed him headlong. Fury gave way to shame – every bit as crimson and engulfing. He saw himself as he had been last night: a big man, drunk and full of threats. A big drunk man, looking for someone to blame for his puny acquaintances – the repressed awareness that his friends' lack of help was a foregone conclusion.

It must have struck echoes.

'Those beans going begging?' asked Muncher.

Mark barely managed a nod. All the stuffing was knocked out of him. As he watched the funny old ex-boxer swapping their plates around, the poignant logic of Clara's band of waifs and outlaws started to become bruisingly apparent. That brutal and scanty past had turned her into a champion of the vulnerable, compelled to sniff out need and answer it. There'd been a dog. Perhaps migratory flocks did indeed touch down twice yearly, to revive on crisps and bacon rinds on the Lisle Street windowsills. An old man, a transvestite, a rent boy, an illegal immigrant, a . . . Geraldine Crowe: Clara had evidently not forgotten what it was to be exposed. She'd maintained a cordon of wariness. She had no choice but to take people in, to create a human shield made of pooled human resources; herself the strength at the centre, the intelligence. And yet, Mark hazarded, in a way perhaps the most vulnerable of all of them.

CHAPTER THIRTEEN

How to Conquer your Fear of Fear

Hemming. Buttonholes. Buttons.

Clara needed coat hangers, lots of them. She needed a clean area without any danger from wet things. French Food & Wine let her have a big coil of wire cheap, from out the back, because it had been there for ever and was dusty and covered in fossil spiders. Clara left it on the kitchen table, came downstairs late from a final ironing session and found Mark Upshaw and Si, sat on the sitting-room carpet making up the hangers; Mark showing Si how to.

'I thought you were clearing a space for the dress rails?' Clara spoke before the order hit her. Sofa cleared of mags and papers, bedding folded. Pillows, cushions and clothing piled concisely, freeing more floor space than you'd ever have guessed lurked under there. The cleaned-up dress rails, ready and waiting.

'You're right, I was, but I finished.' Mark spoke mildly, looking up at her. He had taken to sitting on the floor a lot lately; he'd also started going barefoot and wearing looser T-shirts. His voice seemed quieter.

For two days after that Clara assessed and adjusted in the attic, drinking dreg-made coffee hotted on Bethany's burner, and eating only mini choc bars from a bumper pack (cut-price owing to the holly and snowflakes). There was now no reason for Bethany to restrict herself to this single area of the building, but having got it so comfy she felt little inclination to wander. The kerfuffle and interruptions that usually interspersed any of Clara's attempts to get on with things for once did not happen. In the surprising, unhysterical calm, she and Bethany made speedy progress and wallowed in the gorgeousness of what they'd achieved to date.

Day wear. Skirts and dresses: russets, prunes, plums and apricots. Soft, scoop-necked blouses in grassy emerald, cobalt, chestnut. Easy jackets: old-fashioned rouge, violet, almond. Strolling down Bond Street with your head full of Sotheby's.

Evening. Plunges of garnet. Slivers of oyster. Cascades of salmon.

Clara was starving and hadn't shopped since the mini chocs. The fridge would be a vacuum, Geraldine hyper-anaemic, Si subsisting on stale doughnuts, and Muncher spending all his mazuma on salt-beef sarnies at Cohen's. There was also the question of whether plastic tarps would hold together with Sello, well enough to make the gowns' protective covers. Pierced bin-bags would have been easier, but they'd immediately attract attention. Oh, for the run of a high-class launderette!

The kitchen door was closed. There was even, it turned out, a rolled sheet along the bottom of it. Haddock! Clara slammed the door shut behind her and kicked the insulating sheet back into place, resealing the fish smell away from the clothing collection.

'Kedjerry,' said Muncher. 'We had a whip-round.'

'Rice I can tolerate,' declared Geraldine, 'but pasta gives me nightmares.'

'Y'know what, Clara?' said Si. 'If you put this powder in, it goes yellow.'

'Should there not be any saved for me' – Kim's tight turquoise knee-length indicated that she was off to Gurlz – 'you may kiss good-bye to any future drop-scones.'

'You must be hungry,' said Mark Upshaw. 'I was going to call you as soon as it was ready.' He broke off from chopping a bunch of coriander to check the simmering haddock and monitor Si's egg-slicing. There was a pint mug of not-quite-dead flowers on the table, and a jar of mango chutney.

'No,' said Clara. It came out rushed and loud, less a reply than an exclamation. Had the others noticed? 'Anyway, the dress covers . . .'

'Done 'em,' said Si. 'Me and Maz.'

'Thanks,' said Clara. She made a quick exit, paused and listened to make sure someone pushed the sheet back behind her. They did.

When she descended again some hours later, the kitchen was tidy and deserted except for Muncher, who was drinking a tot of whisky and struggling over the racing pages. Clara looked in the refrigerator. There were two plates of kedgeree covered with clingfilm. She closed it.

'He's a good bloke, luv.' Muncher put down his stub of a pencil. 'Don't be too hard on him.'

'You heard about how he threatened to shop Bethany.' Clara grabbed a bread knife and started to saw at the heel of a loaf on the chopping-board.

'Each of us says things we don't mean after having a few. Not a peep along those lines all day at the Dump. Nor ever since neither, if I'm correct?'

In silence but vehemently, Clara spread butter and marmalade. She left Muncher's question lying where he'd dropped it.

'Strong, our Maz,' Muncher continued, untroubled. 'And I don't just mean physical. He reminds me of those lads you knew from the start was winners. Not just in the biceps, but up here too' – Muncher tapped the side of his head – 'where it counts just as much almost.'

Clara plonked herself down at the table. 'You reckon?' She took an uninterested mouthful, and a sip from Muncher's glass.

'I reckon. It's a complex matter, this business of what makes a fella stand out from his contemporaries. Mostly it's an attitude.'

'What sort?'

Muncher considered this for perhaps five minutes. Clara

watched him, seeing his mind's eye run down the years making comparisons. Probably Mark Upshaw would get lost in all of this, and she'd fetch up with Sugar Ray or Henry.

But, 'I'm not saying the bloke is without his issues,' said Muncher eventually.

'Hardly!'

'But he looks a man to choose the right direction.' Muncher picked up his pencil. 'And he's a gentleman,' he added, returning to his horses.

Clara finished her slice without speaking, made a nest on the sitting-room sofa, switched her senses on to stand-by and fell asleep with – as ever – half an ear open. She woke, semi-tuned-in to a conversation between Mark and Muncher, going on in the kitchen.

'. . . surely worn out?'

'Yeah, but Clara doesn't function in any regular pattern such as you'd notice. Two, three hours and she's up again. Always has been unpredictable in her habits.'

Not true, though Clara smiled: Muncher worked on keeping things simple. After this many years a jerky lifestyle was indeed second nature to her – patterns such as anyone would notice were far from desirable – but it hadn't been that way from the beginning.

'Nevertheless, we should probably keep our voices down.'

'Yeah,' said Muncher, who had a megaphone in place of a larynx.

There was a pause; Muncher presumably thinking that a moment of quiet would dilute the volume of his subsequent utterances.

Mark said softly, 'So I suppose it didn't occur to her that I might be tired the day we went to the Dump.'

Muncher gave a bellow of laughter.

A realizatory silence. Clara waited for outrage, but Mark surprised her by laughing also, then stopping abruptly. 'Clara can't abide me any longer.'

There was a smell of pipe tobacco. After a few cogitative puffs, 'I don't believe she ever could,' said Muncher.

Now who'd sold him that one? Clara was irritated to find herself more than somewhat peeved with her uncle. Part of her would have liked to have got up in all fairness and laid each in-and-out on the table, if only because Mark Upshaw was the first person in WC2 ever to imagine that Clara's eardrums were every bit as disturbable as anyone else's.

'I've been meaning to ask yer something.' The tone of Muncher's voice suggested a pleasing change of topic. 'Actually, it's to see my way to doing you a favour. One of the places I work has got a monster function up and coming. Hundreds of noshers. Ice sculpture. Piped mash taters. Naturally they're crying out for extra washers-up. Thought you might be glad of the cash, so I told 'em I'd put a word in your direction.'

A big pause, into which Clara instinctively inserted the experiences and people that went with clothes such as Mark Upshaw owned. Basement and ground level felt much of a muchness if they were where the majority of your affairs were conducted. But from the perspective of the glittering ice towers where money was manipulated, the penthouses from which you got more than a glimpse of grass and water, Muncher's suggestion must feel like an extra plummet.

Sure enough, Mark's reply came out thin and colourless. 'That would be useful. Thank you.'

There was the sound of footsteps. Clara feigned sleep. The footsteps stopped just short of the sofa.

'Muncher,' Mark whispered into the kitchen. 'Clara's coverlet has fallen off her.'

'Well, put it back. If necessary.' Muncher was out of his depth here – his wasn't what you'd call a detailed affection.

'I think it would be better if you did.'

Then Mark was gone. And Clara was warm enough anyway.

* * *

Though the grand launch would not involve a catwalk – no metamorphosed warehouse, smoke machine and image music – Clara still felt a Crescendo Dress was required. A signature notion which would encapsulate for the hacks, and snap magnificently. Just in case of which, its sizing should be for a female with six inches more leg than Clara had in heels: the kind of glowering, thoroughbred beauty they photographed in *Vogue, Elle* and *Cosmo.* (Clara never could work out what all those supermodels had to look so cross about.)

She went into a stir-fry over the concept; dropped into the National and the National Portrait; visited St James's to study duck colours, absently feeding the pelicans while considering shapes and layers. First, Clara decided, she would construct the dress in shoddy, then she and Bethany could discuss dyes and nuances. Clara thought about Fleur's designer offerings in *Ms London.* Restraint, she supposed, was hard to abandon. Though the biggies might send their models clip-clopping down the runway, all of a billow, all of a shimmer; qualification had always set in by Covent G., South Ken, Regent and Newburgh Street. The way to make an impact was to go for broke.

The only other person in the house who'd have been willing and able to stay put for all the time it took to build a gown *on* a body – undoubtedly the best way to arrive at the spectacular: drape, tear, snip, angle – was Bethany. Such a disparity of girth, however, would only be confusing. Mirrors, though, were available in abundance for the price of a screwdriver. The attic wasn't high enough, so Clara secured a series of reflecting squares and rectangles up one of the walls in the sitting-room by means of a powerful adhesive. In tight shorts and a vest she stood in front of them and fiddled with the permutations of fabric. The job was a sight more difficult than it would have been with a model. Hunching or raising to fold or pin sent the proportions wildly out, unless your bore them constantly in mind.

Clara laboured on the top half first, thinking of feathers, wings and the Middle Ages. To get the height for the skirt she made a platform out of own-brand baked-bean tins, *How to Conquer Your Fear of Fear,* some upturned flowerpots and four knackered videos – though they'd never had a player.

'Would you like the chopping-board?'

'What?' Clara had just managed to prick her thumb securing in place an arum-shaped tuck.

'It would make that more stable. I could level the surface off with newspaper and offcuts and put the board on top.'

Up until then the little rostrum had been just fine thank you. Now Clara felt as if her pointy heels might suddenly go down the holes in the bottom of the plant-pots, or cause spontaneous geysers of tomato sauce.

'I'm just fine, thank you.'

'Do you mind if I take a few of the plastic clothes covers? I'll make sure I replace them.'

'Starting a rival company?'

She hoped that would shoo him off, but Mark sank, cross-legged, on to the floor. In the mirrors, Clara watched him lower his head, stare at the ground a moment, look up again with eyes narrowed.

'I'm selling most of my suits,' he said. 'Perhaps you can tell me the best place to dispose of them?'

'Why?' It toppled out of her.

Mark's smile was a bleak one. 'They aren't greatly needed at present.' He paused, apparently awaiting the names of some up-market second-handers on the King's or Fulham. Then, 'When have you been most disappointed in human beings?' he asked unexpectedly.

'I . . .' Clara stepped down from her platform and perched on the arm of the sofa. She felt like a hedgehog, all spiked and pinned together.

'You don't have to answer. I was doing that cheap thing of asking a question you yourself want to give a reply to.'

Again Mark waited, then seemed to take Clara's lack of comment as an indication to continue. 'I've been let down just recently. My erstwhile friends failed to live up to my expectations. It's left me rather battered.'

Clara hadn't seen that one coming. Her insides crumpled.

Mark went on. 'I'd anticipated so much better from them. I was optimistic. You must know this . . . situation isn't – wasn't – what I'm used to.'

'I smelled the leather.'

'The leather?'

'Of the suitcases.'

'Ah.' Awkward, but Mark shrugged. 'They just got cashed in early. It's hard to believe the money could have been better invested.'

At which, in flew Kim, Si, Geraldine.

'Sunshine,' proclaimed Geraldine, in oracular tones.

'Honeypot!' cried Kim.

'C'n we have some beans for supper, Maz?' asked Si, spotting the tins.

'If you give me a hand with the hamburgers.'

'All right. And mine's Insect. What's yours Maz?'

'I have no idea what we are discussing.'

'A name to put on the dress labels,' said Kim. 'As soon as we alight on an option, we can begin stitching them into the garments.'

'We can't call the business anything to do with Bethany, coz then they'd know we've gotter.'

There was a pause.

'You *can* call it "Clara",' said Mark.

It was a long time since Clara had thought of a bedroom as having any purpose save for storage and sleeping in. Without one, however, there was nowhere to boo-hoo but the bathroom. She couldn't stop herself. She was dripping like spring thaw as soon as she'd got through the doorway.

She hadn't done this in ages. Tears were supremely useless. On the other hand, the swollen, rosy-nosed woman she later ironed out in a powder compact looked as if she might perhaps have given a bit of a scouring to some tarnished bit of her psychology.

Maybe it shouldn't have done, but it pleased Mark to think of the accessibility of glamour. Clenched handbag-tight on the pricier pavements, yet widely available at inauthentic discount.

The dress label trade was apparently a lively one: a niche market far more wide-reaching than Mark would ever have suspected. By putting together snippets gleaned from Clara, Mark was able to extrapolate a thriving, multifaceted, rag-trade black economy woven through with short lengths of ribbon: copied or – better still – originals. Clara veered between being slightly less reluctant to speak and completely unforthcoming. Whenever Mark tried to get details about the grand launch she clammed up. So much so that his curiosity about the event became increasingly intense. Possibly out of genuine ignorance, the others were as uninformative as she was: if you were Clara Hood, sheepdogging such an intractable bunch, Mark could see it would make sense to take things one step at a time. On the other hand, in this household secrecy was second nature.

More and more items of clothing were reaching completion. Dates were being struck off and lists ticked. The labels with Clara's name on were delivered in a supermarket bag around eight one evening.

'Red and green,' said Si.

'Scarlet and peppermint,' said Clara.

Mark continued peeling ginger, which spontaneously transformed itself into colours also – dark, treacly auburn through to palest toffee.

'A triumph of taste,' cried Kim.

'Very nice, luv,' said Muncher.

'I'll show Bethany and get started.' Clara flipped away the door-sheet with the point of her strappy shoe. Her exposed toenails were painted gold. She was wearing a sleeveless dress, striped yellow, brown and orange.

Mark said, 'Some chicken in black bean sauce will soon be ready.'

But Clara had closed the door behind her. Mark heard her running up through the building, to an attic full of finishing touches.

He and the others ate. Si and Kim went off to work. Muncher asked Mark to accompany him to Cohen's, but Mark declined. He went into the sitting-room where Clara's nearly completed Crescendo Dress hung on a tailor's dummy. The dummy had just appeared one day, the way that things did here. Mark suspected it had academic origins.

Though there was no one to tower over, he sat on the ground out of newly cultivated habit. The bare feet and T-shirts had been a conscious decision also. Whether they actually made him less imposing, Mark would have been hard put to say, but at least they made him feel not quite so big around the place. He hated to think that he had once been part of a set that would customarily descend and crowd other people off tables.

From Clara, Mark could of course envision no more than eventual friendship – if that. Nevertheless, such memories of his time with Fleur inevitably led to comparisons. Fleur was the latest example of the type of girl who had recurred throughout Mark's adolescence and adulthood. He had never been involved with any other variety. It was surprising to discover that this fact had been influential in the formation of his character.

In spite of Mark's generalized, school-inculcated regard for the purported weaknesses of gender, he had never before felt an overwhelming protectiveness towards any one individual woman. It muddled him. He wasn't clear how much it was simply to do with Clara's past. He wasn't even sure it was something he was meant to feel. Fleur, who considered herself too feminine to pump her own petrol, had never elicited this kind of emotion. Clara, who – had Mark been an honest-to-God intruder – would undoubtedly have followed her half nelson with a full knockout, left Mark desperate for the trust that would allow him to defend her. His attempts to win it were forcing him to discover and redefine who exactly he was.

How to inspire trust, except by trusting? How to gain the confidence of the wounded, except by allowing oneself to be vulnerable? Mark scarcely had a background where these things were encouraged. Had his misplaced confidence in his friends emanated from an aspect of his personality that had somehow survived his education? Or did they all – himself included – genuinely believe there was a loyalty network, the absence of which was only revealed to those whose chips were down? Was this the first time in Mark's life that he was trusting properly?

He didn't find it easy. It was a fumbling affair, baring his soul to Clara.

Mark returned to the kitchen and put on an optimistic kettle, though hours – days, perhaps – might pass before Clara reappeared. The adjoining door could again be left open; the surrounding streets had sucked the house's cooking smells out of the open window and made them part of Soho's own ever-present odour. Mark leant against the sill, waiting for the water to boil.

From this angle he could see two Crescendo Dresses: the real and its patchwork image. The jumbled shapes of the assorted mirrors made it seem as if they had somehow retained the original reflections that had gone into the gown's design: the ideas, tried and scrapped; swatches of rehearsed pigment; binned configurations. Something about the garment made Mark uneasy. Its bottle-greens and ambers, its romantic Pre-Raphaelite swoops and gathers, represented such an abundance of hope. More than should be selling itself in the classifieds, inveigling a beery upstairs or an anonymous church hall.

Mark had bought a quarter of freshly ground coffee beans in Old Compton Street: once an everyday event, now a little splash of pleasure. He was learning the necessity of treats, how hard-earned cash must also be allowed to buy a single small thing you really wanted. He poured the boiling water on to the grounds and let them steep.

'Kenyan?'

Mark jumped. Clara was standing in the doorway clutching a jade-coloured silk garment. 'Yes. Want some?'

'Only if you've got more than enough.'

'There's plenty.'

Mark poured two cups and sat down. Clara remained standing. 'Look,' she said, suddenly and very quickly, opening her arms and revealing the garment to be an unbuttoned blouse, 'if I'd ever had retail premises, one of the doing-up options would have been scarlet and peppermint. That's why I chose them.'

Mark stared at Clara's name on the label stitched into the blouse's neck.

'Not washed-out mouse, string and crispbread, like Fleur's,' Clara added fiercely before he could comment.

'Fleur's?' Mark was astonished. So wildly was his ex-girlfriend's name out of context in the Lisle Street kitchen that for a few stunned instants he derangedly ran through the decorative schemes of Fleur's house, cottage, lodge, villa, trying to fix on which of these properties Clara must have visited and taken exception to.

'The shop. In Newburgh Street.'

A silence.

'I haven't seen it,' said Mark stupidly.

'You will.'

'Will I?'

'You know we're as good as finished here. So are Fleur's chippies and toshers, if they don't want her imposing that penalty clause for delayed completion.'

'The launch is at Fleur's opening, is *that* what you're saying?' Mark endeavoured to get his mind around the concept. The very idea that Clara could be included in a venture of Fleur's momentarily struck him as impossible. But then . . . Mark's invitation to Fleur's big event was still sitting where he'd left it, on the shelf in his bedroom: a piece of foreign currency, an expired membership card which Mark had shoved to the back of his consciousness without the slightest anticipation of it conceivably resurfacing. Presumably Clara had spotted the news about Fleur's shop at the same time as she'd looked at Mark's other invitations. Presumably it was this which had given her the idea of approaching Fleur with her collection.

An embarrassing thought assailed Mark. 'Is Fleur aware that you and I are . . . er . . . acquainted?' Though Clara using Mark's name as leverage was scarcely different from Mark doing the same himself, and at least Clara had wares to sell. Suddenly Mark was profoundly ashamed that he had ever assumed he could function as his own collateral.

Clara walked forward and picked up her coffee. She dropped the blouse on to the table. It lay there like a stretch of summer grassland or a solid reproach. Mark felt foolish to have imagined Clara would settle for anything inferior when it came to the marketing of her creations.

'Yes, the launch is at Fleur's shop. And no, she doesn't know we're "acquainted".'

'But my invitation to its opening was what drew the shop's existence to your attention?'

Mark tried not to adopt a tone of reproach, but Clara looked at him sharply. Then, appearing to realize that she couldn't logically blame Mark for resenting her snooping in his bedroom: 'My *attention* was there already,' she said, in a tone that implied bizarre offence at the idea of Mark's taking any credit for introducing the establishment to her.

'And Fleur liked your designs?' This Mark found amazing. Not because of anything to do with Clara's dresses, rather because of the change in Fleur it implied. At least as much as the actual objects, Fleur adored the fuss and flurry of making her choices: airline tickets, phone calls, faxes, appointments; most especially, the proximity to those whose mention cut a swathe through the psyches of the stylish. It was untypical of her to show interest in an unknown, virtually just down the road.

Clara said, 'Things came together. Fleur's pretty. Does her hair always curl in the right direction?'

This wasn't something that Mark had hitherto considered. 'I imagine she has a person whose job it is to ensure that it does,' he replied, partly because this seemed likely and partly because he was giddily contemplating the scale of opening Fleur could be expected to have commanded. Fleur did favour rather humdrum colours, now Mark came to think about it, but he knew probably better than Clara the cost of such understatement. Fleur would never countenance any cutting of corners or sparing of expenses. By some happy machination of chance, Clara was going to get the launch she deserved. Mark was relieved about that – he *was* relieved – though the recently invoked inadequate venues for the Crescendo Dress were beginning to feel a deal less emotionally complex, his previous life too close for comfort.

Clara took a big swallow, draining her cup. 'Thanks for the coffee.'

'Won't you stay and have another?'

'Nope . . . thanks.' Clara snatched up the blouse and was gone before Mark could make any other attempts to detain her.

Mark rose, went to the window and breathed in the air. He was altogether dazed by Clara's revelation. He tried in vain to imagine what she and Fleur must have made of each other.

The flat sky was trellised with spotlights. The pavements were crowded. Traffic idled. The night was full of the sounds of occupied people. There was a smell of burnt caramel.

It was disconcerting to think of past and present coinciding. Extraordinary to suddenly realize that the main grid of Clara's existence – the criss-cross of thoroughfares through which she made her runs and dashes – was composed of the same streets as Fleur frequented. Fleur might toy with a salad, or finger possible purchases, only a few doors away from where Clara was talking down the price of an end of salami or poking through some interesting-looking rubbish, yet it must have taken an almighty knock to contrive to slam them together.

Perhaps Clara had strode past Mark himself many times before he knew her, in battered hat or scarf à la Isadora. Maybe she'd nattered with Muncher while Muncher washed a plate that Mark had eaten off. Identical transits but some travelling steerage. Would Fleur even *see* a Muncher Barrow?

And what would she make of Mark Upshaw in his new capacity as partner in a design business? If they were going to have to meet, Mark's situation – if you were unaware of its details – didn't look so terribly bad.

CHAPTER FOURTEEN

A Trial Outing

Eleven o'clock a.m. The gossips over instant or herbal would casually have drifted into the day's outline, looking at must-dos over each other's shoulders, pulling off clip-ons to lean against earpieces and say 'Mmm. Yeah. Sure' into them.

Everyone was out or asleep. White-and-silver clouds dissolved the sunlight every so often, filling the sitting-room with greyish shadow. Clara really could imagine the cool, moist smell of a wet stone floor, thin metal buckets and newly sprayed foliage and petals. She lay on the sofa, wearing a sky-blue cotton, faded in places, drinking what Muncher called a Bloody Shame – tom juice, Worcester, tabasco, lemon, full stop – and turning over page upon page of 'F'.

The phone books really were tremendous value. Letter after letter, volume after shiny volume – and all for diddly-squat. Their annual, gratuitous arrival was one of those small miracles such as must keep the Calaluans heartened. This latest pile of them was recent enough not to have got scuffed yet, but whether the shop would be listed was moot. Usually there was a year's delay at least, and plenty did their darnedest to stay out of the directory altogether (Clara included, for the longest while.) Clara had heard that there were restaurants, clubs and designer stores so utterly exclusive that they kept themselves ex. Which could be about to cause problems.

Not there. Clara reached for the blower, untangled the cord; 192; *Directory, which name please? The number you requested is . . .*

Clara memorized, didn't write. She got up and pushed the sitting-room door shut, then removed the handle. Si or Kim just out of their kip would scarcely sound like credible background customers. By the time they'd tracked down a replacement doorknob, though, Clara would be done, with any luck.

The phone articulated a presumably requisite number of trills.

'Fleur's, Newburgh Street.' Busy, preoccupied, but mega-civil.

'This is the florist.'

'Ah, yes,' scanning some list or other, 'Cut & Dried.'

'That's right.' Right! 'I'm phoning to confirm the best time for us to make our delivery. It was agreed that we should avoid coinciding with the arrival of the last of the garments.'

'During Fleur's meeting with your creative consultant.'

A creative consultant at a flower shop! Blabbing for hours about hothouse compositions. Tossing together wreaths, posies, bunches and arrangements; throwing in the odd cabbage, Far Eastern thistle or colorific discord in the interests of modernity. That must be money for old rope. Though presumably the importation of that trippy exotica upped the overheads, and the temperature you had to keep your cabbages from wilting at.

'During the meeting with our consultant, yes.'

'Let me see. Well, the final two consignments of garments – Yen and Vigilante – are due aaaat . . . around ten that morning. So well after or well before.'

'Ten on the morning of the opening?'

'That's right.'

'Fine.'

'Super. Now, while I've got you on the line, *Country Manner* are going to do a decor snippet.' Well, they wouldn't need a paint-chart vocabulary. 'I think things ended rather up in the air, didn't they?'

Prickle-haired all of a sudden. 'They did.'

'And Fleur got back to you after a jolly good think.'

'After one of those.'

'Aaaand . . . ?'

'And?'

'To save me having to bother her and so that I can get straight back to the *Country Manner* person, did she opt for the lilies and dried wheat or the artichokes and banana blossom?'

'The lilies and wheat, but it was a close shave.'

'These things always are, aren't they?'

'As a rule.'

'Well, thanks masses. You've been awfully helpful.'

'So have you.'

Two days to go, and it was hot, hot, hot. The telly harped on about how in so many years' time the British climate would be like Spain's, as if that was some kind of a problem. Clara twisted a tie-dyed scarf into a coil and knotted it round her head to keep her fringe off her forehead. She opened windows and doors to make cross-draughts. Once in a while she treated herself to a blast of the hairdryer, set to cold. Geraldine put down saucers of water for the mice. Kim made ice cubes of frozen Ribena.

This weather could only be good news, if it lasted. Everything would go better without any rain. No danger of moisture in the distributor or suspiciously soggy frocks. Surely a bigger turnout of both guests and media too: the fashion hacks who issued pronouncements as to what was hip, in the mags and on the clothes progs, didn't look the type to fancy stomping through puddles, and too many typical London torrentials doubtless sent Fleur's chums rushing southwards. Clara could imagine Fleur dictating her meteorological specifications to a jotting assistant: *And sunshine, don't you think?*

So blue skies over the capital. In celebration of which, and seeing as all else was in such good order, Clara, Kim and Geraldine decided to combine a Girls' Night Out with their pre-launch recce. From Clara's point of view, a latish home-coming would also help facilitate the avoidance of solitary encounters with Mark and their accompanying exchanges.

Unfortunately, Bethany had taught Geraldine how to make a turban. Kim wore a tube top and white culottes. Clara had put on a pale pink shift and lots of loops of beads – chunky wood through to diddy seed-pearl look-alikes – and a wonderful jumble-sale pair of high-heeled, between-big-toe-and-the-next leather thongs. She carried a large canvas beach-bag, with her binoculars, bumper pad and *Exchange & Mart* pen in it, for plans and notes and magnification.

They tripped off down Gerrard, with its reds, greens and golds. Dragons. China gods. Powdered medicaments. Luminous pastries. A busker played a high-pitched, sweetly yowling stringed instrument, along to a woolly accompaniment from one of those backing tapes. There was a clown on stilts. The roasting air was thick with competing smells of cooking.

Kim knew the PVC'd punter-puller outside the clip just past St Anne's. Clara bought some speciality sausages from the shop in Berwick for Muncher. Halfway down Broadwick Street Geraldine discovered she'd left her nasal spray at home, and it was the devil of a job to persuade her she most probably wouldn't need it. Clara put herself on stand-by to bundle Geraldine's swaddled head into the beach-bag should she decide to hyperventilate – getting her to breathe into something usually did the trick, and a waft of raw sausage was enough to bring anyone to their senses.

The Newburgh Street jeweller's display had taken on a blue theme: turquoise pendant, lapis lazuli brooch, sapphire hatpin; the three, sat in a bird's nest, like it would be worth hopping down to the Surrey woods with the highest possible ladder and frightening the magpies. It was holiday time at Shoes, Scarves and Handbags – raffia and sandals and a touch of the nautical.

As Clara had hoped and reckoned, Fleur's white-out had vanished. The designer shop's windows were already at full sparkle.

'Here we are,' she announced. For Geraldine and Kim this was a first sighting. It was weird to feel proprietorial about something that didn't belong to you, and wasn't to your taste anyway.

'My oh my,' cried Kim. 'It positively reeks of bulging plastic. And it's so spacious.'

'I find myself intimidated,' said Geraldine.

The shop looked as if every last person working there had simultaneously dropped whatever and rushed off to have nice drinks someplace, swapping one bit of fun for another. This was stylish topsy-turvy, consisting mainly of lots of clean and beautiful articles not in place yet, and balls of white tissue paper. No risk of treading in something sticky, getting snagged on jagged edges, having things tumble on top of you.

Along the far wall of the premises were half a dozen fawn-curtained changing-rooms, some open, some closed. Where they were open the curtains had been tied back like in a theatre, though not with gold tasselled ropes but lengths of hessian. You could have slept four to each and still have had room for a birdcage. They were studded with an encouragingly large number of barnyard-style hooks. Instead of a built-in counter, there was a rough-hewn pine table with a large, awaiting baked-clay vase on it, next to a pile of brown parcel-paper carriers scribbled with Fleur's logo. The chairs for the Cheque Books to sit on while awaiting and making sartorial decisions were movie-star collapsibles in khaki – a mistake, in Clara's opinion, since money and youth didn't necessarily go hand in hand and Big Bucks liked to be comfortable. The lighting was pearlized wall spots.

Quite a lot of deliveries had been made already. (Put a finger on that door handle and the premises would probably go off like New Year.) Fleur's dress rails were now in place along the edges of the retail area – not quite full yet; more clobber to come, undoubtedly. That genre of joint really did have a horror of appearing claustrophobic: there was ample room for a few more racks of garments. Clara's collection should slot in nicely.

After a few moments spent standing on the pavement studying the building, the three friends entered the pub opposite, which had diddy dark windows that weren't awfully easy to see out of – especially with bins. The upside of the small shaded panes, however, was that – placed on stools, with their backs towards the interior – what the three of them were up to wasn't greatly visible. The tenor of the location was also in their favour – folk too cool in and of themselves to be overly interested in what was happening at other people's tables. If anyone did notice the trio's activity, they'd be incurious enough to settle for a simple explanation: Clara, Kim and Geraldine were doing some pigeon-spotting, or trying out a new purchase bought knock-down on the Totty Court.

'Be still my beating heart!' Kim had first go while Clara drew an outline sketch and Geraldine sipped a tonic water. 'Various Melvyn Delves. Six below-knee skirts, dresses, sweaters. Day wear, definitely.'

'How bright?' asked Clara.

'Waving-off-the-hunt sludge and margarine with freckles of rust. Followed by a gap. Then, still day, I think, but . . .'

'Are you sure?'

'Forbear. Yes, too thick for later. Conceived by Puttanesca, the illustrious Italian *enfant terrible* bringing all his accustomed Latinate passion to . . .'

'All right, all right.'

'Hush, dearest. What I'm saying is, pretty colourful – wine and pale mango. Here you could dazzle without being ultra-sore-thumbish.'

'Might I assist?' asked Geraldine, as Clara had been willing her not to.

The next fifteen minutes were taken up with explaining how to focus and get just one image. That accomplished, Geraldine couldn't find the building and started to get teary. Eventually, it was decided it would be better all round if Geraldine wrote – Kim indicated where exactly on the plan she should be writing – and Clara did the rest of the scanning.

A crisp circle of vision. More day wear. Some spicier ranges scattered among steels, bones and navies.

Evening started near the far wall. A selection of sharp lines in muted carrot from United in Life. Citrine shot silks from Co!. A shadowy selection of little black dresses – 'Write "no go" for that area.' And a useful clutch of floor-length shells and plums from Jean-Marie Potiron, after which Clara's full-blown sunsets might look like a natural progression. Potiron, however, was followed by a joker rail of blouses and slacks, which worryingly suggested the whole might be liable to revision – how radical, it was impossible to say. Clara would have slept easier if there'd been something in Fleur's windows to indicate her keynotes. At the moment these were empty aside from some black velvet torsos on sticks. It was the obvious thing, to keep the finished image under wraps till near the last minute; but if Fleur was putting off the luxury of choosing an overall effect, her ultimate decision might necessitate a complete change of tack. Clara was practised at switching direction in midstream, but how well would everyone else?

'Done.' Clara lowered the binoculars and rewrapped them in their duster. 'It is now, I regret, a matter of luck as to whether or not the rails remain in their present order.'

'You lack faith,' said Geraldine. 'Faith is vital.'

'I am star*vink*,' said Kim. 'And it's my turn to order the duck.'

Also hungry, she discovered, was Clara. Besides which, the place was starting to get pretty busy. It wouldn't be long before the bar staff began to consider that the three of them were taking up rather more seating than they were consuming liquid. Geraldine finished the last molecules in her glass – she was good at eking – and they retraced their steps as far as the Canton, their Girls' Night Out restaurant, just around the corner from Lisle Street.

They ordered as usual. A portion of prawn crackers. Three bowls of crab and sweetcorn. Three rice plates: duck, pork and chicken – *in theory* to be shared equally. Seasonal greens with oyster sauce. Jasmine tea. From their upstairs window table there was a view of the flats above the underground carpark, the fishmonger's with its cuttlefish and carp, the pagoda's coloured lights, and the store flogging studded belts and plastic leathers.

'So Clara,' Kim asked, daintily crunching on a crisp white cracker, 'what will you wear for wowing purposes? What have you in mind in order to convey *Designer*?'

'I haven't thought.' Clara ran through the repertoire, as seen on telly: own-label, black-and-white, outrageous, self-consciously crumpled. The accompanying hairdos – from studied casual to downright fantastic, with streaks and gel and zany colorations. Which one should she plump for? The images crashed, and in blew an irrelevant gust of wonder as to what Mark Upshaw liked her best in.

The soups arrived.

'I am fond of these spoons,' said Geraldine.

'All I am is glad things are sorted,' said Clara.

'In what respect?' enquired Kim, adding little droplets of soy to her bowl.

Clara supposed this was how most people talked, spontaneously voicing the edge of an emotion and going on to fill in the details. To her, it felt unfamiliar; as did not taking one of the many alleys she could have backtracked down. 'Mark,' she said. 'I'm relieved he knows about Fleur's.'

'Mostly,' said Kim, swallowing a spoonful of her crab and sweetcorn.

'As much as is needed.' Clara felt defensive. That was the trouble with letting loose your counsel – you got called upon to examine and justify. 'Or completely safe for our plans,' she added.

'Ah, yes. Completely.' There was a pause. 'Do you know what is most difficult about being a transvestite?' Kim asked.

'Tights,' said Geraldine.

'Stockings get round that one, sweetie, *and* they are so very much more sensual. No, it's that sooner or later the fact must be confided. A hurdle at which some fall, and some don't. Like Mark Upshaw.'

'Mark guessed.' Though Clara could see this was a technicality and didn't really address Kim's point. It wasn't that she couldn't imagine a person taking *one* other chance – just like she could more or less picture Calalu Island before its current griefs – but there was dogged history. A man making amends had too many resonances: a million second chances granted, none of them worth a shred; a bellyful of negated reparations, each starting out by looking quite equally sincere.

The finished soups were whisked away. Kim gouged tobacco-red dollops of chilli sauce out of a ramekin with the end of a chopstick. Geraldine inhaled the steam from her teacup. Clara tried to think about how she could modify her eyebrows with a very dark eyebrow pencil.

The main courses arrived. 'Bags I divide,' cried Kim, already starting to scoop and ladle, covering the paper cloth with a flurry of rice grains. 'Though you'll be disappointed, I warn you, if you're hoping for perfection. Duck-wise, in fact, I shall take flagrantly unfair advantage. True friendship can cope with an ultimate test, can't it?'

Mid-afternoon on the eve of the launch the sky turned saucepan grey. The air was alive with static. Whenever Clara touched a plastic dress cover, her hair flew up and there were sparks and crackles. She was removing the gowns for pricing, the amounts to be written on ordinary old baggage labels, which would scarcely look out of place among Fleur's hooks and hessian. Once a sum was decided, the idea was to secure the label with a little gold safety pin somewhere deep inside the garment: punters were always made to delve – perhaps because it gave the floggers a chance to strike with their sales pitch.

Fixing the rates was no easy matter. It required works of reference. Spread out on the floor were scrounged, ex-hairdresser copies of *Woman's Journal, Cosmo* and *Elle* (unlike stingy quacks, the chichi Soho stylists kept their magazines up to date). There was also the Fleur edition of *Ms London,* which had to be Clara's primary source. Cross-legged and barefoot, leaning against the sofa, Si looked through the extracts from Fleur's collection for items similar to the ones Clara held up to him. If there wasn't anything close, he searched through the other mags' fashion pages.

Len Semerraro had broken a rib falling off a wall, so Mark Upshaw was conveniently out of the way, picking up the van. Though Mark would probably have been able to throw some light on this business of assessing values – had Clara been able to ask him.

Using the plug socket located farthest from the mould, Geraldine ironed ball-gowns. Kim hung finished packages in their allocated places on the rails. Muncher sat on the sofa cleaning his pipe and making the odd comment, not helpful.

In spite of all the familiarity, Clara felt marooned and weightless in this fracturing atmosphere. She was about to step into a world that was new to her. Where to pitch herself within it? How to fight the impulse to underestimate her worth? She'd had to compromise for so long it was part of her nature. It was wild to contemplate a realm where you didn't need to bargain, or start by naming a figure that you never imagined anyone would accept. There was a lively danger of selling herself short.

'Ninety-nine,' said Muncher. 'It's deceptive yet classy. Put down four ninety-nine for that shirt thing, and none of 'em will think to think it's a penny off a cockle.'

'It says here "model's own",' said Si. 'But there's another like it in this photo at one forty-five.'

'Must be overpriced jumble,' said Muncher.

'One *hundred* and forty-five, I surmise,' said Kim. 'Such a curious sum, neither one thing nor the other.'

Clara had a grapple with her instincts, which yearned to tunnel deep below those elevated digits. 'We'll say a ton thirty.'

She wrote it down quickly, hid the label up a sleeve and replaced the blouse inside its cover. The plastic shimmered glassily. Clara handed the hanger to Kim.

Kim consulted the diagram plan Clara had made, based on their gathered info. 'Let me see. Here's where it goes. Rail number two.'

'Rail number *three.* Do try to get it right – there's only five of them.' Clara experienced a lightning surge of haphazard irritation. Not only with Kim, but with Geraldine, Si and Muncher also. Suddenly it seemed virtually inevitable that they would mess things up with their higgledy-piggledy, prevent anything whatever from making a difference. In a wink Clara would find herself returned to the days before Mark Upshaw, just as broke as she'd been then.

'That's right, beloved. How wrong we get things sometimes! Pardon my slipshod moments.'

Geraldine said, 'It is not unnatural to be overwhelmed by geometry.'

'Happily I'm only the driver,' said Muncher. 'Though Len says she's prone to die on you now, unless you give her constant choke.'

Oh yes, it was nerves, and this was nervy weather.

'Let's take a breather. I'll go and make some squash.'

Clara marched into the kitchen, slammed the door shut, and stood at the window, hoping for a whiff of cooling breeze. You'd think all those moving feet would swirl one up, but not a tremor. Back behind its shield of cloud, though, the sun was evidently trying to break through. The black slabs of movie poster along the front of the Prince Charles were giving off yellowish reflections. Buildings and passers-by were outlined in lime green. The greased hair of a couple of gawpers was ridged with steely light. Sunshine or downpour tomorrow, to dowse one of her many strategies? In the face of a mesh of variables, serenity or mayhem?

More dauntedness than jitter, and still this terrible sense of solitary; a nagging inclination to spill every bean in spite of many trouble-free years of keeping her mouth well shut. Was it really in the end desirable to be up-front *whatever*, as Kim maintained? Or was the thought of launching yourself enough to make anyone yearn for the very chancy possibility of a reliable other to grasp?

No answer from On High, of course, but a series of explosions from the grubby distance. Like they were dynamiting quarries down Trafalgar. Like a twenty-one-horsepower salute. Clara swung round on her heels, opened the fridge door and grabbed the squash bottle. Time to get moving and finished with labels. Fasten final poppers. Button last buttons. Zip zips and hook hooks. Quit agonizing, slip *Ms L.* PDQ under a concealing cushion, and price to the utter do-what-you-will skies.

Driving a van proved to be a lopsided experience, involving a lot of mounting of pavements in order to squeeze between obstructions; trusting, all the while, in the uncertain efficacy of the vehicle's balding tyres. Small wonder that the paintwork had a new scratch – gained since Mark's outing with Muncher – deep and wide, and stretching nearly the full length of the driver's side. Negotiating narrow back streets must make such accidents a common occurrence, and Len didn't have much intrinsic reason to be careful. Mark's precision driving was executed more with a view to avoiding inflicting damage on anyone else's automobile than fear for the aesthetics of Semerraro's own.

Mark did rather wonder how Fleur would react to Clara's collection arriving in such a derelict means of transport. Clara existed in a landscape so fugged with compromise and alienation that Mark sensed it was only through strength of will and sheer necessity that she sometimes forced herself to perceive its abnormalities. Maybe the vehicle's inappropriateness was something Clara hadn't thought about. The Christian minibus would also have looked odd – though better – and its interior would at least have been clean.

The filth of the back of the van was something that weighed heavily on Mark's mind as it jumped and backfired its way through the toiling traffic. He hated to think of any of those dresses getting soiled. It was the kind of thing Fleur and her clientèle would notice. Their sifted lives – like Mark's once had – involved sparse encounters with grime. The few that did occur impinged and rankled. There would be pointings-out and removals. Major aspects of all Clara's loveliness might be consigned to a storeroom owing to ash and dust and oil.

By some miracle, and by dint of virtually crawling the van's wheels halfway up a wall, Mark managed to park near to home, a little way down from French Food & Wine. He opened the back of the van and surveyed its interior, aware that his ritualized Corps sessions with kit, the regular and exacting school-dorm inspections, had left him with little idea how to tackle hardened squalor. He was surprised, however, to discover that the prospect of doing so was rather appealing.

It was hot but the threatening cloud was beginning to dissolve. Some women who worked in one of Lisle Street's well-stocked Chinese supermarkets were crouched on orange boxes, chatting. People lolled and gossiped, bare-shouldered, unencumbered. There was a symphony of city noises – sirens, music, shouts, pigeons. The streets used to be no more than conduits leading to set, predetermined destinations. The outdoors was a strictly green and leafy notion. Having a go at the van would include enjoying the air, though, every bit as much as when wandering through fields.

Abruptly, Mark paused in his thoughts. He had the distinct sensation that somebody was watching him. He glanced up at the windows of Clara's house. If by any chance it was her, she'd bobbed out of sight. He studied the road and the pavement opposite. The mermaid-tattooed Australian from the White

Bear, who had evidently been observing him, loped towards Mark from across the street.

'Got a bit of a job on there, mate, if you're fixing to blitz it.'

'What would you do?'

'I wouldn't. No. Yeah. I'll tell you what, you won't get it pristine – no way – but I can lend you a big paint-brush for the surface dirt. Then you'll need plenty of soapy water and a scrubbing-brush. Come over for them too – you don't want to be lugging buckets up and down. Shacked with Clara, aren't you?'

'Well, I . . .'

'And what I'd do is not go bothering with washing those walls. Just line them with heavy-duty – try Food & Wine for some – tack it to the wooden slats.'

'Thanks for the advice.'

'Oh, and loads of tinnies, and the radio on full blast if you reckon the battery'll take it.'

'Sounds like a good idea, but I don't imagine it will.'

'You're probably right. Stick with a regular bevvy, though.'

Not regular, but Mark did have a can of cold lager from Food & Wine, who were able to equip him with the plastic sheeting he needed and some nails to secure it, which Mark hammered in using a brick he'd spotted in the front of the van. The sky turned a glittery eggshell blue. Mark worked up a sweat. Len Semerraro's motor got as good as it was ever going to, and the man with the mermaid tattoo, whose name was Rob, looked on from time to time and so did the occasional other.

It was near six when Mark finally locked the back of the van shut – though there really wasn't much point, and nobody in their right mind would consider stealing it anyway. He ached, was grubby, thirsty and needed a cool bath; his soaked T-shirt clung to his body; but it was a job well done and that was overwhelmingly satisfying. Satisfaction in simple achievements was actually becoming quite a familiar sensation. He would put the kettle on for some lemon tea and then suss the availability of the bathroom.

Mark mounted the staircase and entered the sitting-room. He paused, embarrassed. Clara was alone in there. The dress rails were full. Each item of clothing hung in an icy shroud filmed with white, mercurial light. There was a smell of ironing. Clara was wearing loose, cream drawstring trousers in a gauzy material, and a rose-and-cream top with big red buttons. She looked so clean and Mark was such an unspeakable mess; awkwardly conscious of this and also moved, in the same way he had been the first time he saw the workshop in the attic. It crossed his mind that perhaps all over the land there were such valiant endeavours. It crossed his mind that now was when somebody should be able to book a table, and order champagne without bothering to enquire about its price – like he used to do every piddling time he or Fleur fancied it.

'Clara, I . . .' How to express what he felt about her achievement? She was staring at him and starting to blush; doubtless embarrassed too at witnessing his sweaty, dishevelled state. 'I've been cleaning the van for tomorrow,' he finished lamely.

There were skippy footsteps on the stairs. A tedious interruption – though surely it was easier to be interrupted?

'Oooh, my! It's Mark, our Man of the Month. Which hulky calendar did you step out of?' Kim was carrying a pair of shoes. She placed them on the arm of the sofa, put a hand in each and made them do a little tap-dance along it. 'Clara, my sweet, a gift for tomorrow: for luck, and so that you can *look* the part. Blue-and-green watered-silk mules, only slightly scuffed, with – see them? – kitten heels.'

'They call to mind a Monet,' said Geraldine, who had glided in while Kim was speaking.

'Thanks.' Clara glanced at Kim sharply, though, an apprehensive expression on her face. Mark sensed that for some reason she was having to make an effort not to let herself become rattled.

'Better leap to it, Marky-boy, and get washed up,' said

Muncher, behind him. 'Toasts in the White Bear in twenty minutes. And final talk about the a.m., more than likely.'

'An' peanuts an' scratchings,' Si's voice added.

'Why don't you put the shoes on?' asked Kim. 'Give them a trial outing?'

Clara said in a loud voice, 'Why did no one tell me about this?'

'We wanted to surprise you, luv,' said Muncher.

Until a moment before, Mark had heard nothing about any kind of celebration either.

Things were as slippery as chiffon.

No room upstairs and the conversation would have been drowned out by heavy rock, but the same table was free that they'd sat at following the Bethany Smile evacuation rehearsal. Clara glared out the window at the crinkly light, and mentally cursed Kim for giving voice to her own, spontaneous reaction to the way Mark Upshaw had looked after his van session – especially since she knew she'd been blushing. Also, that dig – or *was* it? – about not looking like a legit designer. Now, in the seething, fireworky climate, Kim was knocking back G-and-Ts like they'd quench her thirst and jostling against risky topics. Clara had the sensation of being boxed into a situation that was inexorably pulling away from her grasp.

'It's the order of those dress rails. Such a lot to remember!' Kim rattled her sharp, painted fingers in everyone's direction, but mostly Mark's. Clara had hoped Mark wouldn't come, but he'd bathed and shaved and was drinking a long whisky and soda.

'I'm just glad I'm only doing the driving,' reiterated Muncher, like they were some sort of double act. Hitherto there'd been no whiff of any last gossips about arrangements, and all this relief, to Clara's way of thinking, struck more than a slight off-note. As did the way Geraldine kept informing the table in general of her state of agitation when she contemplated the morrow. Although

Geraldine was usually agitated about something or other, it did seem to Clara that such excessive jitters might well appear unmerited by what was purportedly due to take place.

'Remind me again, luv.' Muncher's pipe tobacco hung motionless on the unbudging air. 'Where is it the van goes?'

Si said, 'Outside the Coffee Café, 'less it rains, then . . .'

Clara said swiftly, 'For *loading,* as near to the house as possible.'

'Pity *that* bit can't be done the night before,' Muncher grumbled to Mark. 'Used to be folk knew better than to touch merchandise left inside a familiar vehicle – particularly when acquainted with the status of the driver. Still, Clara reckons you can't trust anybody.' And yes, Mark turned and looked at her, with a contemplative expression she could see out of the corner of her eye.

There was a jagged crackle of lightning.

'Y'know what, Maz? That's when the clouds bang together.'

How could the Calaluans truly believe the heavens chucked gratuitous fortune down to average mortal beings? Soon the skies would splinter into trillions of thin slivers of hampering rain which wouldn't have ceased by morning. Everyone was wiping brows. Geraldine's turban had slid down the side of her head and was threatening to collapse. Si crunched ice. Muncher's bristly cheeks were purple. Kim's mascara had gone panda, her lipstick was smeared. Clara's entire body was damp and suffocating. Only Mark Upshaw seemed unaffected by the stifling atmosphere; talking to Si in his soft, measured voice, drinking slowly, exchanging comments with the barstaff when they came to gather glasses. It felt like he occupied a calmer, more pleasant place than Clara – wired to edgy undercurrents and hounded by forebodings.

Kim leapt to her feet. 'We've been sitting here all this while without a single toast. A round of tequila slammers, on me, and each person must make one.'

Mark said, 'I'm doing fine with my whisky, and Si's all right with his rum and Coke.'

'Oooow.' But Si didn't protest further.

'I could be on for that,' said Muncher.

'Tequila should cause me to become incapable,' said Geraldine.

Clara said, 'I'm about done.'

'Well, you spoilsports. So be it. Two only. But Clara, don't you stir until we've heralded. It will only take a shake.' Once poised with salt and lemon wedge: 'I'll go last. Who wants to begin?'

'To fate,' proclaimed Geraldine, raising her ginger ale.

'Lots of dosh!' Si's glass waved and slopped.

'No hitches,' bellowed Muncher, spilling into his lap half his grains of salt.

Mark ducked his head, raised his eyes to Clara's briefly with a diffident smile. He lifted and tipped his glass a little, like they did in films. 'To you,' he said.

Clara's voice wouldn't kick in for a second. After all, her friends were benign. They didn't mean to irritate. 'Thanks . . . very much . . . for your help.'

'Now me.' Kim scrabbled unsteadily to her feet, stood rocking for a portentous moment, then cried in a loud, unmistakable voice: 'To tomorrow's launch! *And* to the unsuspecting Fleur!'

CHAPTER FIFTEEN

Lost Souls

Back at the house, not a long time later. The fidgety weather had resolved itself into long, warm strands of rain. Up from the street rose smells of wet dust, drains, cardboard and orange rind.

'The *unsuspecting* Fleur? Am I to understand that she doesn't know your collection will be at her opening?'

Forcing himself to remain aware of the resonances an interrogation by him might have for Clara, Mark emphatically *sat* at the kitchen table, resisting a compelling impulse to raise his voice, pace and gesticulate. This unforeseen piece of blurted news had thrown him completely off balance. He was horrified, ashamed, shocked beyond all measure.

'Fleur hasn't an inkling. That's the sum of it.' And Kim, whose fault this was – not to mention the aiding and abetting others – had simply scurried off to bed like homing dormice, leaving Clara as per usual to deal with the flak. Now, uttering the honest, Clara vowed to herself that never in a squillion years would she confess to Kim, etc. that this admission afforded her the tiniest bit of relief.

Clara's face remained impassive but not set against him – or so it seemed to Mark – though who was he to judge? If he hadn't been mortified to the extreme, he might have found his own continued credulity touching. Fair but hard-nosed, he'd always styled himself; and yet, with the unambiguous cards laid blatantly before him, he had stubbornly persisted in misinterpretation. Fleur's supposed compliance on its own should have been enough to alert his suspicions.

'So when did you meet her?'

'Fleur? I haven't.'

'That's not what you said.'

'What I said was that she's pretty. I saw her photo in a magazine.'

'In a magazine?'

'I didn't want to lie to you.' Clara swallowed. She very much hadn't meant for that to stumble out. Surreptitiously she crossed her fingers, willing the statement not to get pounced on; far from sure she could adequately explain such an assertion to herself, indubitably convinced she didn't want to make a fist of doing so to Mark.

'And the magazine was where you found out about the penalty clause in the builders' contracts?'

Clara was relieved. Less, however, than she would have expected. 'No, I got that info off the sparks – the guy who put in the electrics. I'd visit and monitor progress. He let me have the run of the place, then he'd stop for a cup and a chat. It's the sort of moan blokes on a job like to put about.'

Yes, Mark supposed it must be. With something not a million miles from panic, the way things worked this side of the tracks was brought home to him afresh. Didn't they always say that conjurers relied on where you weren't looking for the success of their tricks? Mark was on the outside looking in, but persisted in viewing himself as on the inside looking out. No need to lie to him when he was so eminently capable of lying to himself. Bereft of his familiar standpoint, though – what? The thought of total separation from one's own kind was numbing. In spite of all that had taken place – in spite of his acquaintances' wilful and systematic abandonment of him – Mark found it impossible to categorize the class he had been born into as alien. Fleur and Mark had been involved, for God's sake.

Unable any longer to prevent himself, Mark sprang to his feet, strode to the window, leant his back against the frame and waved a hand towards the ceiling.

'You gave me to understand Fleur liked your designs.'

'I told you things came together. There's lots of ways they can do that.'

'Oh, are there? Then please enlighten me as to how precisely you intend to incorporate your collection into Fleur's most carefully purchased range of designer clothing without her knowledge.'

A pause.

'We're smuggling it in.'

The sheer audacity of the statement rendered Mark momentarily speechless. 'You're smuggling your gowns into Fleur's shop?' he eventually managed to gasp. 'Hasn't it occurred to you that is *stealing*?'

Actually, it hadn't. Nor had it occurred to Clara that anyone could be so morally hypersensitive.

'Define "stealing".'

'Really, I . . .'

'*Define* "stealing".'

'All right. Stealing is taking away something that belongs to somebody else.'

'Aha! 'But we're not taking away, are we? What we're doing is putting in.'

For an instant Mark was at a loss. Then, 'You're stealing space,' he said, lingering on the words, remembering how his own supposed trespass upon Fleur's mental territory had been used to justify his dismissal.

'Space? Fleur's got more of that than she knows what to do with. Just take a look at our charts.'

'*Charts?*'

Who'd have predicted it? Suddenly Clara felt proud. 'Diagrams of what's going where along the shop's walls. While other deliveries are being made and unloaded, we'll just slip our rails of schmutter in too – the plan is to put it next to the garb it'll best harmonize with. Hopefully the punters will reckon our clobber stands out from the rest, but we *don't* want it spotted and ditched before the joint even opens. The charts will become defunct, of course, if Fleur opts for a last-minute reshuffle, so I've also memorized the contents of the rails we're putting ours alongside.' Clara came to a slightly startled halt. The words had positively poured out of her, but really, why not? Mark had the powder keg and matches, courtesy of Kim. He could already blow her project to smithereens if he wanted.

There was a silence.

'Let me get this straight,' said Mark. 'You are going to insert dress rails containing your garments among the ones that are already in there . . . ?'

'Like I say, the shop's scarcely crammed and there's only five of them. Others'll be wheeling full rails in and empty ones out. We'll simply leave ours in situ.'

'You don't think you'll get noticed?'

Clara shrugged. 'A lot will be going on. You don't normally attract attention when you're doing something similar to everyone else.'

The pressure of the window frame against Mark's spine reactivated the aches caused by the afternoon's cleaning. Reluctantly, mesmerized by the epic scale of Clara's strategies, 'What about the van?' he asked, sorely aware that the inappropriateness of that too should have screamed scam at him.

Blurred and woolly summer rain still fell cussedly outside the window. Clara imagined its diamante beads on her stuck-together sheaths of plastic. 'If it's dry Muncher'll park up round the corner from the premises, and we'll deliver our stuff as soon as we see Yen and Vigilante unloading theirs.'

'You know when they're due?'

'I pretended to be a florist.'

'Ah.'

'If it rains, Muncher will try to get as near to the premises as possible and see if he can double-park to hide the van.'

'Newburgh Street is narrow. That could be pretty difficult.'

'I know.'

'And then later you go to the opening and see if your collection has provoked enough interest to make it worth Fleur's while to do a deal with you – presumably using my invitation?'

Clara's look was a bizarre mix of scornful and offended. 'Not using your invitation. Besides any other considerations, that going missing might get you thinking. No, I just put on my posh togs and tell whoever's doing the door to check out my design name on the dress labels. Glad it's not Honeypot or Insect. If the punters like what they've seen and Fleur knows that, maybe she'll fork out.'

There was a silence.

Mark's turmoil had dissipated somewhat as he'd become caught up in Clara's narrative – the schemes to avoid alerting Fleur or her assistants, the paths Clara had wangled around Mark himself. Watching Clara's plot circumlocute his own, apparently cumbersome, presence was like looking at a reflection in a mirror: the position Mark occupied in life was different from the one he held in Clara's mirror world.

'What if I suddenly decided to attend the opening?' he asked. 'Mightn't my suspicions be aroused if I spotted you engaged in negotiations? Or maybe Fleur would tell me what had happened?'

Clara said, 'If you'd made like you were going to the bash I'd have taken away your screwdriver.'

'You'd *what*?' Mark's sense of aghast humiliation welled up again. 'Good God, woman, have you never heard of habeas corpus? That would be tantamount to kidnapping me.'

The force of Mark's response took Clara by surprise, coming plum in the wake of his being so matter-of-fact. Abruptly, Mark turned away from her and stared fixedly out at the street, almost as if he could see himself down there. Something about the rigidity of his stance made Clara bristle. Surely even your average, run-of-the-mill prosecutor, who boozed down the Coal Hole, wasn't this quick to bandy disparaging legal definitions. 'How can you be kidnapped in your own bedroom?' she demanded.

Mark did not reply. Instead, 'Fleur used to be my girlfriend,' he said as softly as he could, but with considerable bitterness. Incarceration in an illegally rented lodging in Lisle Street while his former friends were partying was just too neat an emblem of this newly revealed situation to be wholly bearable. Somehow, without being aware of it, all the way through his recent experiences Mark had harboured the notion that he would never be completely sundered from his past. One day, he would be back at the Queen's School, Pitsbury, again. One day, his father would still be alive, and a whole catalogue of wrong moves would not have been made yet. Mark would be on the old side of the divide, behind the restaurant frontages. Misty: the future era would be as misty as tonight's lavender veil of rain. All the lights would still be lit. They would shine off the patent-leather handbag, the shoes, the hair of Fleur or another like her. Mark would not be in imminent danger of encountering an ex-girlfriend while delivering dress rails to her wondrous new establishment. He would not be obliged to pretend that doing deliveries – rather than working as a partner in a (paltry enough) design business – was his current job. He wouldn't be on the brink of consolidating allegiances that might set him forever beyond the pale.

'Till when?'

'I'm sorry?'

'Till when was Fleur your girlfriend?'

'Until just before I met you.'

'So you do know about her hair!'

'Her hair?'

'Whether it always curls in the right direction.'

'No I don't, not definitively.' The conversation was taking such a bizarre twist that, still mired in his own thoughts, Mark had the surreal sensation of not being totally awake. He faced into the room again, returned his fuddled gaze to Clara. How – and why? – explain an intimacy than studiously avoided any exposure to the nuts and bolts of daily existence? 'It wasn't that sort of relationship,' he said.

'You mean you didn't . . .'

'Of course we did.' Mark was amazed to discover he had any pride left to be affronted.

There was a heated silence. Clara imagined the two of them, Mark and Fleur, strolling across Covent Garden together; dazzling.

Mark said suddenly, 'I suppose there is a definite risk that I'll be noticed by Fleur when we make the delivery. That might attract her attention to your garments.' He was suffused with relief at having found such a quick and easy get-out.

'Fleur won't arrive till later,' Clara retorted immediately.

'Can you be certain?'

Clara sensed in Mark's voice a reluctance, a drawing away. 'It's guaranteed. She'll only waltz in for the plaudits.'

Nettled both by the failure of his escape attempt and the unshakable confidence of Clara's pronouncement: 'You sound as if you know her,' Mark said.

'And you sound as if you don't.' Snapped out in reaction to his tone.

'I bow to the superiority of your insight into the personality of my former lover,' Mark responded coolly. Though in truth he probably hadn't known Fleur awfully well – one didn't – and the word 'lover' was jarring. Previously it would have been adequate enough, but here it came across as obtrusive and not altogether accurate.

Clara leapt up and started to fill a noisy kettle. Spilled water rattled down its battered metal sides and fountained off a couple of unwashed bowls. She was sick of being confronted with images of perfection.

'Who ended it?' she asked rather loudly, watching him over her shoulder.

'Fleur. It was amicable.' Mark gave a slight wince. Heartbreak or damaged ego? Either way, it didn't matter a fiddle. Clara wondered what Mark had done to displease Fleur, decided probably nothing enormous: likely it was just another typical example of a member of the Fortunate chucking out, casting off, for no obvious reason. There was many a thing Clara had gone through for flaws and been hard pressed to find any but the odd negligible one.

'Why didn't you tell me about you and her?'

'It didn't seem relevant.' That wasn't exactly what Mark meant. Of course, in one way it was relevant – much more so than Mark had hitherto realized. On the other hand, the relationship between Fleur and himself had no influence whatsoever on the way Mark currently lived his life. Fleur had not, for example, cracked Mark into dozens of pieces which he had been obliged to glue together again. Overwhelmed by a surge of diffuse resentment, mingled with hope that Clara might now confide in him, 'There are things *you* haven't told *me,*' he added.

Clara clanged the kettle on to the gas and glanced out at the sheeting rain. Mark's reproach suddenly made her feel as if she had spun a gauze and wrapped it around her spirit. She was a shuttered house whose furniture was cloaked and hooded. There was one thing in particular she had told nobody about, though Muncher had known at the time, and possibly remembered. Spontaneously it seemed to Clara that her wretched marriage had delineated and determined the phases of her existence, like Muncher's Henry Cooper and Sugar Ray. Where did you find the right tools to unpick and unravel something as confining as a bandaged past?

Mark was surveying her more intently than Clara was comfortable with. The kettle began to exhale a thin trail of transparent steam. She switched it off.

'We have a partnership,' said Mark. He felt short-changed by her silence. Disappointed. It was foolish to have imagined he might gain access to whatever thoughts moved through Clara's head. Nevertheless, 'You cannot possibly expect me to be a proper partner to you if I'm not in touch with the full picture,' he persisted.

Beneath his relentless gaze, Clara's cheeks reddened and her arms tensed. One hand curled into a fist. To his surprise, Mark realized she was extremely angry. All thoughts to do with himself fled away: anger was a kind of trust. As the deep flush spread to Clara's lips, blinkers seemed to be falling from Mark's vision. Facts he had overlooked before became explicable, relevant. He recalled Clara's abrupt revelation that her launch was to take place at Fleur's shop: the ferocity with which she had delivered the information, how she had appeared to avoid him thereafter. Mark had put it down to dislike, but maybe Clara had simply been afraid of saying more. Maybe she had actually wanted to. Perhaps, after all, at some buried level, Clara did feel a need to trust and confide in him. She knew and saw so many things; it was inconceivable that some subconscious crevice of her being hadn't registered and admitted that she couldn't keep him in the dark indefinitely. Even had Kim remained the quintessence of secrecy, even had the launch and any subsequent negotiations passed off without Mark becoming aware of anything untoward, he and Clara were in business together: one day a face-off was inevitable.

The drumming rain sounded like heartbeats. If Clara wanted a confrontation, she could have it. Mark wanted it too, if it meant they were really talking.

He waited.

'You aren't a proper partner.' Clara spat the words out. Sham and copies, tacky reproductions of the real thing: that was what she'd got palmed off with. She had a drawer full of enough museum postcards to know that they didn't do justice. 'I was forced into a deal I never wanted. Remember?'

Mark looked down. 'I remember. So why didn't you tell me I was a bastard?'

'I . . .' Clara thought of fear. She thought how much of her life she had spent forging it into something else.

Mark said, 'Why don't you tell me now?'

'You . . .'

'Were a bastard.' Mark kept his head lowered but raised his eyes. 'Come on, Clara, you can do it.'

Clara's emotion trickled away. She shrugged. If she could tell him what kind of a man he was, it would cease to be the case.

Mark appeared to sense her change of mood. 'Then how about I apologize?'

'You could have done that sooner. You could have said you were sorry the next day, straight off.'

Mark raised his eyebrows. He gave a half-smile. 'I did. Actions mean more to you than words.'

'They turn out to be a heap more reliable.'

'Though they aren't wholly predictable, are they? And that's the essential problem with your way of life.'

'I'd have said it was the "essential problem" with everybody's way of life.'

'Granted.' Mark nodded his head. 'Except that most of us don't have to set things up so that they're in constant danger of going out of kilter.' Clara couldn't help but note the keen, interested expression on the man's handsome face. Was this what it was like to have a rational debate?

'I don't understand what you mean.'

'I mean that to surround yourself with lost souls might ensure that you are the strongest – the only one who's really needed, the person in charge – but it also means there's never anyone else to turn to. I know how that feels.'

Quicksilver sensations tore across Clara's frame. Through Mark's wide, questioning eyes she caught a flashed image of her cack-handed companions, her makeshift life, before, out of reflex, leaping to their defence – just a second too late.

'They aren't lost souls. They're A-okay. Things hold together absolutely fine. It works. And nothing on earth buys you the right to despise us.'

'I don't despise you. On the contrary, I sincerely respect and indeed like every last person who resides in this house. But admit it, Clara, you're making do. You're making do because you're too damn frightened to let anyone of a capacity equal to your own anywhere close.'

As he'd been speaking, Mark's voice had grown louder. The vehemence that had possessed him left him troubled and confused. He'd got carried away somehow. Unthinkingly, he had pushed Clara considerably further than was appropriate. Why did it seem so imperative that he should?

There was a drawn-out silence between them, interrupted only by the rain's slow handclap.

Clara said, 'I've never had particular reason to trust people much. You included.' Her voice was an icicle. 'Whether you planned it that way or not, *you* don't seem to have made that impressive a show of handling *your* affairs either – witness having fetched up lodging with freakish old us . . .'

'God, Clara, I . . .'

'Nor do I notice the place exactly thronged with *your* nearest and dearest. So don't make like it's only me that's got problems.'

Another pause.

'Touché,' said Mark quietly. He attempted to arrange his features in such a way as to conceal how her retort had made him feel.

Again, that rigid posture, as if his jaw was chiselled rock. Given which, why bother trying to bestow a little insight? However, 'Listen,' Clara said. 'There's two ways of doing things: the straight and the not so. One's the prerogative of those with an abundance of choices, who never have to settle for anything. The other's what's left over for people like me. And like you now, perhaps.'

The temperature had fallen, but anyway Clara's last words would have chilled Mark to the core. Instinctively he recoiled.

Clara continued, 'So I'm sticking with precisely what I've got planned for tomorrow, and you can come along or not, as you please.'

Nothing had been irreparably concluded yet. Social stigma notwithstanding, Mark still had the chance of a foothold in at least the middle-class camp. It occurred to him that there must still remain various avenues he hadn't explored. He could walk down the stairs and out of the door. Was Clara unaware of the radicality of the options she was setting before him? Didn't she see that in order to go along with her way of doing things, Mark would have to say farewell to his past and send much of his attitude to existence up in smoke?

Clara knew what she'd uttered had sounded calm as calm. Most times she could do that: it was a necessary talent. Inside, however, she was malarial. She'd have liked to have rushed across and slammed the draughty window, stopped the meddlesome hunger for change from puffing at the cobwebs of her means of coping. She'd have liked to have put a 'discontinued' sign on the blowtorch line of thinking which ended with the conclusion that she might relate to others differently.

'What's on offer involves more risk than you're accustomed to,' Clara said to herself out loud.

As when she had appeared to doubt his usefulness in unloading material, Mark was offended. And this time with more cause. Then, the aspersions on his physique had been a diversionary tactic. Now, Mark's nerve was genuinely being called into question.

'I think I have proved my mettle frequently enough to quell any doubts as to my courage,' he said in a clipped voice.

Clara was startled. 'So you're with us?'

Mark was thrown. 'I didn't say that. Frankly, I don't know which side I'm on.'

'Which *side*?'

'What do you think coming with you tomorrow would imply for me, Clara?'

Clara felt distanced. 'I imagine I'm about to find out.'

An irritatingly reserved expression came on to Mark's face. He waved a hand in a non-committal gesture. 'I am perfectly confident that I possess every bit as much valour as the next man and, I reiterate, I have on occasion given evidence to this effect – albeit unwittingly. But there is the crux. Now my involvement in what I have been accustomed to view as chicanery is required to become conscious and deliberate.'

With which he gave Clara a meaningful look, as if he'd said it all, and that was that. Clara sprang to her feet. Two could turn their backs. She pulled open a cupboard and started to cram anything and everything within reach into it. Wet crockery. An apron. A saucerful of pins.

'You mean it's okay to break the law as long as you aren't aware you're doing so?' she enquired.

There was an exasperated pause.

'Of course not. I mean that you're asking me to become a completely different person.'

A length of ribbon. A box of tin tacks. A half-burned candle. A tape measure.

'And you haven't the stomach for it? You lack the guts?'

'It's not a question of guts.'

This was nearly shouted. Clara had got him riled, but she was angry too. By what arrogant right did Mark Upshaw think he could airily imply that Clara should break the habits of a lifetime, while at the same instant balking at the small prospect of putting one over on a hyper-cashed ex who'd finished with *him*?

'Yes, it is about guts. That's what it is. It's about guts all round.' Clara twirled to face Mark. 'It's about nerve and commitment, which you apparently don't have.'

The kitchen china rattled. The drenched road sizzled. The light outside the window was the colour of trees caught in headlamps. Clara and Mark both stood motionless, glaring. Fury had frozen them. The whole tortuous, fragile world teetered on a table-edge.

Mark's face was pale, his eyes shone black. 'I can make no promises,' he said, and strode out of the room.

* * *

The rain had stopped, or only paused maybe. From the sitting-room Clara could hear voices out in the street.

Water racketed through the pipes, then Clara heard Mark's footsteps on the landing, his bedroom door open and close, a floorboard creak.

She'd thought it had grown cooler, but now it seemed to be boiling up again. Clara was choosing clothes for tomorrow and the temperature was something to bear in mind, what with short staff and possible extra shifting. Camouflage gear for a.m. Clara worked her way through stacks, hangers, stashed piles, and there seemed to be little there that would irrefutably keep her hidden. Though what was the point of muted khaki when Geraldine would look like something escaped from a string quartet and Kim would undoubtedly be done up like the fairy on the Christmas tree? Good it was custom to borrow the sheen of whatever glam business you worked for, if you did. Clara reckoned ninety per cent of those you saw in Old Compton with their mobiles, tunic tops and flatties really spent their working days hacking at the keys of a PC. Not choosing film scripts or faxing LA.

Thinking about that weighed Clara down. She was hot. There was a short satin slip, parchment-coloured, hanging from a picture hook. She unbuttoned her damp top and let it fall to the ground. Her bra felt as if it were glued to her; she unclasped it and let it fall also. Thirties screen star: it left an imprint of sensations on her body. Clara finished undressing and stood naked a moment, letting the air breathe upon her flesh. She heard pigeons twitching in the eaves, Mark's footsteps again, the sash window thrown open wide.

Her forehead was covered in a cold sweat. For doing the delivery she would wear a thin Indian skirt and a sleeveless cotton top, mottled moss and burgundy. Yes! For the evening . . .

How could a place this crammed feel so very empty?

For the evening Clara would wear a Clara. Her fingers clicked along the dress rails, trying to decide which one. On the arm of the sofa, static in a dancing pose, were Kim's watered-silk mules, only slightly scuffed. Something to match them perhaps? Something lavish and luxurious, lest one appear paltry (apparently there was a danger). Something to prevent the incursion of the idea that Clara's project on its own was no longer enough, that tomorrow would have aspects of simply going through the motions. The blab you got doled about the subtle misery of possessing lashings of wealth had always struck Clara as the most utter tosh, but now she could a bit see that buyable joys mightn't entirely suffice.

Clara's mind swivelled back to the time when there had only been herself, the other four and Bethany. They still didn't look like lost souls to her, but in the light that had been shone on them since then, they did look like misfits. Clara knew a fair amount about those. You could chuck them out, make them fit, or build around them. Clara had done the latter. Had it been, she wondered, in crackpot anticipation of some piece that would fall into place and therefore make everything else jar less?

Clara rarely gave head space to the rest of her life. The future seemed no more than a hand-to-mouth scrabble from one day to the next. For a Mark Upshaw it evidently wasn't like that, which would probably be the reason the prospect of things not already taken into account appalled him so hugely. Even with mess and compromise to look back on, more of the same suddenly struck Clara too as quite a lagging. With calm and symmetry and known quantities behind – an environment of certainties and long-term projections – perhaps it was right to see Clara's outlook as pretty awful. Awful was what it seemed to her at that moment. Depleted. Nothing left up her sleeve. Reincarnation, no kind of rebate. Everyone getting some use out of Clara's life except for Clara herself.

She hadn't wanted Mark Upshaw along for the ride, and there he'd been. She wanted him now, and there he wasn't. Clara imagined Mark lying up above her. She imagined him sleeping the sleep of the just: all that had looked willing to stretch and open having bounded safely back whence it came.

Mark would not be there in the morning, that Clara knew for certain: it was par for the course.

Mark peeled off his T-shirt, wiped his brow with it, threw it to the floor and lay down on the bed. Hands clasped behind his head, he stared at the wall, feeling his chest cool and the smoothness of the coverlet against his bare feet.

He was a smart guy. Surprising how easy that was to forget. But then he'd occupied a world where money was often a smartness substitute. It paved ways which, if necessary, you could pave for yourself. Fortunes had been lost and found again many times over. One could start small. Get a job. Invest. Mark had thought he possessed nothing, but he had knowledge, nous, experience, plus a hell of a good education. Capital made these things look like small details when in actual fact they were everything. Self-reliance could render a world less hostile: no power to its refusals or its favours then. Oh yes, it was easy enough to identify with that.

Windows were open and Soho was hushed. Mark could hear Clara doing things. The clattering of coat hanger against coat hanger. Her stomping feet. She played the building like a giant orchestral piece. She was all slams, reverberations and echoes. Mark thought of a crescendo of falling, smashing objects; the whirring tumble of a house of cards; the deep hollow of an empty cupboard.

Moving would be much more difficult without suitcases. Anything could be got round, though.

It seemed ironic that he'd spent so many of his days recently wishing he knew more, only to arrive at the state of wishing he knew a whole lot less. Perhaps the ultimate layout of Fleur's establishment was already finalized and sorted. Maybe Fleur did have a blueprinted 'arrangement concept', as it had been styled when she was having the villa done over: as thorough as the Ten Commandments, as unnegotiable as present-day Islam. Nothing but *this* conjunction of tile and marble. That, *and that only,* size of pond and pot in the courtyard. Fleur would have kept the flowers from growing and expanding if she could. She'd have restricted certain birds from entering the arbour. The same attitude to her latest venture was at least possible.

There was a second distinct possibility also, however, and it was the one which went much more with Fleur's British mode – conceivably, it suddenly occurred to Mark, because the two contrasting approaches each required in their context the maximum pains to execute them. The Pyramids could scarcely have involved more convoluted rigour than Fleur's Tuscan rose garden. On the other hand, the tortuous aspect of her New Forest cottage's conservatory and greenhouse extension had had much to do with Fleur having put it in place, disliked the effect, and started the entire thing again from scratch. Which could well be the case with the dress rails. There would be Fleur, imposing artificial chaos upon order. There would be Clara, imposing artificial order upon chaos. The results could be unspeakable.

Mark wiped the sweat from his forehead. His arms and hands felt heavy and useless. He wished he could be out there with the van again, with a bucket of soapy water and a task to be performed.

Putting things in place: how succinctly that summarized the subject-matter of an awful lot of the conundra that were raising havoc among Mark's beliefs and instincts. It was tantalizing to go all the way with Clara's argument about what it would mean to deposit unsolicited garments into Fleur's collection. One could, if one had a mind to, view the deed as a charitable act, a form of giving: the parody of a fair exchange, in fact, for Clara, the rest of the time, having to make a life out of objects that Fleur and those such as her discarded. And besides, should Clara's items sell, would that be anything less than grist to Fleur's mill?

Mark shifted on the bed, closed his eyes and opened them again. It wasn't precisely lack of guts which was stopping him from being true, nor yet the queasy scruples that Clara was probably right to despise. Mark like his friends, was afraid that lack of fortune was contagious. It was not brave or forgivable, but surely it was understandable to want to close ranks with the immune and rely on the strengths of one's own inoculated history.

CHAPTER SIXTEEN

Alchemy

'One should never be naughty on an empty stomach!' Kim and Si were sharing a bag of pink and white marshmallows. 'Look, Clara.' Kim pointed a fingernail at the flawless sky. 'The gods have been cleaning.'

Clara poured herself a black coffee. 'They forgot to do the bathroom.'

Eventually she had got it together to grab a couple of hours' kip, after which she'd bathed and togged up. Her hair was soft and bouncy and still damp at the tips. It smelled of oranges from the free-gift sachet. Clara had put on high, plaited-leather sandals to match the Indian skirt. No rings or pendants, though, because they might catch. She'd studied the charts again and tested herself to be sure that all necessary intelligence was well lodged in her head – panicked it might have done an overnight flit. She had made an impeccability check on each and every garment, ascertained that Geraldine was awake, and taken a morning cuppa up to Muncher.

The weather *was* being co-operative, and the street did have a newly washed look. Almost, it was too bright. Standing at her window, Clara felt spotlit, scrutinized. The lemon beams had an interrogatory air. She wouldn't have been surprised to have seen a silver plane shoot out of Heathrow and write a fuzzy question mark against the blue. Distances seemed distorted. She could have reached out and nicked chips from the cartons of the two men leant against the opposite wall, chomping; clicked the shutters of the rubbernecks taking pictures.

Clara glanced back at the clock, the black seconds frog-marching around the dial. Twenty minutes for loading and twenty-five minutes in the van, she had calculated. Arrival time round the corner from Newburgh and rendezvous with those making their way there on foot: 9.45. Assembly in kitchen: 09.00 hours, and they'd be hard pressed now. Light a joss for no serious jams. Flashing blue lights really should be standard issue for all vehicles, to be used in the case of dire hurry. When the whole operation was over and done, Clara would get a sunflower for Bethany; such a lot of bloom from such a little seed. The time at present was 8.47. (Clara had set the clock exactly right before her bath, so it wouldn't be misleading.) When oh when would Muncher appear? When would Geraldine? Should she chase upstairs and make a lot of noise in the corridors?

Heavy footsteps. The sitting-room door opening. Muncher in overalls. Overalls would have been a good idea for the others probably. Overalls or lab coats, which wouldn't have been hard to come by. Something, anyway, that would have presented an image of consistency. Kim wasn't too done up, considering, but the lemon rah-rah, white cotton blouse and almost matching yellow scarf still didn't amount to understated. Si, on the other hand, looked positively designer, which might prove an asset. He'd tied his shiny black hair into a ponytail, secured by a leather thong. Si had grown taller and broadened out of late. Perhaps he'd turned sixteen? He wore faded black jeans and grey espadrilles, a khaki T-shirt with a red star. His slightly Chinese eyes always looked as if they'd been outlined in kohl.

Eight fifty-eight and thirty seconds. Geraldine: saturated in essential oils, looking like cheese at fourpence.

'Did you have any problem getting access to the bathroom?' Clara asked quickly.

'I am not late, I trust? I set my Baby Ben.' Geraldine's eyes started to fill.

'No, no, no.'

'Marky-boy's cutting it a bit close,' said Muncher. 'Time for another cup of tea, then, luv?'

'No there is not.' Clara took a whopping breath, as if she were a Calaluan about to dive fast and deep. 'And as for Mark . . .'

Muncher sang 'Ten Green Bottles' all the way to Newburgh Street. To him they might as well have been some merry coach trip off to the Derby, rather than a wound-up – and in some cases grim-faced – set, riddled with apprehension. There were coils of barbed wire and bundles of springy stuff in Clara's chest and stomach. She felt like compressed cotton wool, popcorn about to pop, a champagne cork on the very brink of busting out.

So far so good. They'd loaded the van efficiently and fast – first in, last off. The ancient motor's interior was so squeaky clean Len would think they were worried about a dusting for fingerprints. No hem was going to collect so much as a speck, no sleeve the merest smudge. Kim, Si and Geraldine ambled off on Shanks's. (They could hole up in the Coffee Café once they got there, but mustn't even think of making any stops *en route.*) There was an awkward squeeze into the front of the vehicle and then they were moving, Clara virtually sitting on the handbrake.

'And if *wun* green bottle should accidentally fall,' bellowed Muncher joyfully over the engine – in spite of the fact that the whole West End was one big clog, and by the time they got to Newburgh there'd probably be nothing there to meet them but empty wineglasses and the ghosts of adulation.

'Cut down Wardour. Cut down *Wardour.*'

'There'd be *five* green . . . Wot?'

Leaning over and flicking the indicator. '*Cut down Wardour.*'

Brakes and hoots and yells of abuse. Clara felt Mark's body

tense. He muttered an exclamation under his breath. Mark had spoken barely a word – and none to Clara – since his eleventh-hour appearance. He had worked smoothly – effortlessly competent – interpreting Clara's plans in a businesslike manner, and spotting mistakes before they could happen. Why had he come, though? The look on his face was leaden, and he certainly gave no indication this was something he in any way wanted to be doing. Clara felt the weight of a massive concession that she might have got up the pluck to ask about, had chance allowed.

It was a gorgeous a.m., so what was the entire population doing converging on London? Why hadn't they gathered together their spades and flippers, rugs and Thermoses and headed for the south coast? At least it wasn't raining, at least it wasn't raining: the national anthem, the Brit refrain when making the best of things. Still, however, there were those lively sensations in Clara's insides – part spangles, part drawing pins; fear and excitement making a novel sort of rumpus.

There was a delay where the council had suddenly decided to gouge the road up. Two blokes were working with pneumatics at the far end of twenty foot or so of a cordoned-off length of highway, leading up to the intersection between Wardour and Broadwick. The van sneezed and gasped and hacked as it waited to snail along the bit of narrow tarmac that remained open to traffic.

They crawled down Broadwick then into Marshall Street, their designated meeting point.

'What time is it?'

A pause.

'Just gone a quarter to ten,' said Mark.

There, glimpsed between parked motor, parked motor, parked motor were Kim, Si and Geraldine sitting at one of the Coffee Café's outdoor tables.

'There's a Porsche right up the back of me,' said Muncher. 'I'll have to go on round the block.'

No deliveries happening yet in Newburgh, but another clagup: press and Fleur's employees doubtless, not about to budge until they'd secured parking places, the traffic at a complete standstill. When the van at length turned into Marshall again, every vehicle still looked as anchored to its spot as the lions in Trafalgar. *Including the one with the Coffee Café's logo plastered all over it.*

'There'd be *no* green bottles . . .'

'Muncher, head back to Wardour. Stall at the bit of road-works that's farthest from the navvies.' Clara turned to Mark. 'As soon as Muncher stops, jump out and grab as many witches' hats as you can handle.' Mark said nothing; perhaps he hadn't understood her. 'Traffic cones,' Clara persisted urgently. 'As many as you can get. Traffic cones.'

Mark stared straight ahead. 'I'm aware of what you mean. I am just not too crazy about the idea of appropriating from a pair of sixteen-stone workmen, in broad daylight . . .'

'They won't notice. They've got earplugs.'

'And blindfolds also?'

'Here we are,' said Muncher.

The van door flew open. Without a word Mark hurtled out and had gathered up six traffic cones before the navvies' eyes could send a message to their brains.

Six! 'Back to Newburgh, Muncher. Fast as you can make it.'

'Hold on ter yer seats. Ten green . . .'

The others had drained their paper cups and were looking thrown. The street remained chock-a-block. Once he'd dropped Mark and Clara off, Muncher was obliged to recommence circling.

'Grab hold of these.' Clara deposited the orange-and- white-striped plastic hats with Kim, Si and Geraldine. To Mark she said, 'We're undercover rozzers wanting the café's parking space for a reconnaissance vehicle.'

'Won't they ask us for identification?'

'Only if they've got something to hide.'

'I suppose you know that impersonating a police officer is . . .'

'Better than being one. Look, if you're here, you're here, and that gets taken into account. Coppers always come in pairs.'

'Okay. Okay.'

As it turned out, Mark made a highly convincing plain-clothed. Not quite burly enough perhaps – too muscular and well formed. And a single gold hoop earring would have added to the effect – actually, it would add to the effect anyway. But Mark did mimic really well that seemingly diffident way a rozzer could make a command sound like a request. He also managed to suggest that what they were at was terribly important and awfully hush-hush, which went down a treat. Thank heaven for the load of telly stuff which made coppers' dull lives look agog with ingenuity and risk. Once their story had been bought, the pretty staff would fit the sight of Clara, Mark and the others moving about with dress rails into whatever dramatic scenario they'd jointly managed to concoct for themselves. The boy who moved the café's van did so with a mixture of barely contained thrill and civic virtue on his face. Scarcely had the spot been vacated when a white open-top attempted to nip in. Just in time, Mark held up a hand and Clara filled the space with cones.

Then there was nothing to do but wait for Muncher to return and put everyone on stand-by.

'Kim, you go into Newburgh and see if any deliveries have started to arrive. Geraldine, put yourself where Kim can signal to you. Si, stand where you can see both Geraldine and us.'

'This is ace!'

'I fear ambiguities.'

'There won't *be* any, dearest. I shall simply shake my head for no and nod it for yes.'

As Clara watched them take up their stations, 'What time is it?' she enquired, dreading the reply.-

'Quarter past, but bear in mind the traffic is bad for everyone, not just us.'

'It doesn't feel that way.'

'Never does. But look.' Mark pointed at Si, who was indicating an encouraging lack of action.

The blast of the horn made them both jump. Len's van was bigger than the café's, but Muncher did a series of forwards and reverses until he'd got it in with half an inch to spare front and back; by which time Si's gesture had changed to a positive and he was running towards them, followed by Kim and Geraldine, approaching at a trot.

'We're on,' said Mark. Briefly, his eye caught Clara's. Then he was lifting dress rails out.

Muncher was to stick with the motor: however unlikely some of its legit denizens, no one was going to mistake Muncher for even a peripheral member of the fashion world.

'Remember to slow down just before the entrance and check your charts,' Clara shouted to the others as they raced the rails along the road in approximate order, round the corner and into Newburgh Street, where everything was happening at once.

A massive puce lorry with Vigilante written on its side was stopped plumb outside Fleur's shop. Behind it was Yen – white on black with a tinted windscreen. Parked parallel to Yen was Cut & Dried, the florist. The pavements and road were thronged with stylish people. Folk had come out of the neighbouring establishments to watch the show. Slowed by the crush, Clara got a chance to study the velvet torsos in Fleur's windows. She had been hoping that they would be clad in day wear, which would keep day logical for the front section of the shop and suggest that the layout still tallied with their maps. What she saw, however, was inconclusive (and oh so *safe*): a dress-up-or-dress-down, mid-length, office-to-nightclub (by way of striking brooch). Clara's heart began to sink.

'Now?' asked Mark.

Clara rallied. 'Yup. Go for it. And we'll need to push.'

The crowd had momentarily thinned a fraction. They surged forward, timing it so that they entered the building shortly after a consignment from Yen, delivered by minions in buff T-shirts with Chinese characters on.

Inside the shop the atmosphere was clenched. The place was crammed and everyone was being agonizingly polite.

Damn! Damn! Damn! Could nothing on the planet be trusted to remain consistent? What, for heaven's sake, had been wrong with Fleur's previous layout? And when had Clara's schmutter grown so bright and Fleur's dissolved into undertones? Could Fleur's shades have been distorted by Clara's binoculars? In spite of the new difficulty of locating their chosen spots, it was vital that they still attempt to blend. Everything from now on was going to be infinitely more complicated.

As if he'd read her thoughts, Mark turned to Clara. 'All changed round, I guess?'

Clara nodded. She would have liked to have to torn ahead, got Plan B into motion, but now they were halted in their tracks by a blond-haired assistant with a stuffed headband, like ear-phones.

'Could you lot be absolute angels and wait a little bit?' Clara recognized the voice from the telephone. 'There's been a teensy mix-up I'm just trying to deal with, and Vigilante *himself* is having a look around at present. We weren't expecting him, of course, or Fleur would have come up from Hampshire last night. But she did fax us from there first thing with all her marvellous new ideas about where to put . . .' The assistant paused, suddenly seeming to become aware that most of this was only relevant to herself. 'Golly, that's rather colourful.'

'We're okay to wait,' said Clara sharpish.

'Worry thou not,' put in Kim.

Mark said nothing. Clara glanced in his direction. To her surprise Mark was looking startled, as if a new idea had suddenly struck him or only this moment been assimilated.

'Can I at least put these down?' asked the apparent agent of the teensy mix-up, a man in a grey workcoat carrying a mammoth bouquet of spiky things, and twigs with little flowers on.

The assistant's attention returned to him. 'Well, look, you *said* you wouldn't be coinciding with the designers' deliveries, and you also said wheat and lilies. Which is what *I* told *Country Manner.*'

'That isn't what I've got written down here, and if I drop them there's a danger someone'll get hurt.'

'But they're *not what Fleur wanted.*' Betwixt snarl and wail.

There was an almighty flurry. A man with egg-yolk hair tied in an upward-pointing sprout above his tanned face, and a little yellow arrow of beard, had appeared and was leisurely wending his way towards the exit flanked by a a multitude of lovelies. This was – couldn't be other than – the celebrated Vigilante, chief squeeze of the beau monde. He must have been having a poke around the storage area out back. Vigilante was wearing crimson jodhpurs, a black string top, a red suede jerkin and high black suede boots. Everyone – but *everyone* – paused for a moment, broke off, gawped, admired.

'Let's make our way forward, nice and slowly,' said Mark.

Exploiting the glamorous distraction, they glided around the assistant – her attention mopped up by designer and flora – and interweaved themselves between unpackers, deliverers and note-takers; tacking on to the tail-end of the posse of Yen.

'*There,* for yours, Geraldine,' murmured Clara, as they edged parallel with a range she recognized.

'It's all different,' cried Geraldine, fanning her map around.

'I know.' Softly. 'But your rail goes over there. Next to those greens.'

'There's no room.'

'You'll need to push the other dress rails along to make some.'

With the air of a nurse about to put a screen around a hospital bed in order to do something very unpleasant to its occupant, utterly incongruous and nearly in tears, Geraldine moved towards where Clara had indicated. Clara flicked a look the way of Vigilante, who was still occupying a helpful number of eyes.

'Where'll I go, Clara?' Si was just loving this. 'Tell me where'll I go.'

'Calm down,' Mark instructed him. 'Don't try to do anything too fast.'

Each of them should have quietly glided into their allotted slot. Instead, they were now forced to stop, confer and cluster. At any minute an agreement would be reached between Fleur's assistant and the bloke from Cut & Dried. Vigilante would disappear into a waiting limo and people would start looking around more. (Celebs always came and went in a rush; it ensured you never got quite enough of them.) Clara's mind had transformed itself into the sludge-grey blank of a switched-off telly.

'Where do you want *me*?' twittered Kim. 'No, it's all right. I think I can see where it was planned these would go.'

Clara looked at Mark, who was looking at her.

'Probably the most important thing is to get ourselves to the edges of the room,' he suggested. 'We can place the things after.'

'Right!' said Si.

'Yes, I *do* remember,' said Kim.

She and Si started to move off in opposite directions. At that same moment there was a pair of high-pitched yelps. Two girls went flying; one collided with the florist's man, who fell forwards on to his banana flowers and artichokes with a prolonged, muffled cry which sounded something like 'I told you!' Every gaze flew to Geraldine, who must have given a big shove to one of the sets of rails she wanted to get between, thus creating a domino effect which had thrown the girls – presumably engaged in hanging things up – completely off balance.

There were a few seconds of stunned silence, immediately followed by an almighty crash as Kim and Si's rails collided. Geraldine's position centre-stage was instantly supplanted as all eyes leapt to Kim and Si.

Another silence, and some powerfully resolute, let's-get-a-few-things-cleared-up-right-now expressions beginning to form on the faces of those in charge of making sure things ran smoothly.

Then, 'What is *this*?' breathed Vigilante into the hush,

freezing everyone in their tracks and causing the employees' expressions to switch to confusion, since they no more than Clara had the foggiest what the International Genius was referring to.

Vigilante raised a manicured finger, pointed it at Si and beckoned. 'Come here,' he commanded.

The multitude goggled and craned as Si strode forward until he was standing slap in front of the famous designer.

'Are you a model?' Vigilante enquired.

'Sort of,' said Si.

'And you are how old?'

Si shrugged.

'You will get taller.' Vigilante turned to his entourage. 'He will get taller.' Every member of the entourage nodded madly, like Si *would* now get taller, whether his genetic material had planned it that way or not. To Si again, 'You are a boy of great beauty,' Vigilante observed. 'Has anyone ever told you so?'

Si smirked. 'On occasion.'

'There will be more such occasions, I think. Yes, many. Get yourself an agent.' The designer paused, presumably to let everyone prepare their gasp. 'Tell them to send you to Vigilante!'

With which he swept out like the Demon King.

This moment of complete exposure – when surely the game must be up – should have been the point at which Mark's confusion as to the reasons for his continued participation in Clara's affairs reached a climax. All the requisite ingredients for a nightmare scenario were securely in place. The worst had come to the worst, and Mark had no idea what to do next except watch the whole appalling business play itself out. His inner questioning, however, had ceased. Which was in direct contrast to the way things had been when he had woken that morning, seen clear blue sky in the gap between his curtains and heard the familiar sounds of plumbing, thumps and voices.

Mark should have known that he wouldn't oversleep. Punctuality had been dinned into him virtually from birth. No possibility of Mark's biorhythms baling him out or taking over the decision-making process. And that, apparently, was still in full operation: the situation which had seemed pretty much settled the night before proved open, moot, far from concluded.

Mark had lain there, perplexed. A sunbeam touched his bare chest, both bathing him in warmth and at the same time making it plain that days such as this were not to be wasted. Perhaps Clara kept a stock of summer mornings in a bag somewhere and used one very occasionally, spreading it out like a tablecloth with a parachute flourish.

Mark was aware that he was smiling.

In had marched duty, looking rather different from usual. One's duty? To break the law in subtle ways? To tot up what could be salvaged from the past, then draw a line under it? To be free and new again? There was Clara, standing where class and clan had been, arguing as vehemently as they ever had that you didn't let people down. This was unwelcome. It hadn't been planned for. *Nothing* had been planned for: that was the burden of it.

So then Mark was in T-shirt and jeans, drawing the curtains back, feeling excitement and dread trace fizzy lines along his muscles. Unwilling. Unwilling. This wasn't fair and Mark was resentful. Hands other than his had pulled off the covers. As he stood there in the morning light, Mark felt watched, assessed, as if he were in the presence of an audience surveying him from outside and monitoring his actions. He didn't want to like his reconceived self, the fired-up man who checked the time on the face of his carriage clock and evidently couldn't bear the thought of not being a part of whatever was going to happen. Perhaps his motives could be explained in terms of some sort of natural outcome? So many events had built up to this. Opting out would be like going home before the final act. Anyway, Mark didn't have to be pleased about his prospects. He merely had to be cool and efficient.

Which hadn't worked out either. Now, confronted with imminent disaster, Mark realized that the heat which had first galvanized him had been increasing ever since.

He had held himself in check, been aware of the restrained impression he was projecting. But there was something in his soul that began to enjoy the thought of Muncher's smashing green bottles. If need be, Mark could have whisked away every witch's hat in the capital once he actually got started. Zest was catching: it was that, wasn't it? A citrus mix of animation and fear. He couldn't not feel Clara's pounding eagerness – each nerve alert; full of purpose. Mark had tried to remain sardonic but he'd got progressively caught up in the task of making things work – if they only would, if they only would.

And then had come the information about Fleur, relayed by an assistant schooled to swallow her resentments – the fact that Fleur wasn't there, the implied problems caused by her instructions having changed at the last minute. Clara's confident prediction about his ex-girlfriend's movements galloped back to Mark: *She'll only waltz in for the plaudits.* Clara really did understand Fleur substantially better than he ever had. Or she noticed different aspects of her. Or things jarred on Mark that at one time wouldn't have. Yes, Fleur would only waft in for the accolades. The realization hit Mark with a shock, though it was only consistent with what he already knew of Fleur's behaviour, and had his own life worked out differently he would doubtless have been her approving consort. There was just something uniquely inappropriate about the sight of all this effort on behalf of what was no more than a plaything; these real people putting in real labour for the sake of somebody's hobby. It was heart-wrenching to witness Clara – who spent every waking minute planning and striving – being obliged to claw for her piece of the action. Last night Mark had viewed Fleur as whimsical but somehow participatory. In truth she wasn't either and never had been. Fleur's role was performed by proxy. Never need Mark have feared that Fleur would be there to witness him making his delivery – Clara had been spot on about that – and fortunate though this was, it was also an affront to Clara's labour.

Albeit of an unconventional variety. The two women whom Geraldine had catapulted backwards were now being helped to their feet, apparently embarrassed at having cried out, murmuring over and over that they were 'absolutely okay'. The man from the florist was exhibiting less stoicism, though from what Mark could make out of his comments he did have an excuse, being studded with prickles. Geraldine was sniffling audibly. The impact of the collision had knocked Kim's rail over. Some of the hangers had come unhooked. Clara's Crescendo Dress lay sprawled across the floor.

Mark wondered how things would pan out. Might they just be hefted from the place, or could they expect someone to call the police?

At his side Clara said, 'Could we please have some *help* here?' in a loud and imperious tone which suggested it was small wonder things had gone awry, in the light of this establishment's massive inefficiency. Immediately, to Mark's gaping astonishment, clipboards were hurriedly put down, phone conversations curtailed, tasks abandoned. There was a general apologetic rush in their direction, mostly centred on Clara, who brushed this off as yet more waste of time when there was so much still to be done. 'That's all right, but could this set of rails go over there please, next to the Puttanescas. You'll need to make some space. And these . . .' Clara feigned a show-stoppingly irritated sigh. 'These should already be alongside the Jean-Marie Potirons. Yes, like I say, in that corner.' Then, breathtakingly, pointing at Geraldine, who was beginning to rally, 'And can we have a glass of water for my assistant, please? Sparkling.'

Mark's rail was whisked from his grasp. Kim's was lifted back on to its casters and the Crescendo Dress spirited away to be ironed. Under Clara's instructions her collection glided into place, for all the world as if its arrival had been completely anticipated. When eventually they were ushered out, it was with additional profuse apologies and the promise of a better performance in future.

The whole interlude had been like a glimpsed image of how things were meant to behave. Mark was entranced, impressed, at a loss to explain how Clara had worked her alchemy. Indefinable changes had been wrought in unsuspected locations. Clara was reshaping everything.

CHAPTER SEVENTEEN

A Merry Dance

How many fingers and toes would you need to cross in order to guarantee that kind of outcome? Small wonder Clara was still hyper keyed-up. (The handbrake really was too uncomfortable to sit on completely, especially for an extended period: with this ton of traffic the others should have got the tea well brewed in the pot by the time Clara, Muncher and Mark got back to Lisle.)

Was there a word the fashion world understood better than *endorsement*? Folk employed in a biz that would pay millions for the privilege of displaying a logo on a range of sportswear or undies could be virtually guaranteed to respond automatically to anything that one such as Vigilante lent his seal of approval to. Clara was familiar with guilt by association; its opposite was thinner on the ground, but that was what they'd harvested when Si's striking looks had snagged the interest of the Designer to the Stars. Invisibility was usually an only option. To be made visible and simultaneously legitimized was beyond the dreams of avarice. Vigilante had thrown back the door for Si and they'd all trooped in behind him. The Designer's good favour had rendered them kosher in that context.

Two birds with one stone as well: Si *would* grow taller if Clara had to hang him from the ceiling with weights around his ankles. He'd get to be photographed looking sulky and bad-tempered in the glossies. He'd have a flat and friends and a mobile telephone.

Mark would know enough about the look of a nice tight legal contract to ensure Si didn't get sold short by anybody.

There was no rush any more, but Clara nevertheless felt as if she was in one. There was nothing chasing her at present, but still she felt chased. If cars had wings like aeroplanes you could simply fly them out of traffic jams. If people had wings, using them might produce the same sensations that were fluttering through Clara at this instant. Or even more so, the ones that had overwhelmed her when Mark had appeared in the kitchen – in spite of everything and on the dot.

You couldn't reasonably resent a bit of extra congestion you yourself might possibly have helped contribute to – though why did they always wait to bring out their pneumatics till the sun was ultra-bright and the city saturated with tourists? Wardour Street trembled at its foundations and Clara thought how, single-handed, she still could have made things work out. Though that would have been another world, wouldn't it? Pull one thread and the whole weave unravelled. There didn't exist a version of this summer's morning in Soho in which Mark hadn't been in the van beside her, with Muncher singing up a storm. (Mercifully, he'd stopped that now.) The witches' hats were gone, leaving the traffic muddled. Mark had apparently loosened up enough not to come over all responsible and insist they were put back. Or he'd forgotten about them. His face when Clara glanced at it was . . . too many things to go into. Clara could smell Mark's sweat. A lock of hair could have done with brushing back from his eyes. Her fingers itched to deal with it.

Whatever he'd had to steel in himself to come along, whether or not it was only out of wounded male pride, Mark had been an asset. Perhaps a professional partnership was possible. For a long while it had been as if Clara was driving a dodgy jalopy with a pile of squabblers in the back seat and no one except her in the front. Arms linked was way more effective: that was why coppers did it when dealing with protesters.

* * *

Mark remained silent. He felt tense. Quite suddenly the streets seemed an anxious place, rife with threats to happiness. Perhaps it was a reaction to their narrow escape, but the anonymous faces on the teeming pavements had an intrusive aspect. Mark could almost feel against his stomach a metal turnstile freeze in its revolutions and block him off. An unbudging bulk of elbow and shoulder was ready to impose itself between Mark and whatever he dearly wanted. At the same time, however, the colours around him had become more compelling. Buses had turned a fleshy red. The few leaves on the few trees imposed their noisy greens upon the pale buildings and the azure sky. Mark was breathing pure oxygen. Something had become much too precious. The van was transporting a cargo of gold bullion through a sea of pirates.

Lack of sleep coupled with an intense experience, Mark told himself. The realization that nothing was anchored. Not even Si, who Vigilante's brief words had given an opportunity that might so easily have been missed had metal not hit metal. Mark outwardly smiled and inwardly sighed. He eyed Semerraro's lurid orange dice and ran through what it might take to bring Si's particular chance to fruition. The world was full of impediments. Possibilities would leap away if not handled with care.

The portals of Gerrard Street reminded Mark of an Indian temple. Two policemen in navy uniforms spoke into walkie-talkies, their backs reflected in the windows of an all-you-can-eat Chinese buffet. Lisle Street was a fretwork of blinding light and dingy shadows.

'Here we are, Aitch Sweet Aitch,' said Muncher, finding a parking place where Mark wouldn't have expected there'd be one: right opposite the house, between a grubby blue van and a dusty grey car. As Muncher manoeuvred into position, Mark watched a woman from one of the supermarkets taking handfuls of loose coriander from a plastic bucket and tying them into generous bunches. The woman looked up, caught sight of him, and it seemed to Mark she gave the merest shake of her head, though probably that was only his unsettled brain playing tricks.

Mark turned to Clara.

'What?' she asked, responding immediately, a strange sort of eagerness to her tone.

'I just wondered if . . .'

'Outyer jump,' said Muncher. 'I could kill for a cup.'

Semerraro's doors didn't so much open as dislocate. Mark blinked. The sun was in his eyes. He wiped his brow with the back of his arm. He heard Muncher slam the driver's door and stomp on ahead. He heard the light click of Clara's heels hit the pavement. She smelled of sandalwood. Mark wouldn't have thought his heart could accelerate, but it did. The sun went behind a minuscule silver-and-white cloud and the shadows took on a damp appearance. Muncher was opening the door to Clara's building. There were lots of people simply leaning against the walls and frontages. Among them, a burly man with greased-back blond hair, wearing fawn trousers, a loose green tie and a white nylon shirt. There were razor cuts on the man's face.

Mark stopped dead in his tracks. He very lightly touched Clara's arm. It was warm and downed with soft hairs. Mark felt Clara struggle not to flinch. 'Your landlord's over there,' he murmured.

'Where?' Mark sensed in Clara's voice an adrenalin rush similar to his own. He was aware of the stiffening of her body, its preparedness to act. Clara swung to face him in an ostentatiously casual manner. 'Tell me exactly. Make like we've just stopped for a chat.'

'At the far end of the White Bear. Next to the entrance.'

Clara laughed, nonchalantly tossing back her pretty chin to get an angle on the man. 'That's not my landlord,' she said. At that moment, Mark's nose was assailed by the sweet smell of coriander. A body brushed against his. 'Immigration,' a voice muttered in his ear. 'Immigration offisa.' And then the woman was gone.

As if Mark had been staring at a picture for a long while without knowing what it depicted, the scene suddenly composed itself. Not one of the strangers in Lisle Street was there for idle reasons. Nor were the studiedly anonymous vehicles or the policemen on the corner of Gerrard. This was a swoop. The area was positively riddled with immigration officers. They had come to arrest Bethany Smile.

Mark didn't think. He didn't stop to weigh up the consequences. 'Fire!' he yelled, charging forward. 'Fire!' he shouted at the top of his lungs. 'Somebody dial 999.' Under the kitchen window, bellowing up at it in the hope that the others would hear and register: 'Fire! Fire! Fire! Get out! Get out! Get out *as soon as possible!*'

It would never have occurred to Mark that the forces of law and order might buy his ruse, but it seemed that for the moment they at least partially did. Immigration evidently hadn't expected anything other than an easy removal of Bethany Smile, and this change of circumstances appeared to catch them on the hop. Of course, they had no way of knowing that he'd sussed their presence, Mark realized. As far as Immigration was concerned, maybe there really was an emergency. While Mark stood clamouring, he saw out of the corner of his eye a number of the officials form small, loose clusters, apparently unsure whether to converge on the building, block off the street or do a check to ascertain whether there actually were any flames.

'What the fuck's going on, mate?' It was Rob, the Aussie barman, who'd run up to Mark with a tinnie – presumably in order to dowse the inferno. 'I've got one of the guys calling the brigade.'

Mark took a risk. If they could create a diversion in the street for as long as it took for a fire engine to arrive, perhaps when it did Bethany would be able to slip away in the ensuing confusion. 'There is no fire. 'We've got a problem with some unwanted officialdom.'

'Oh yeah?' Rob made a rolling-back-sleeves gesture, though he was actually wearing a black vest with a marijuana leaf on it.

'Hey, boyos,' he bawled in the direction of the White Bear, at a volume even louder than its deafening music, 'Rumble!'

Where was Clara? Mark glanced frantically around. Then he spotted her near the other end of the street, which was suddenly absolutely flooding with people. Some of them looked purposeful, others merely confused. Clara must have run from building to building, both creating panic and soliciting speedy support from those she reckoned would be sympathetic.

This great torrent of humanity was rendering it increasingly difficult for the immigration officials to group and form strategies. A couple of bunches of them appeared to make a unilateral decision to advance on Clara's building from opposite directions.

'Those the buggers?' asked Rob, who was now flanked by four or five brawny fellow Aussies, who looked like they ate bowls of car batteries for breakfast. Mark nodded. 'Right, mates. Get 'em.'

Before there was a chance for battle to commence, however, there was a dramatic increase in the expanding commotion. Grapefruit, sugarcane, a thunderous cavalry of watermelons were being emptied out of their containers by the women from the Chinese supermarkets. The immigration officials – and others – were tripping, toppling, slithering. The ground was an ice rink of squelched melons, a log-jam of slippery sugarcane. Some of the officials did make it nearly up to Clara's door, but Rob and his fellow bar staff intervened between them and it. There were punches and outbursts of swearing; bodies went careering into the populace or sat down abruptly. Meanwhile, in the other direction, French Food & Wine had scattered a large box of ball-bearings into the road, bringing movement in that area to a virtual standstill.

The air resounded with a pandemonium of alarms and sirens. The street was being inundated with ever more people, the news that something was up probably having spread to Gerrard Street and Leicester Square. Not entirely ridiculously, Mark was reminded of Muncher's birthday party. Although the drainage ditch had long since been filled in, and there were no boas or sequins, they could all have been assembling for an enormous hokey cokey. The mood was oddly like a Mardi Gras. When oh when would the fire engine arrive, though? Mark tried to imagine what was going on inside Clara's building; he hoped to God the others would pick the best moment for Bethany Smile to make a dash for it.

Where was Clara? She seemed to have vanished.

The street spontaneously filled with scarlet reflections. A fire engine had appeared on the corner of Lisle and Wardour. Blue light bounced off the walls and windows. The siren's wail reverberated in Mark's eardrums. Slowly and gradually the waves of individuals parted as the fire engine turned into Lisle and edged its way towards Clara's house. Coinciding with the rescue vehicle's arrival came a new preponderance of navy. Police reinforcements. Were they there as an aid to Immigration, or only to support the firemen? Both, Mark feared. Though unable to say by whom, he sensed he was being pointed out. The massive influx of people had made it hard to know any longer who was working for the authorities and who was not. The fire engine lumbered nearer. At the same time, and to Mark's joy, another one appeared from the Charing Cross Road direction. The firemen in their yellow helmets shouted at the crowd to get out of the way, and yelled instructions to the police to do their best to set up a cordon. Their only concern would be to get the inhabitants out of the building – very definitely *not* to let anybody into it. Surely, surely that made escape more likely for Bethany?

Watermelons exploded under the second engine's tyres. In the opposite direction there was a terrible grating sound and a few cries, as the side of the first encountered the metalwork of Len Semerraro's van. Long metal ladders were extended. People watched and cheered. Mark made a mental plea that no macho fireman would decide to carry Bethany down a ladder over his shoulder, in full view of police and Immigration and bang slap into their awaiting custody. Bethany's size was on her side there, however. Such a feat would be foolhardy, fraught with danger and probably in the end impossible. A vast roll of hose was uncoiled. Two firemen applied their axes to Clara's front door.

'Time to skip it, matey,' said Rob at Mark's elbow. Rob's vest was torn. There was an ugly bruise along one of his biceps. He was covered in sweat and looked as happy as Mark had ever seen anybody. Scattered among the seething crush, Mark glimpsed some of Rob's fellow bar staff; most of them were in a similar condition. 'Pretty soon now the shit's going to hit the fan,' Rob continued. 'And once it sinks in that there's no flames and all, you're going to be the subject of too bloody much attention for it not to make sense to scram while you're still able.'

'I can't leave without Clara.'

'Where is she?'

'I don't know.'

'Then it looks like she's left without you, mate. Besides, a sheila that can't look after herself isn't worth bothering with 'cept for recreation.'

Mark said nothing. Desperately he scanned the multitude of faces, hoping to locate Clara's. Just as it had done earlier, the true image of what was going on sprang nastily into focus. Mark was part of the throng but there were police on all sides of him. Not close – not yet – but definitely present. Their positioning should have been random. It wasn't. Mark was also being stared at by a couple of short-haired men whose gaze felt more than casual. His throat tightened. Prickles of fear ran up and down his spine. If he tried to slip away unnoticed there was no doubt he'd be surrounded.

'I think it's too late to make a quiet exit,' Mark murmured.

Rob's eyes circled. 'Jeezus, you're right. Okay.' Rob raised his voice above the rock music, the yells, the alarms and sirens. 'Scrum time, fellas! And *you* owe me a pint, matey.'

'Done.' Mark paused. 'One. Two. Three. And I'm out of

here.' As fast as he possibly could he plunged through the ocean of bodies. Destination: Leicester Square Tube. Immediately, the circle around him contracted. Immediately too, Rob's chums surged, ducked, and made rugby sorts of dives, which could just conceivably have been passed off as inadvertent – the pressure of the pack; unfortunate tumbles – into the legs of the coppers. Mark felt a hand grab his T-shirt and heard the material rip. He shook away from its grasp. He was being pursued from behind, that was for certain. No one had managed to cut him off, though. The swarms of people on the Charing Cross Road when Mark reached it were only the usual mixture of Londoners, shoppers and tourists.

As casually as if she were there to meet an acquaintance for a natter and a lunch, Clara strolled into one of Old Compton Street's open-fronted cafés; not panting any longer but soaked in sweat. There was a big, gilt-framed mirror behind the bar. Clara placed herself at a table with her back to the street and trained her eyes on it.

'What can I get you?'

Clara jumped, then quickly made another jittery gesture to suggest that acting nervy was something she always did. 'An espresso, please.' As she spoke, patches of dark blue appeared among the pale leaves of a giant reflected pot plant. The two rozzers who'd been chasing her appeared in the glass. Clara watched them slowly walk past the café's frontage, behind wine bottles, beer taps and shelves of glasses. They looked angry and overheated. Gradually they disappeared off the edge of the frame, but were followed almost immediately by the couple of immigration officers who'd been on Clara's tail also: speed dropped to leisurely, ears pricked up, alert, gazing around more than the police had done. The hairs on Clara's arms tugged at her skin. She was X-marks-the-spot. She was an enormous ginger vixen, reeking of fear.

'Would you like a biscotti with that?' The waitress pointed a long finger in the direction of a jar full of rusks. She was wearing the whitest shirt Clara had ever seen in her life.

'No, just the coffee.' The immigration men had paused.

'Double or single?'

'Single.' They exchanged a couple of words then moved on. Clara began to breathe again, shallow little gulps that had to be wrested out of her lungs and immediately got tangled up in a hot lump of rage that suddenly formed in her throat. It seemed she had always been in some version or other of this situation. It seemed she had spent her entire life being hounded or dogged, or feeling like she was. Time, yes, time right now for that to stop. No reason to scarper unless you really were being chased.

The coffee came with a thin square of choc and a small, waxed-paper tube of sugar.

'Anything else for you?'

'No thanks.' Clara kept her eyes glued to the mirror. In spite of the precariousness of her cover, in spite of the fact that she'd been within a cooee of getting nabbed, her lips kept twitching into an itchy smile. Were her pupils always that big?

The sirens were still screaming like crazy. Strange that setting things in order made such a gloriously anarchic sound. Lisle Street had gone wild, and when Clara had last sighted Mark he'd been right in the thick of things. The thought spontaneously made Clara's body go icy. Next minute, however, she was molten hot. An identikit yo-yoing took over her brain also. Clara was alternately freezing solid and burning up. She could have wept and laughed and wept again indefinitely. She had led Mark Upshaw such a merry, merry dance, but none of that had stopped him from coming through for her. Clara knew instinct when she saw it in action: whatever he'd said, Mark's personality had given him no choice but to defend Bethany Smile. The thought of him tearing forward yelling 'Fire! Fire!' set off major detonations in Clara's chest, stomach, toes and heart. (Actually, the thought of

Mark at all did that.) What was going to happen to him, though? What kind of heinous ructions were taking place at this very instant? What was going to happen to any of them, for that matter? Were there no-win-no-fee lawyers who did criminal cases? Clara didn't suppose . . .

Her thoughts ceased. The duo of cops and the blokes from Immigration were in the mirror again. Centre-frame. Bang slap behind her. Clara imagined the back of her cotton top, stained with South Americas of sweat while everyone else in the establishment looked as innocent as cucumbers. All Clara's nerves went on to action stations; every muscle prepared for flight. Sometimes a pursuer could look right into your face and yet not register it. This didn't appear to be one of those occasions.

Clara's chair crashed sideways as she advanced towards the officials, tearing a track straight through the middle of them which – she'd calculated right – wasn't what they'd been expecting. One of the rozzers got it together to stick out a boot, but Clara managed to leap over it. She hurtled in the direction of Brewer, the four men snapping close at her heels. Some worthy citizens did their best to catch hold of her. Clara twisted from their grasp. One she managed to get in the shins. She would not be brought to ground like this – no, she would not. She'd take rights and lefts, and lefts and rights; loop round and double back. She would create false trails by running clean through shouting restaurants, front to rear and rear to front. She'd scoot down narrow alleys that smelled of rotten veg and scorched tyres. Guard dogs would bark and jangle their chains. The beggars are coming to town! The beggars are coming to town! There were things that Clara wanted too much to tolerate being taken. How many of them were on offer she refused to be prevented from finding out.

Were the men gaining on her, or were the advancing footsteps just echoes of Clara's own? Had reinforcements been asked for? Was an invisible pack of police officers encircling Clara and about to close in? From almost directly above her head came the deadly chop, chop, chopping sound of a helicopter.

Mark was in Camden Market and he was worried sick.

Obviously he couldn't return to Lisle Street. Nor could Clara. If Clara hadn't been arrested she might be absolutely anywhere, which was why – though it was against the odds – Mark kept thinking he'd seen her, only to have woman after woman with short dark hair obtusely metamorphose into someone else. (Had any study been done on the disproportionate number of brunettes in London?)

It was as hard to imagine Clara in a prison cell as to envisage a genie inside its lamp. On the other hand, it was hard not to imagine Clara in a prison cell also. Mark kept finding himself staring dumbly at painted African masks with white-ringed eyes and red lips, dusty old valve radios, brown leather jackets; recalling every story of police brutality he had ever read, all the inordinately long prison sentences that had been handed down in order to make an example of somebody. Make an example of Clara? Would that one could. Would that one could point to Clara in her cast-offs, her high heels and jaunty headgear and say, 'Better that! I challenge you to better that!'

Though such an approach wouldn't go a long way in court, and the fees of Keele, Warren & Masters rivalled the mileage on Semerraro's van. Perhaps in lieu of payment the law firm would permit Mark to clean their offices free for the rest of his life – assuming he didn't get a custodial sentence, or if he did when he came out.

Supposing Clara hadn't been apprehended, maybe it would be wiser to stay on the run indefinitely than to trust in the skills of solicitors? Mark had chosen Camden as a place that could be expected to be thronged with enough people for him to lose himself, and it was. He hadn't been there for years. In different circumstances he would have enjoyed it. There were worn cobblestones, and stalls selling antique clothes. There was freshly squeezed orange juice and a shady café doing falafel. They could have sat in the sun with takeaway cheese crêpes and a couple of cans of lager, and watched the ripples on the olive-green canal. After that they could have walked along the towpath to Regent's Park and listened out for the squawks of exotic birds and the roar of the lions in their cages.

Mark *could* go to a police station and ask if anyone named Clara Hood had been arrested that morning. No he couldn't. That would be utter madness – akin to Mark turning himself in and at the same time admitting their mutual guilt.

People claimed London was expanding. It was true. Why did England need such a massive capital? Paris was so much more manageable: a location where you were infinitely more likely to bump into those you knew.

What precisely *did* Mark know about Clara? Perhaps going through that would offer some guidance as to how to proceed. He leant against a bit of wall outside an old stable block full of stalls doing glass and china, vinyl records, second-hand books and prints. He knew that Clara could vanish, which must be a kind of comfort. She'd done it before, she could do it again. The upside of London being large was that there were endless nooks and crannies a resourceful woman could disappear into if necessary. And Clara was resourceful, God knew: she was nothing if not that. Mark had never encountered another who could have brought out of their hat a fully formed plot to infiltrate Fleur's establishment.

Beyond the wall was a view of Camden High Street's wild shopfronts, plastered with murals and effigies, giant kicking boots, enormous faces.

Clara would go back to Fleur's! If the authorities hadn't caught her, surely she must. It had been planned that she should, and it was beyond Clara not to carry through any task she had set herself – an aspect of her character that Mark was well acquainted with. His best chance of finding Clara again was to go to Fleur's that evening and, since his invitation was still on the mantelpiece in Lisle Street, bluff or beg his way in there.

Mark felt a rush of joy surge through him. A torrent of happiness inspired by that one small dose of hope. He knew Clara was beautiful too. And kind. She made things beautiful around her as well. The scraps and leavings of this sorry world turned into food, clothes and decorations at the touch of her hand. Who but Clara would have taken in Bethany Smile and patiently put up with Geraldine Crowe? Mark ran a hand through his hair. This burst of happiness suddenly wasn't a million miles away from torment. He positively ached to be with Clara now. He wanted to watch her pick up an embroidered shawl and hold it up to the light. He wanted to be beside her while she inspected a sweater for moth. If Clara were here she would bargain and haggle and spot gifts for Si and Muncher. She'd find a hideaway caff that was better value than the ones on the main drag. Mark would be able to sit and watch her drink black coffee and wolf down chips with salt, vinegar, ketchup and mustard. He wouldn't want to eat or buy things or do anything himself except watch Clara discussing, buying, examining, eating.

The sun was bright and high overhead. It didn't look as if it ever planned on slipping down that long length of sky and being replaced by twilight. Mark sighed. He wandered on aimlessly, still thinking about Clara. Eventually he twigged that there was a name for what he was feeling.

CHAPTER EIGHTEEN

Paying for Mess-ups

Even with all the lights of London to drown out the sky, there was still one lovely planet visible, poised in the blue. Newburgh Street had lost its frenetic air and was sleek and elegant, purring almost, luxuriating in the glamour of Fleur's big night. Jeans and a T-shirt in and of themselves were not entirely inappropriate to the occasion, given that fashion events were customarily anything goes. Mark wished he looked better groomed, and that the T-shirt wasn't torn, however. He hadn't been able to have so much as a shave.

Fleur's premises were radiant. The street was full but its movements unrushed – perhaps owing to a sizable media contingent, which was popping camera bulbs at the suitably glamorous and shoving microphones into the faces of the well known. As Mark paused near the entrance, awaiting some opportunity to gain admission, a cab dropped off supermodel and animal rights campaigner Tina Wood, plus her on-again-off-again film star boyfriend, both wearing sunglasses. A group arrived that Mark assumed must be from Yen, at its centre a chillingly chic woman with a short slick of lacquered black hair and one pointed black eyebrow. The dress she wore was black also, save for a single white dot. It trailed along the ground. Out of another taxi emerged Sam Thorne, Managing Director of Wassen UK, followed by a very young woman whom Mark didn't recognize. Mark hesitated, then decided against approaching Sam. The companion of his Oxford days might prove to be his ticket of entry or he might not, and Mark wasn't banking on any second chances. It was difficult to believe that he and Sam had ever known one another now.

There was no sign of Clara.

A pink, open-topped Cadillac pulled up, driven by a chauffeur in peaked cap and full regalia, also all in pink. Vigilante, who was seated in the back, had changed into white Renaissance-style breeches with a pink codpiece, white calfskin ankle-boots, a puce silk waistcoat and an inexplicable white eye-patch. Had Si not been a rent boy, it might have crossed Mark's mind to wonder just how good an example the designer might be to a young mind.

Various dinner-jacketed gentlemen crossed Fleur's threshold, and lots of women in short velvet dresses.

What had Clara planned to wear? Mark wondered. It stabbed at his heart to think of her having to arrive crumpled and dishevelled, like himself.

'You've got a tan. Been away?'

Pods Morris. For a second Mark felt dazed by the curious mixture of familiarity and distance. He could have been looking at Pods through water. Pods was staring at Mark with a bemused expression, evidently rather startled by the lack of even a tie.

'I'm sorry?'

'Tan. Swanned off somewhere?'

'In a manner of speaking.'

'Bermuda?'

'No.'

'Well, I must say you've got thoroughly into the spirit of this do. You make me feel positively old hat.'

Pods did come over as somewhat defunct.

'Shall we go in?' asked Mark.

'S'pose we must. Is Charlie coming, do you know? Or is he busy being Home Sec?' To the person on the door, 'Friends of Fleur's.'

'Can I see your . . . ?'

'Oh tosh.' Pods gave a dismissive wave of his pudgy hand. 'Speaking of which,' he continued to Mark, 'and damn me if I hadn't forgotten about it, but whoever was that funny little man at Rumbles? He smelled like a water rat.'

'A friend.'

During the embarrassed silence that followed, Mark glanced around. No Clara, and maybe there wasn't going to be. Most of the day, Mark had managed to cling on to hope by keeping himself from contemplating that. An abundance of his old acquaintances were in attendance, though. Charlie was indeed present, talking to the two MacIntyres down from Scotland.

'Champagne, sirs?'

'Ra*ther*.' Pods relievedly grabbed two glasses and handed one to Mark. 'And what are those?' Collaring a young man who was carrying a tray of canapés.

'Lemongrass skewers of deep-fried tofu or monkfish, sir.'

'Oh, I say. Good idea.'

The flowers had been changed. On a pine table sat a large vase of white arums and dried ears of wheat. Either Mark's presence here earlier in the day had been sufficiently quiet for his face not to have etched itself upon the memories of Fleur's staff, or his arrival as a guest had erased him from that context. Whichever was the case, he thankfully wasn't attracting any unwelcome interest.

Mark spotted Cavendish and Miriam Collet, sipping still mineral waters and looking very bronzed and West Coast. They were deep in conversation with a couple of Fleur's friends from school and the Foreign Secretary, who was here also; he was married to one of Fleur's cousins. Others of Fleur's chums and cronies were absorbed in studying the outfits. From various points around the room Mark could hear high-pitched sounds of appreciation, but it was hard to tell whether any of them were for Clara. Mark willed that they were. Dotted among the guests were various PR people who looked as if their brief was to monitor reactions.

'Oswald!' Pods desperately beckoned the financier over.

'Pods!' With a handshake. 'Mark.' With a stiff nod. Oswald was accompanied by his wife – a handsome woman who rode to hounds and drank – and a thin, completely bald man attired in a costume that put Mark in mind of an undertaker, whom Oswald introduced as the designer, Melvyn Delve.

'This decor speaks volumes,' Delve said.

'It does,' ferociously agreed Oswald's wife.

'Fleur is a clever little girl,' said Oswald.

Mark thought of London's drains and sewers. The Underground that had shunted him off to safety. Surely, surely, surely . . .

'That's the mind behind Co!,' said Oswald's wife, lolling her coiffed head in the direction of an individual in a yellow-and-blue-striped suit, who was surrounded by a number of women, some of whom Mark knew.

'If you can *call* it that,' said Delve.

Mark had been a fool to blind himself with hope. Clara, Bethany – and probably the rest of the household too – were incarcerated. Mark should be moving heaven and earth to do something about that, rather than standing here listening to these vacuous exchanges. His eyes moved to the dress rails. He caught a glimpse of one of Clara's creations; its colours were those of the last rays of a sunset before it melted into night.

The place was swarming with press. They weren't hard to identify. They carried notebooks and had a workaday air. Most of them wore boxy, thick-framed spectacles and were dressed in nuances of black. As Mark watched, a female journalist unhooked Clara's gown from the rail, studied it inside and out, replaced it and jotted something down. Mark wondered what. He wondered whether it might be possible to go over to the woman and elicit her opinion. If she were ill disposed to Clara's offering, it would be impossible not to remonstrate. Her approval and admiration, on the other hand, might give Clara sufficient leverage to force a deal – should Clara ever show.

There was a tap on Mark's arm. He whirled round.

'Oh. Fleur.'

'Nice to see you too, Mark. And *un*expected. *Jeans!*'

Fleur's dress was blue-grey. She had on thin silver earrings. Her blond hair was curled into identical sharp points on either side of her face – the expression on which indicated to Mark that she had been fully appraised of the gargantuan extent of his fall from grace, and didn't think it reflected too well on herself. It was patently obvious that Fleur would very much have preferred it if Mark had not come. She was doubtless regretting that, though one might easily *drop* a shamed individual, it didn't cross one's mind to *disinvite* them also. If Mark had any decency and self-respect, Fleur's features telegraphed, he would have known to crawl into an ignominious hole and never come out again.

'I wanted to see your new space,' Mark said.

'Yes, well, I hope you've found it nice.'

'Very.' Mark smiled. Fleur couldn't choose but to tolerate his presence. It would be infinitely more embarrassing to have him thrown out. Mark could see her calculating the most fitting candidate to get a rocket for this unforeseen vexation. An easy one that, he could have told her. Blame Life: its inclination to twist on you; the impossibility of securing it entirely in place.

There was a frigid pause. During their relationship, Mark realized, he and Fleur had been no more to each other than sketched figures who adequately fulfilled a social purpose.

'My flower, my flower, but this is quite superb!' a grey-suited man with a tangerine tie proclaimed in a heavy French accent. 'The taste. The knowing-how-to-do. I find it really incomparable.'

'But why did this not happen in Milan?' asked a pouty-faced youth with auburn locks. 'London? I spit on it. You should have opened in Milan.'

'Perhaps I shall,' said Fleur. Kisses were exchanged.

'Jean-Marie Potiron and Puttanesca,' slurred Oswald's wife in Mark's ear. 'He's out*rage*ous.'

'Which?'

'Puttanesca, of course.'

Mark thought of Clara. 'How does this manifest itself?'

But, 'Fleurie!' cried Oswald's wife. 'Congratulations on your overwhelming achievement.'

'You must have been to hell and back,' put in Pods, who was beginning to sound plastered.

'Yes,' Fleur agreed. She aimed a cross little look at Mark, as if to suggest he should do roughly the same thing but dispense with the return ticket.

An assistant approached. 'The *Sunday Times* would like a word.'

'Ah, yes. Excuse me, please.' Fleur and the assistant moved away. Mark watched Fleur shake hands with a tall, dark-haired woman dressed in a long-sleeved black top and a brick-red skirt in a softly flowing fabric – Clara would know what it was. The journalist made an appreciative gesture at the room in general. Fleur made a comment in reply. The journalist consulted her notepad and said something. Fleur nodded.

'In London I am always misunderstood,' said Puttanesca.

'Don't let it get to you,' said Pods. '*I* wouldn't.'

Events such as this didn't go on late. The newspaper people would be departing shortly; they usually left as soon as they'd got their copy. The other guests would take this as a cue to drift off to their dinner reservations. The opening would be over, with nothing out of it for Clara. Should Mark attempt to negotiate with Fleur on her behalf? Had Clara's gowns received lots of positive feedback, or would Fleur simply laugh in Mark's face and order them to be removed? When Clara was present, nothing seemed like a shot in the dark. When she was not, her aspirations felt as if they were pitted against the entire organization of the universe.

Desperately, Mark surveyed the room. '*Why* aren't you Clara?'

he mentally demanded of the more likely faces. All his hullabaloo over what future to commit himself to had died away and seemed in retrospect ridiculous. There was only one possible course for Mark's life now. He could only move in a single, unambivalent direction. Nothing else that might ever have been on offer came anywhere close to what he was currently experiencing. Depending on how Clara felt, he was on the brink of being happier than he had ever been in his life.

Fleur and the *Sunday Times* journalist had been joined by Tina Wood. The supermodel was enthusiastically pointing at a rail of ball-gowns on the other side of the room – Mark could just make out glimpses of them – apparently in complete agreement with whatever the journalist had just said. Wood was taller than she looked on the billboards – six foot one at least. Mark's eyes returned to Fleur in an attempt to assess whether there was anything at all amenable in Fleur's face, anything to suggest that she might respond sympathetically to a sales proposition if he made one. To his surprise, a blank and rather panicked expression had fallen across it. Fleur was asked a question that she seemed to be at a loss to answer. Excuse me, Mark read on Fleur's lips. Wood and the journalist made brief assenting gestures, then continued a discussion that was evidently becoming increasingly excited. Fleur hurriedly moved away from them and beckoned one, two, three, four assistants over. Sporting ominous looks, they followed her, weaving slowly through the crowd towards the section of clothes that Wood had pointed at.

Instinctively, Mark started to head that way also. He couldn't have said why exactly, but he had a hunch that whatever it was that had got Fleur puzzled and displeased was somehow linked to Clara's collection. The Parting of the Red Sea. Shoulders and backs. There was little difficulty in making your way through a bunch of people you used to know when your name had turned to mud, Mark discovered. 'Oh God, there's Upshaw,' said Sam Thorne's voice. 'Upshaw who?' asked his young female friend.

Fleur had summoned another two employees and a PR

person *en route*. Mark stationed himself behind her, out of sight but near enough to hear the hissed and murmured conversation that was taking place. He wouldn't have been likely to attract Fleur's or anyone else's attention anyway, it transpired. Shielded from media and guests, Fleur's mask had been whipped off. Her staff were a picture of mystified dismay while Fleur herself was a combination of distraught and livid. 'What do you mean, you don't *know*?' she was furiously asking an assistant.

The assistant consulted a printed sheet. 'There's no mention here of this gown, or of its designer.'

'So what is it doing in my shop?'

Mark held his breath. Fleur shoved her finger into the folds of Clara's Crescendo Dress, which responded with a wave of ripples – early autumn sunlight on reedy shallows; scrumpy cider glugging slowly out of a green bottle.

'There must have been a mess-up with the orders,' the assistant offered.

'Or the deliveries,' added a disconsolate male.

'But I don't pay for mess-ups. In fact, I pay for them *not to happen*.' Fleur turned her back on the worthless bunch for an instant. Mark swiftly adjusted his position. 'And what is *that*?' she raged, obviously having beheld something else that incensed her. As one, Fleur's employees stared at where she'd been looking.

'You mean the lilies?' cautiously asked the assistant.

'This is a disaster. An absolute disaster.'

The PR person said, 'The ball-gown *is* very pretty, and the others by that designer are going down phenomenally well also.'

'Others? Others?' Fleur didn't carry it through, but made as if to stamp.

'There appears to be a full range.'

A menacing silence followed. Then, 'This is the situation I have on my hands,' Fleur said. 'Over the other side of the room is Tina Wood. With her is Renee Parr from the *Sunday Times*. Renee wants to do a write-up on this dress, accompanied by a photograph of it being worn by one of the top three models in the world. Renee wants to know all about the designer and all about the label. *You* have no information for me on either, because of which I am going to lose my reputation and probably my write-up too. I want the situation dealt with. I want this . . . this . . .'

'Clara,' said the PR person.

'I want this Clara, if you have to magic her up out of thin air.'

The tirade met with clueless expressions.

Eventually, 'Perhaps we could distract Ms Parr with Melvyn Delve for the moment,' said the disconsolate male.

'Not Delve,' said the PR person briskly. 'Puttanesca. He can talk about himself for ever and might do something outrageous.'

'I'll get more canapés and drinks going around to stall people,' said another employee, hurrying away.

'I'll try to locate Clara via the Net,' said the assistant with the sheet.

'Do that.' And Fleur was in the midst of her intimates again, all smiles.

Briefly, Mark wondered whether to reveal that he had an association with Clara. But then what purpose would that serve? He could scarcely do the interview with Renee Parr in Clara's stead. He knew relatively little about Clara's designs and methods – only what he'd gleaned from watching her work and asking questions; probably no more than Renee Parr could figure out for herself. A credible gloss would need to be put on the true nature of Clara's set-up. Clearly, to say that her collection emanated from a building that was currently flooded with water and being gone over by the police would not produce the effect required. But what would? How small and low-key could a clothes design business be without declaring itself of negligible interest? On this as well, Mark was at a loss. For him to inform Fleur who Clara was, but then go on to say that he knew nothing of her whereabouts (unless she was in jail) was likewise without any point. All Mark could do was go and stand not too far from the shop's entrance, so that he would quickly be able to brief Clara on the remote chance that she should arrive.

Which she did. Sailing unchallenged through the unmanned doors, Fleur's staff being otherwise occupied.

Ironically, Mark didn't recognize her for a moment. After so long spent seeing mirages – so many hours during which he had hallucinated Clara's features on to pale imitations of herself – Mark's mind found it hard to accept the reality of her presence. Also, he had been looking out for green and maroon, the busy pattern of an Indian skirt. But Clara had changed. Her whole attire had undergone a complete transformation. Whatever form it might take, Clara evidently did not intend to be deprived of her moment.

She was wearing a glorious, high-waisted, neoclassical-style dress in thin, ruby-coloured silk. A fabric rose was pinned to the garment's left shoulder, securing in place a gold-and-black shawl that cascaded down Clara's back. Crowning her head was a plait of claret-and-black gauze and gold ribbon. On her feet were a pair of pointed black shoes with ankle straps; she carried a large beaded and embroidered bag. Clara looked as fresh as a daisy. Mark caught a mingled aroma of wet meadows and citrus fruit.

Clara's eyes were here, there and everywhere. Her excitement was palpable; her body seemed to quiver. She scooped a flute of champagne off a proffered tray and took a big gulp. Her eyes alighted on Mark. Mark felt as if silvery bubbles of wine were burning his own lips. What, he wondered, was she wearing underneath?

Fleur had a fringe you could have cut ham with – the smoked foreign kind that they flogged a million varieties of at Hodge's. She was even prettier in the flesh. Clara could see the attraction of the woman's looks, though her personality was more than a little bit tight at the seams. Until informed who Clara was, Fleur had come over as none too keen to meet anyone an ex might dredge up: something Clara found hard to comprehend – unless there'd been acrimony, which Mark said there hadn't.

They'd crashed a conversation between Fleur and a corporate type plus bimbette.

'Please forgive the interruption. Fleur, there's someone here I'd like you to meet.'

'Oh yes?' Like she was chewing rind.

'Yes.' There'd been a sort of flourish in Mark's voice. 'I would like to present to you Clara. Clara Hood.'

'Clara?'

'We're in business together. Clara designs dresses.'

'She designs dresses?'

For someone in possession of a ton of cash, Fleur seemed ill at ease with the nitty-gritty of it. Given the leisure to, Clara guessed she would have had a minion negotiate on her behalf. Fleur's favoured way of dealing was probably via personal assistant, and that fax to fax rather than nose to nose. (And Clara thought *she* lived a second-hand existence!) Nevertheless, after some ascertaining and a – refused – offer of more glug and some nibbles – cubes of white stuff or fish on a stick – Fleur had spirited Clara away for this 'chat'. Presumably Mark was excluded because Fleur imagined that as a woman Clara would be the more amenable. (Ha!)

Last time Clara had been in this tucked-away office it had smelled of sawdust. Now the walls were painted bleached-bone. There was a grey cord sofa and two grey cord armchairs, a glass table with a vase of white roses on it, and a diddy grey desk with a high chrome chair behind it and a lower one on the other side. Clara was deemed worthy of the sofa. Fleur placed herself gracefully in an armchair and her pleats fanned out around her. Clara fought it, but she couldn't help feeling a bit thrown together. Fleur was so much all of a piece. She even matched her furniture. Clara's bargain-bin shawl concealed a badly mended tear. The fabric flower had been salvaged from a past-it hat. The ribbon Clara had plaited into those offcuts and tied round her head came from an empty box of peppermint creams. Her bag kept shedding beads.

'What a coincidence you're associated with Mark,' Fleur said in a lulling, buttery tone.

'It's a small world.'

Clara was relieved, though not surprised, that in Fleur's scheme of things Clara trolling in all convenient couldn't be anything other than a matter of chance. Putting two and two together was an activity that women such as Fleur probably left to their accountants. Whatever Fleur's feelings about Mark, she would be unlikely to imagine him involved in anything that wasn't strictly above board. Besides, Fleur was used to good luck.

'You didn't mind Mark asking me to meet him here?' Clara asked to underline the randomness.

'On the contrary. You have plans for the rest of the evening?'

'We're going to take it as it comes.'

'What fun!'

'I hope.'

There was a pause. Clara wondered when they were going to get down to discussing hard cash.

'I think I might have mentioned already that a number of your super gowns seem to have found their way on to my dress rails, by virtue of some extraordinary mistake?'

'Maybe you did. I spotted them anyway. I wandered around to see exactly what of mine you'd got. I was flabbergasted.'

'Of course, you *would* be. I felt exactly the same.'

'I wonder how it happened. A muddle at the warehouse to do with deliveries, most likely. Somebody must really have messed up.'

'Oh, tell me about it. You can't trust a solitary soul to do a thing right these days.'

That had obviously struck a chord. For a minute or two Clara reinforced it – no sense in not kicking over the traces as thoroughly as opportunity allowed. Fleur's conviction about the utter inefficiency of underlings handily provided an additional blinker to the possibility of any alternative explanation.

'Well, no prob,' Clara concluded. 'I'll just get the items picked up and out of your way as soon as possible. We're putting a big order together right now. Some of the clobber that's fetched up here I think is earmarked to be part of it.'

Fleur looked momentarily thrown. 'Oh. But, I mean, funnily enough your collection looks just so . . . I don't know . . . so *right* alongside my other designers.'

Fleur definitely planned on keeping the hack and the runway queen hush for the time being. Clara would have done the same herself. When it came to bargaining power, they put Fleur at a distinct disadvantage. Within certain parameters – which it was imperative she calculate right – Clara was in a position to name her price.

Clara tossed Fleur a grateful look. 'Thank you. That's a generous thing to say.'

'I'm not being generous. Honestly. I really am interested in purchasing your range.'

'You're serious?'

'Absolutely.'

Clara did a big sigh. 'I'm flattered you like my designs, I really am, but there is that other order I mentioned.'

'Can't you just get your staff to work harder?'

'They're as shiftless as yours are, given half a chance. It would mean overtime.'

There was another pause. Why did folk wonder how come the economy was in a shambles, when those with the serious spondulicks were so maddeningly dithery about coming to the point?

'Suppose, just for the sake of it, I suggest a sum?' Fleur shifted in her chair a little, apparently highly discomfited by the squalor of having to name an actual figure.

At last! 'For the lot?'

Head down, Fleur nodded. 'Mmmhmm.'

'You've seen the retail prices of my garments?' Clara thanked heaven she'd had the nerve to opt for astronomical.

'I have of one of them. I could get an assistant to do a quick overall valuation, if you like?'

'Don't bother. As long *you've* got an idea of the kind of money we're talking, and *I* know the quantity of my stuff you've got in stock. Make me an offer, just for the sake of it.'

There was an embarrassed silence, then Fleur rose to her feet, went to her desk and wrote down a number with a nice quantity of zeros but not quite enough digits. She returned to her chair, pen still in hand (a strategic mistake). 'I was thinking somewhere in the region of this.'

Pull the other one; You're having me on; Let's get serious: none of the classic responses for this stage of the game felt quite right to Clara in such a setting. Nor did pretending to be on the point of walking out. Fortunately, Fleur added, 'And that would be with the understanding that you'd be willing to do any media interviews that might arise as a result of your designs being on offer in my establishment.'

'*Media* interviews?' Clara coated the words with horror.

Fleur looked startled, as well she might: though you did read of designers whose purported desire was only to create, the rag trade didn't strike Clara as exactly thronged with shrinking violets.

'Would that be a problem?'

'I'm quite a private person.'

'Oh.'

For a second Clara feared she'd overplayed her hand. But, 'Perhaps this would be adequate compensation?' Fleur asked, adjusting her offer in the appropriate direction, clearly of the opinion that there was no problem that wouldn't go away if you threw enough money at it.

'Done,' said Clara, a tad too fast.

Fleur didn't notice. 'You mean you agree?'

'Yup.'

'Good. Invoice me for that amount, then.'

'I'd prefer to have it now.'

'Now?'

'For my books.'

'Oh, of course. Let me write you a cheque.' Which Fleur duly did, seated at her desk. Then, while Clara was still blowing on the ink, 'Actually, it just so happens that one of my guests here tonight is Renee Parr, who writes for the *Sunday Times*,' she said.

Constantly replenishing people's glasses had indeed delayed departures. Many of those present were now well drunk, and having such a good time that they persuaded their soberer companions to stay on. Mobile telephones kept being brought out as dinner engagements were cancelled or postponed. The tempo of the occasion had gone up several notches. Even the press seemed disposed to stick around. Puttanesca stripped off the blouse thing he'd been wearing and showed to anyone who cared to look his gold-and-diamond nipple-ring.

'Can I give you my phone number? It's nothing to me that you're broke,' slurred Oswald's wife. Mark smiled politely, feigning not to have understood.

A dispute broke out between Vigilante and Melvyn Delve.

'I say,' said Pods, whose face was as shiny as a billiard ball, 'these fashion chappies are different from other people, I think. Can't fathom what most of them are on about. Cummerbund and a bow tie sees me through most that arises.'

'I hear you did something really rather awful, but nobody will tell me what,' said Sam Thorne's girlfriend, who could barely stand.

'I lost all my money,' said Mark.

'Golly! As awful as that!'

The journalists clustered together and began telling loud stories. Tina Wood's film-star boyfriend left in a rush, shortly followed by Tina Wood.

Mark watched anxiously for Clara's reappearance. As soon as she had arrived, he'd appraised her of the situation in a minimum number of words – she caught on to things with such lightning speed! – and then he'd immediately introduced her to Fleur. Now it was difficult for him to keep hold of the knowledge that he really hadn't imagined Clara's presence. He was terrified something would wrest her away again. He pictured the back of Fleur's building as a sieve of open windows and unlocked doors, through which anonymous hands might snatch and grab.

'Yellow!' announced the Frenchman in the tangerine tie. 'Take it from me: spring will be yellow.'

'In my house it will not,' cried Puttanesca.

'Can we quote you?' shouted someone from the press contingent.

There were raised eyebrows from the Home Secretary and from the Foreign Secretary, who appeared to be among those who had been prevented from leaving by others in their group who would rather remain.

'Dammit, I'm sure I know that girl from somewhere,' said Pods.

Mark's eyes flew to Clara's. Clara gave him a surreptitious thumbs-up. Mark's gaze accompanied her through the crowd. Fleur presented Clara to the writer from the *Sunday Times.* Clara didn't look nervous, but she did look very much on her mettle; flushed and beautiful. Fleur left Clara and the journalist alone to talk. Mark wondered whether he should join them. After watching for a few minutes, he decided he should not. Clara was speaking with joyful animation. She unhooked one of her dresses from its place on the rungs, shook it off its hanger, turned it inside out. The journalist was clearly fascinated. She jotted a few notes. Clara said something that made the journalist laugh. This was, Mark realized, possibly the happiest moment in Clara's life. When she told Kim and the others about it there would be whoops and exclamations.

Mark became aware of a slight disturbance. Quickly, he glanced around with a sense of foreboding. He couldn't think of any mechanism by which the authorities might have tracked him and Clara to Fleur's shop; nevertheless it was dangerous to linger too long in any one place. As soon as Clara was done, they must make an exit.

The disturbance appeared to be centred upon the two members of the Cabinet, who had joined one another and were both being spoken to by men in grey suits who'd only just arrived and looked as if they might belong to the Civil Service. Charlie and the Foreign Secretary listened, consulted together, spoke some words to those they were with, then left, flanked by the grey-suited men.

Clara and the journalist were shaking hands. The journalist put her notebook into a leather bag. Fleur returned to them, shook hands with the journalist and ushered her out.

'Goodness,' said Pods. 'Wonder what all that was about. Must be a bloody nuisance being an MP. Living in constant fear of getting your evenings messed up like that. My old man wanted me to give it a try, you remember? Bloody glad I didn't.'

'Any idea *why* they suddenly had to go?'

Clara's face had the biggest ever smile on it. The tips of her pointed toes were performing a little dance. *A good deal! A good deal!* they said.

'Oh, some international emergency, I expect.'

'Good-bye, Pods.'

'Bye, Mark. We must meet up some day. I'll be in touch.'

Mark moved towards Clara. He wanted to run. He wanted to ensure that nothing would ever separate them again. The place felt more crowded than it had done earlier, and Mark's ignominy appeared to have slipped from people's thoughts – he found it harder to make his way through the crush. It was impossible not to believe that the departure of Charlie and the Foreign Secretary spelled bad news for Clara and himself. Though surely that was paranoid? Mark was merely making jittery connections between things that were in actuality unrelated.

It wasn't until he'd reached Clara that he saw all the police.

[illegible] shop [illegible] it was dangerous to linger [illegible]

[illegible]

[illegible]

[illegible] Bonnet [illegible]

[illegible]

[illegible] after the [illegible]

[illegible]

CHAPTER NINETEEN

Living on Duck Island

'You have questions for my guests concerning the whereabouts of someone who might be known to them; this person being suspected of conspiring to harbour and conceal a foreign dissident, who is wanted in their own country for *extremist political activities?*'

Fleur's voice was more high-pitched and louder than usual but everybody would have heard her anyway. The arrival of the police officers had created a deathly hush, which was only intensified by Fleur's outraged repetition of the explanation she had just been given for their presence. Mark could well appreciate Fleur's horror. Described in such terms, Bethany Smile did sound extraordinarily dangerous; Mark recalled the image he himself had fostered of her before making her acquaintance. He could appreciate Fleur's indignation also. Even if this was revealed to be a scandalous mistake, the affluent and illustrious here present were unlikely to forget the event's more unusual aspect. Who, moreover, among Fleur's impeccable guests could the police honestly look at and genuinely believe capable of this variety of illegal act?

Glancing around, Mark conceived a desperate hope that the officers might indeed agree that Fleur had a very good point, apologize and go. Though the MacIntyres had ample room in their Scottish residence for any number of rebellious foreigners –

and their extended families also – who could attribute a trace of guilt to Rickie and Kirstie's astonished faces? 'Steady on!' exclaimed Pods, incapable even of hiding his drunkenness. Puttanesca's nipples plus ring were exposed for all to see. Sam Thorne and Cavendish Collet were so visibly irritated at having got caught up in such an infernal incident – Mark could almost see the falling share prices in front of Thorne's eyes – as to remove them from suspicion. The same was true of Oswald. Mark looked at Clara and was reminded of one of those angels of the High Renaissance that he had admired in Florence.

Would Mark's jeans strike the policemen as dubious?

To his dismay, the senior officer gave no appearance of possessing the slightest doubt as to the validity of their being here. 'That is indeed the reason we have come, madam,' he replied to Fleur calmly.

'I think the lady should be given more extensive details, Sergeant,' said an eminent-looking elderly gentleman, not of Mark's acquaintance.

There was a pause.

'This is becoming a bore. Please excuse me if I depart,' said the mind behind Co!

'Me also,' said Jean-Marie Potiron.

'I too do not choose to involve myself,' proclaimed Puttanesca.

'I am afraid I cannot permit anyone to leave the premises for the moment, sirs,' said the senior policeman.

Mark's heart began to beat fast. His muscles tensed. He sensed a similar reaction in Clara. He moved closer to her.

'I am under arrest?' asked Potiron. (Mark was suddenly bitterly aware of the, doubtless suspicious-seeming, ubiquity of non-British accents. Though surely even the police knew that the fashion world was international?)

The senior officer smiled with grim politeness. 'Let's just say we're making sure there's no reason why you should be.'

'Unless you count that tie,' said Melvyn Delve bitchily.

'It is my feeling that the lady should be informed of the circumstances which have led up to this,' reiterated the elderly gentleman.

The senior policeman appeared to come to a decision. He gave a brief nod to one of his men, who duly produced a notebook and started to read from it.

'Members of the Constabulary were today summoned to a building in Lisle Street, which undercover surveillance had led them to believe was the location in which the aforementioned foreign dissident – namely, Bethany Smile – was secreted.'

Bethany Smile! A frisson passed round the room. There were gasps. '*Who?*' drawled Thorne's girlfriend. 'Any chance of something more to drink?' asked Oswald's wife. Mark looked towards the exit.

'Unfortunately, at the same time as the Constabulary was due to enter the premises a small conflagration broke out within.'

Mark was amazed. Had there been a *real* fire, then? He heard Clara draw in a tiny breath.

'In the confusion resulting from the extinguishing of said conflagration, and also caused by some incidents in the street, it is our belief that the alien escaped. The police officers found the building deserted, though we do have details as to the identity of the tenant; these having been given to us by the building's owner.'

Escaped! Mark grinned at Clara. Clara grinned at Mark. Whatever happened next Bethany was, for the moment, safe. And so were Kim, Muncher, Si and Geraldine. Abruptly, Mark's joy subsided. He felt as if he had stepped straight under an icy shower. The others were safe but Clara wasn't.

'I fail to see how this has anything to do with me,' cried Fleur in a fury of impatience, glaring at various members of her staff as if the ghastly situation might somehow be their fault.

'Damned if I do either,' murmured Pods.

'Thank you for that, Constable,' said the senior policeman. 'I'll take over.' He turned to Fleur. 'Naturally a search was made of the building. Owing to the work of the fire-fighters, my men were rather hampered in their endeavours to unearth anything of significance. They did, however, find in one of the rooms an invitation to the event you are holding here this evening.'

'An invitation to the opening of my shop?' Fleur squealed, aiming further livid regards at her assistants. 'It must have been stolen.'

'That is a possibility.' The police officer nodded.

'Look here, even if it wasn't,' said Cavendish Collet suddenly, in a voice designed to cut through all this Englishy bullshit, 'even if the invite was really sent him, what kind of a guy is going to help a felon escape then go on to a party after?'

'In *LA* that would be extreme,' agreed his wife, Miriam.

'Your bird has flown,' cried Puttanesca.

'The invitation was *stolen,*' Fleur yelled. 'I do not have friends, or even distant acquaintances, who live in rented accommodation *any*where, let alone in Lisle Street of all places.'

Pods was staring at Mark, a thought-beginning-to-dawn expression on his corpulent features. 'I say!' Pods waved an unsteady hand in Mark's direction.

'Can you divulge to the assembly the name of the tenant of the building where these events took place?' asked the elderly gentleman. 'It may serve to throw some light on things.'

'The name of the individual we are endeavouring to trace is Clara Hood.'

'I say, Mark,' shouted Pods. 'Didn't that water rat fellow at Rumbles say *you* lived in Lisle Street?'

That bastard landlord! It just went to show what Clara had always known, and mostly adhered to: you should never put anything down on paper. There was only one way to guarantee than dodgy folk would play Simple Simon when the Bill came a-snooping, and that was by making sure you were no more to them than footprints on sand. You'd have thought you were safe enough with an invite, though; the tanned Yanks were right about that one – those who sailed to the windward did customarily curtail their social lives for a while thereafter. But then rozzers were so methodical. No stone left unturned. Not because there was anything under the majority of them, but because the Force had never worked out a better way of doing things. And granted, this time their plodding methodology had paid off.

Indeed, these must be awfully law-abiding people. Clara hadn't witnessed this level of shock in her entire life. Saucer eyes. Jamjar mouths. Staring at Mark mainly, as if being about to be put under arrest indicated anything conclusive. With moral judgments and knickers alike: make Clara's brand new, please. London was full of trapdoors and some of them were big enough to accommodate Bethany Smile. Mark Upshaw could not have achieved better than this day's work.

The police had got the front exit covered, of course. And the back ones, doubtless. Both probably in proportion to the degree of optimism they'd have had about making an arrest here, however; and that couldn't have been enormous.

'Clara Hood, Mark Upshaw, I am informing you that you are . . .'

A cat, they said, could fit its entire body through a hole the width of its whiskers.

Once before – a world ago, it felt like – it had seemed to Clara that she and Mark were in sync as they were at this minute. Muncher-taught Clara; Mark, probably schooled by instructors at some big-lawned establishment: it was lucky they'd had the opportunity to get the measure of each other's movements; now there was no need even to touch. Clara could sense Mark's physical preparations, because she was making them also. Would Mark remember that Clara had inside knowledge of the shop's layout? (Thanks to the builders. Thanks especially to the sparks. Hooray, hooray for a particular little cupboard.) Clara could get the two of them out, she was mighty confident, *if* they only started off in the right direction. Surprise was on their side, they were both conscious of that. Personages with big lawyers and the prospect of open prisons wouldn't usually bother to resist arrest. High profiles made for mitigating circumstances.

Clara had no intention of seeing Mark swiped away from her. It was time to have a good long talk. The Beautiful People assembled were looking on like they'd never before seen a pair of handcuffs – even Puttanesca. In circles such as Mark's, Clara didn't reckon this manner of occurrence easily dissolved into anecdote. Shame, she supposed, must from here on Sello itself to the name of Mark Upshaw. She didn't sense Mark himself felt any shame, though.

Aaaand . . . go!

Angry coppers and lots of shouts and screams. A nicely timorous lot, the Fashionable, however. No one, but no one, made the slightest attempt to weigh in. They all looked dead scared, as a matter of fact, and rather pulled back to allow Clara and Mark through: *Let others crumple their linens; uniforms are* designed *for the purpose; I am creative, I never claimed to be courageous.*

Of course Mark had the intelligence to follow Clara. Of course he did. Into the storage area, which smelled of wool, cashmere and mohair: hand-knitteds, stashed away waiting for the weather to get nippy. Into a tiny staffroom with leather handbags dangling from hooks, an aroma of perfume and coffee, and a window that would have accommodated Clara but was much too small for Mark. Pursued, natch, but not too closely as yet, they hurtled onward and entered a redundant-looking area with a sink left over from some long-ago usage. And here was that cupboard. Clara leapt up on to the draining-board, flung the cupboard's door open and – hey presto! – the establishment was plunged into darkness. Just so as the lighting wouldn't be able to be restored in a hurry, she also ripped out the fuses.

Fresh and more panicked shrieks met the snuffing of the pearlized wall-spots. Panic was a friend. Panic was a diversion. It wouldn't exactly be a coalmine out there but Clara was relying on the Hothouse Flowers not to respond well to a sudden change in environment; some of the guests, besides, struck her as considerably more than half cut.

Bull's-eye! Bewildered, drunken footsteps blundering around every part of the building.

In some ways it was obviously a disadvantage to be unaccustomed to things going wrong.

The champagne wasn't champagne really, nor was it particularly cool, but it was complimentary, as were the chipolatas on sticks and the stuffed olives. The gurlz welcomed Clara and Mark literally with open arms, and found them a nice table from which to witness the show – each gurl taking a turn at donning an exotic costume and miming to songs by Barbra Streisand, Shirley Bassey and other such vocalists, while giving the audience the occasional full display of their slim, muscular thighs. None of the gurlz had received any word from Kim, but they got quite excited about the idea of relaying secret messages should she get in touch.

In the nightclub lights Clara's robe turned into a stained-glass window, a kaleidoscope. Her cheeks were stroked with pink, blue, white, yellow. 'Where did you get that outfit?' yelled Mark, above the strains of 'Hey Big Spender'. 'It's . . .'

'The dress is from a charity shop near Berwick,' Clara yelled back. 'What I had on earlier is in my bag.' She gave it a pat and a hailstorm of beads shot off in all directions.

'The shop is where you were able to change?'

'No, I did that at the Oasis Baths. I needed a shower after all the running. A woman there let me have a couple of squirts of her Wash & Go.'

And the sharp, citrusy perfume that put him in mind of an April garden after rain?

'I went to Camden Market,' shouted Mark.

'Did you buy anything?'

Mark smiled and shook his head. Perhaps it would have been

appropriate to have reached out and touched that little hand tapping its fingers to the music. Perhaps not. Mark watched Clara's profile and the criss-cross of lights on her hair.

After a while they moved on.

At the deserted cashpoint area of a closed bank Clara filled in a deposit slip and popped the envelope containing Fleur's payment for the dress collection into the deposit box. She placed the credit card from which she had read the account number back among her wad of others. Mark had never seen anyone in possession of such a wealth of plastic.

'Now we can do everything by cheque,' Clara said.

She was apparently known to the proprietor: a way was somehow found of *squeezing* Mark and Clara into the Patio Restaurant in Shepherds Bush; a part of London Mark wouldn't previously have expected very much of. The restaurant's cuisine turned out to be Polish, the set menu less than ten pounds a head. Mark was starving, he discovered. They ate smoked salmon blinis and roast duck with red cabbage. They ate crumbly pastries dusted with icing sugar, and pancakes stuffed with cream cheese. They drank lemon vodka. An accordion band entered in a mad rush and played a series of wild mazurkas, each of them faster and more frantic than the one before, then exited in a jangle of loose change, leaving Mark feeling as if a fairground had pitched camp in his head.

There were bags of stars in the sky above South Kensington. In a small, grassy, private square an event was taking place. There was an open marquee festooned with fairy lights, and a food and drinks table. People were seated on rugs and rolled-up cardigans listening to a jazz band. Some of them were wearing hats. All had a lopsided look, as if they'd started out upright some time back, and had gradually slipped. There was a big lacy bride with a skewed veil and smeared lipstick, and a smiling groom with a wonky carnation. The atmosphere was mellow.

Clara fished the Indian skirt out of her bag and she and Mark sat on it, fairly close together. Mark would have liked to have done a filmic scoop now – Clara's hair brushing the grass, Mark's arm about her shoulders, their lips meeting; no need for Mark to speak, or fear he presumed too much. He was aware that words must be exchanged before such a thing could happen, however – if, indeed, it did. Too much damage had been done, both recently and in the distant past, to proceed with anything other than infinite care. Until permission was granted Mark and Clara's bodies mustn't touch, even by accident.

'Hallo,' grinned a long-faced, youngish man with big teeth, slopping droplets of wine around them. 'We haven't met, I don't think. How long have you two known Rosalind and Toby?'

'Not very,' said Clara.

'Lovely wedding,' said the man, staggering off.

'Yes,' said Mark softly to his receding form, 'truly wonderful.'

Later, in Curzon Street: 'Once,' said Clara, 'this city must have been full of fairs and markets.'

They drank espressos in an extraordinary basement bar-cum-café that didn't look as if it had changed at all since the early seventies. The walls were painted black and studded with LPs. The tables were made of black Formica. The guy who served them had a beard and wore a kaftan top and small, round-framed glasses. The place smelled of mildew and patchouli oil.

'Do you know Sheila's in Covent Garden?' asked Clara. 'Their chairs are a bit like these ones.'

'I don't think so.'

'We should go there some time, perhaps. It's Australian.' Clara spoke rather loudly. 'The pawnshop's still got your cases,' she added.

St James's Park was deserted except for wildfowl, drunks and lovers. Couples kissed on benches, and geese, swans and pelicans roosted under the willows. Mallards made tiny clucking noises and the drunks snored in the sprawling shadows.

'Sometimes I used to wish I could live on Duck Island,' said Clara.

There were drunks and down-and-outs too sleeping on the paving stones around the entrance to Westminster Cathedral.

'It's a good thing Fleur didn't go for candles. It would have made getting out of there a sight more difficult,' said Clara, staring at the building's red-and-white brickwork.

With sudden inexorable force, as if a potent but short-lived spell had been broken, the events of the day came rushing back to Mark, bringing with them a vivid recollection of the rocky nature of the future. It was like being given a hefty shove and told to get on with finding out whether happiness was possible. Midnight had long since run out on him and yet Mark Upshaw – experienced, sophisticated Mark – was so very frightened of what Clara might say to him that he was acting as if they had the promise of tomorrow.

He took a quiet breath and turned to face her. 'Do you think we should find somewhere private where we can talk – and sleep if we want to?'

Slowly, Clara nodded.

The hotel room smelled of dust. There was a bedside lamp with a pink, ruched nylon shade. There was a kettle, and a tray with thick white cups and saucers on it, and light, thin teaspoons. There were teabags and sachets of instant coffee and small containers of UHT. Clara filled the kettle and put it on; it would be a shame not to get their money's worth. Probably, at this time of night and in this location, she could have talked the bloke down, but her mind had been on other things.

They were near Victoria. The open window looked out over the rails, silver where the illuminations hit them. Clara listened to the sound of a train slowly creeping into the station, the relieved sigh it gave as it came to a standstill. She listened to the uneven flow of water from the shower in the tiny bathroom. Clara had nipped in there and rinsed her skirt and top through. They hung from the curtain rod to dry in the night air – evening gear in the a.m. would be bound to attract attention.

Could you feel calm and fearful, happy and apprehensive all at the same time? Did conflicting emotions cancel one another out as some folk seemed to think, or was it possible to experience a job-lot of sensations – a bit of this mingled with a bit of that?

A train came out of the station now. In a hurry, this one: it sped up almost straight away.

The bedspread was made of pink candlewick. An old television set had been placed high up on a ledge in one of the corners. For the best possible view of it you'd need to stand on the pillows. Clara leant her back against the headboard and picked up the remote control. She managed a picture but no sound, which was absolutely fine.

In the bathroom the water was switched off.

With only about a third of the screen visible to her, Clara channel-hopped. She saw the tops of palm trees against an unbelievably blue sky. Part of a fizzy drink can. The eyes and hair of a politician she couldn't remember the name of. A brightly coloured turban. The ears of an Alsatian dog. The roofs and spires of the Houses of Parliament, and four of the hour markers on the face of Big Ben.

The bathroom door opened. Clara extinguished the telly.

Mark came into the room looking clean and refreshed, though also somewhat ill at ease. He walked over to the window as if with the intention of making a serious study of the railway tracks. His clothes gave the impression they'd ironed themselves while he was getting washed. Portentous, the atmosphere was portentous. Clara felt like one of those circus performers running on a great big coloured sphere. 'Coffee?' she asked, but it didn't help. Mark shook his head, and the quietness of the gesture made the situation take on even more potential nuances. At the thought of what might be about to come, Clara felt as if she'd had a sauna and emerged from it into snow. She was scrubbed and in a very white place where warmth was an echo. Raw truth:

that was in the end the best and all Clara had to offer – the best anyone had, perhaps. She sensed Mark was struggling with similar notions.

Which of them was going to break the silence?

'Mark . . .' said Clara, before she could change her mind.

'Clara . . .' said Mark, sitting down on the end of the bed. Then, hastily, 'Please go on. Do go on, please.'

Clara hesitated. She decided to make this as speedy and as matter-of-fact as possible; keep her voice clear and valiant, and only stop to draw breath. 'There's something I want to tell you about, something that happened to me a long time ago. It wasn't my fault, you know, but as much as anything explains anything, it probably makes some sense of why I haven't been able to . . . to *trust* you even after I knew I could.'

This was even harder than Clara would have reckoned. Emotion forced her to pause, but she willed her eyes to meet Mark's in a bravely prolonged gaze. Mark looked immeasurably moved. His expression was extraordinarily gentle. Clara got a snorty sensation as if she'd had to come up for air ultra-fast. Trust, it transpired, threw you every which way. Clara simply couldn't cope with the sight of Mark's kind, handsome face. In a minute she would be one almighty sob with leapfrogging shoulders and a runny nose, and who on earth was going to be charmed by that?

But, 'Clara,' Mark said quietly, 'there's no need to continue. I think I know what you're going to say.'

The shock whacked Clara back to her senses. She experienced the funny kind of hot relief you got after tears were over and done with. 'Are you sure? How come?'

'Muncher told me about your troubles.'

'He remembers?' Part of Clara found that hard to credit. Part of her felt much less abandoned.

'Yes, he does. He feels guilty.'

'Muncher told you everything that happened?'

'Some of it. Probably not all. And I am so . . .' To Clara's surprise, Mark's voice went husky. He had to wait a moment before he could continue. 'So very *angry*. So very *sorry*.'

'Why didn't you mention any of this before?'

Mark swallowed. 'I thought it was more appropriate that you should raise the topic, when and if you ever believed that I was a person you wanted to confide in; when and if you ever felt that the nature of our relationship was such as to *invite* intimate revelations.'

For a moment Clara experienced a lurching sensation. She steadied herself by staring out of the dark window in the direction of Sussex. From way down the line there came the vibrations, the whispers, of a terribly distant train. Then it all came spilling out of her: details of the marriage; followed by descriptions of a whole ton of other things – both good and bad – that had happened to her also; finishing with the financial straits that had led Clara to put round ads for another lodger.

'I didn't want a man, and when you first arrived I found you proud,' she blurted.

Mark smiled. 'In practice, I probably was. It wasn't how I felt internally. I found you haughty.'

'I was scared.'

'I know.'

There was an awkward pause.

'Forgive me for last night,' said Mark. 'My hesitancy to help you carry out your scheme strikes me now as incomprehensible.'

'Even given what's happened since?'

'*Especially* given that.'

Mark's reply set Clara's pulse sautéing. She gave a shrug, as nonchalant as she could manage. 'I spend all my time trying to grub up a better existence,' she said, looking down but sensing Mark's eyes upon her. 'How can I blame you for being chary about turning your back on the same thing?'

The end of this sentence came out rather hoarse. Clara stole a peek at Mark and, yes, he was looking at her meaningfully. She dropped her eyes again and felt the bed shift slightly. She watched Mark's hand move slowly towards hers until he was just touching the tips of her fingers, which immediately went sort of pins-and-needlesy.

'Clara,' Mark said, 'let me love you. Let me love you as you deserve.'

'Meaning what?' asked Clara before she could stop herself. It almost hurt, happiness.

'Meaning I'd like to share your life. To be your partner in every sense. Is that possible?'

In every sense. But Clara must have nodded because Mark's lips were suddenly on hers and the plait of ribbon was undone. His T-shirt had been thrown on to the floor and Clara could feel the contours of his chest muscles against her dress, against her cream silk bra, against her breasts, which then were being kissed and nuzzled. There was the sound of a zip, of Mark's warm breath, of Clara's own little gasps. Mark pulled the bow of Clara's apricot muslin drawstring knickers.

Spontaneously, a whole pile of dormant terrors shook themselves awake in Clara. There was a pause. Mark shifted into a sitting position, with his back towards her. Clara looked away. She was naked bar a slither, but she'd have liked to have been bundled beneath coats, jackets, leggings, woollen socks, thick cardigans. She couldn't bear this onslaught of male flesh, she simply couldn't stand it. She felt like a shell-less snail, a hermit crab between habitations; and all those other vulnerable creatures that were used to being able to gather themselves into their own, small, private places. The pause continued. Clara rolled on to her side, crossed one cold arm over the other, and waited for the thing she didn't want to happen.

Mark didn't move, however. He simply continued to sit on the edge of the bed. Clara could feel the heat emanating from his body.

Eventually, 'I've been insensitive. This is happening too fast for you, isn't it?' Mark said. He left space for Clara to reply before continuing. 'Passion and desire, those are the explanations. Wanting to *make love* to you with a level of intensity I've never felt towards anyone before. But I'm not about to frighten you, Clara. If this doesn't feel right at present, we'll wait until it does.'

A bit of Clara's brain uncrumpled. She was cold because Mark was no longer touching her. 'It's awfully bright in here,' she said.

'Isn't it?'

Mark switched the bedside lamp out and then there were only the lights above the rails, and perhaps a moon, making nice soft shadows. Clara rolled back over to face him. Mark turned to look at her. He was naked and his evident unselfconsciousness about that made it seem easy and natural. Mark reached out and stroked the hair back from Clara's forehead. He really did have the most beautiful body.

'Perhaps,' Clara suggested, '*I* could make love to *you* first?'

There was no need for Mark to speak in order for Clara to gauge his reaction to her question.

Early morning. They hadn't really slept, just lain on the borders of sleep during the intervals between lovemaking. Towards dawn the trains had become more frequent, murmuring and rocking their way into the city. There'd been a heat haze, which was burning off now; pale lavender mist and orange sunlight. Mark and Clara had showered together, watching the water run down each other's hair, neck, shoulders. Mark's limbs felt relaxed and heavy, as if he'd been swimming in the sea for many hours. When they left the hotel it had been hot already. It was going to be a scorching summer's day.

And what would that day bring? Mark found it almost impossible to nurse fears when every aspect of existence was alive with the new excitement of loving and being loved. Sitting opposite Clara – who was avidly studying a menu – Mark caught the sandalwood aroma of her skirt and blouse, which were crinkled and stiff to the touch from having dried in the night air. It seemed to him than Clara's clothes smelled of steel too – the smooth metal railway tracks that dawn had turned molten. Everything was part of a whole. The world felt entire, sane and rational. Automatically, by falling in love, Mark and Clara had corrected the balance of things. There were no tripwires. No horrors hid in doorways. Instead, people were packing picnics for boating on the Serpentine. Pigeons rose in whirring, grey arcs above the fountains of Trafalgar Square and settled on the public buildings. Flower-sellers peddled multicoloured blooms in the markets. Mark Upshaw and Clara Hood were, of course, in love. It was the school holidays.

The restaurant they were sitting in was harmonious also; Mark could sense its regular rhythms. Every day, surely, the windows were cleaned as they were being cleaned now, and these very customers ordered their usual orders.

A coffee-making machine hissed. A griddle spat and sizzled. Dried sausages hung from the ceiling. There were large baskets full of different-flavoured bagels; bowls of olives and pickled cucumbers; platters of cooked meats and pâtés; baked cheese-cakes.

'Up to nine-fifteen they do a Special Breakfast Offer,' said Clara. 'Two scrambled eggs plus lox, toast and a bottomless mug of coffee.' She looked at Mark and, evidently struck by some memory of the night before, started blushing.

'Sounds good to me.' Mark grinned and raised his eyebrows. Whatever had caused this sudden bashfulness would have to be repeated. He reached out and traced the outline of Clara's chin with his fingers. She smiled. Their hands interlaced.

The food was ordered. The coffee arrived. The pavement outside the clean windows became fuller. The restaurant's proprietor clicked on a little radio: '. . . *Island, where last night* . . .' 'Ach!' The proprietor made a weary gesture and clicked the radio off. 'Nothing but news, news, news these days. Like there isn't anything *else* that ever happens.'

More customers entered carrying morning papers. Mark saw the upside-down face of Charlie, presumably photographed while busy being Home Sec.

The food arrived, and Mark would have given anything to know where they purchased that smoked salmon and the excellent rye bread. '*CAL*', read the beginning of a drooping scrolled headline. Was that *CALLS FOR RESIGNATION*, wondered Mark? *CALCULATES WALL STREET*, perhaps? Or maybe some sort of *CALAMITY*.

Clara said, 'Not often, but sometimes, you feel you're getting a bit of a respite.' She swallowed a forkful of scrambled egg. She took a gulp of coffee. The conversation in the room dissolved into murmurs. What Clara had just said pealed in Mark's ears. He had the sensation that he was sitting among slowly falling things: meteors in their timeless trajectories, being pulled towards Earth; Celtic coins fallen from wooden boats, floating to the seabed; iridescent feathers sashaying on the air; cherry blossoms. Mark looked around. He spotted on the front of another newspaper, folded into a rectangle, a swatch of ultramarine waves with frothy, cotton wool crests.

'We must go,' he said to Clara. 'Straight away. Now.' Then, seeing Clara's face and body leap into alarm mode, 'It isn't bad. In fact, I think it's completely all right.'

Rather wildly, Mark waved for the bill. Clara scribbled a cheque. And then they were out in the street. Hurrying but not running, so as not to be too noticeable. Moving quickly, though. Almost running. Clara's heels clattering on the paving stones. Mark's heart pumping in his chest. As a rule there was a newsagent every ten feet or so, a news-stand on every corner, people positively clamouring to sell you their papers and journals.

Abruptly, Clara stopped dead in her tracks, bringing Mark to a sudden halt beside her.

'Is *that* what we're looking for?' she gasped, pointing across an intersection of about seven major roads, boasting several dozen sets of obstructive traffic lights. On a large white sheet of paper imprisoned behind a grid of metal a headline was displayed, written in black felt-tip.

Mark nodded. Spontaneously, all the traffic lights turned to crimson.

'Daily for you, sir? Madam?'

Breathless, they tumbled on to a bench. Mark put his arm around Clara. For a while they could take in little more than the words, *PEACEFUL COUP ON CALALU ISLAND.* Then Clara read out loud from the leading article:

> *Calalu Island has been celebrating far into the night the peaceful ousting of its unpopular government, which has been replaced by a socialist party that appears to have the full backing of the Calaluan people and has declared its intention to call a democratic election at the earliest possible opportunity. It is apparently for this reason that, in spite of Britain's previous support for Calalu's overthrown regime, the Home Secretary and the Foreign Secretary have both made statements welcoming the news and condemning Calalu's former government as undemocratic.*
>
> *Calalu's first election – which ushered the ousted government in – was uncontested, and the electoral process did not appear to have been fully understood by the country's people.*

When Clara had stopped reading she and Mark remained there on that bench for a long, long time, feeling the warmth of the sun on its splintered paintwork and watching the ebb and flow of the traffic.

It was strange, Mark reflected, that although he had experienced affluence, prestige and success, this was the first time in his life that he felt he had been singled out for particular good fortune.

EPILOGUE

Gatwick Airport

A grey, overcast day. Cold, too. Sopping fields and every tree leafless. Semerraro's van must have thought it had died and gone to heaven, though; what with the best part of half a tank of juice inside it, and all that repair work paid for by the insurance Len had been able to claim after the motor's unfortunate encounter with the fire engine. The van's doors closed properly now, there was glass in every window, and the dents had been knocked out of the front bumper. The old jalopy was positively bowling along towards Gatwick.

Really, barring the mess, encounters with fire-fighters had worked out pretty well all round. Kim having possessed the good sense to start a credible blaze in the bathroom (clothes and towels hanging above joss-sticks and candles: a recipe for disaster), the brigade hadn't been able to say they'd been called to Lisle Street for no purpose. The mayhem caused by the firemen hacking the door down, then running amok throughout the building while simultaneously filling it with water, apparently made scarpering unnoticed not too much of a problem; though it *was* a monster task to get things shipshape again once Bethany had turned herself in and the rest of the household judged it safe to go home.

Since surrendering to the authorities effectively amounted to doing their job for them, Clara guessed it was policy to make it relatively easy. Bethany must have gone to a copshop pretty much the minute she got wind of the changes in her homeland. By midday she was second item on the TV news. Clara and Mark watched the report on a telly in a kebab-and-pitta caff. A press conference, no less! Millions of reporters firing questions. Bethany registering her support for the new set-up in Calalu and saying she'd spent her time in London living rough, which the press, etc. evidently bought. Clara had found it ticklish to keep from sobbing. So much like London buses, this sudden cluster of things going right.

Because of Bethany's statement, all the rozzers had been able do Clara and Mark for was resisting arrest. A hefty hunk of cash found its way into the account of the hotshot solicitor Mark insisted they hire to defend them – but then how could they have run the risk of being forcibly parted? Somehow the solicitor had got them off with a fine and a lecture. Holes in her pockets! Clara didn't mind the lecture – air was free and the beak's wig a wonder to behold – but bang went more of those readies. It also seemed only right and proper to pay the fines of Rob and the other White Bear bartenders, and those weren't exactly a song – that not having been their first such barney.

Bethany was deported. One chilly morning some weeks later, when autumn was beginning to bite, Clara found a luminous postcard on the doormat. Sky and sea trying to outdo each other. Sand, coconuts, bananas. The postcard wasn't signed but on the back of it was written: 'Thank you'.

You could tell it wasn't England!

Now, as Muncher accelerated to pass a forty-footer, a thin drizzle began to fall. Clara thought she heard Geraldine give a small wail and Kim respond with reassurances. Hardly ideal for people to travel in, the back of Len's auto; but the others *had* insisted on coming *and* on Mark and Clara riding up front, and Clara had provided Geraldine with a triple thickness of carrier so there was no danger of her being sick on Si's new trainers. Si was pretty thingy about those rubber shoes, but they were the first purchase he'd made after doing the commercial.

Inspired by Vigilante's interest in him, Clara had read a library of dietary information on Si's behalf; but all the volumes did was outline ways of getting or staying fit. Geraldine and Clara combed the Charing Cross Road for a volume entitled *How to Grow Taller,* which Geraldine was convinced must surely exist since there was so obviously a niche. Clara measured Si's height twice a week, but there was no progress. In the end Mark had suggested Si should go and see an agent anyway. The agent liked the look of Si, put him on her books and got him a low-budget cinema ad – though more and better was expected to follow.

'Mind yer hats!' shouted Muncher as a massive plane screeched overhead. 'Nearly there now.'

Despite the puffing heater, Clara felt herself go cold. There was a tonic-water tingle in her stomach. She stared out across hangars; terminals; a control tower with something revolving on top of it; acre after acre of carparks; runways bordered with lights; a close, steely sky.

'You're sure you'll be okay doing the market on your own?' she asked Mark.

Mark's arm tightened around her; his lips brushed her hair. 'It's only for a couple of weeks, and Si's said he'll put in a few hours.'

Clara fell silent. She made her mind fix on their recently opened prime-site stall in the Jubilee Market, Covent G. Lease established courtesy of the bulk of what had remained of Fleur's cheque after the legalities.

Lucky the *Sunday Times* journalist left Fleur's premises before the Bill made their appearance! Because of the newspaper puff, Fleur had been obliged to keep Clara's clobber on the rails for a while, but unfortunately that was where it ended. Although Clara's collection sold well in Newburgh Street (She knew that for a fact: she'd made enquiries), Fleur opted not to reorder. Cross about the rumpus and the rozzers, probably. Or maybe she'd made her own investigations and discovered Clara was only small-time. Access to any other chichi stores seeming for the moment unlikely, it had made sense to establish their own retail outlet. Clara cut out the *Sunday Times* article and accompanying photo and put them in a frame. She hung it from a nail in the nice little changing-room she and Mark made at the back of the stall (a couple of sheets and some curtain rails from the Dump). Business wasn't at all bad.

The colours, though, the designs and patterns: punter satisfaction notwithstanding, Clara could never get them quite as good as Bethany had.

'Up we go,' said Muncher. The van turned into a multistorey, which was chock-a-block, mean on room to manoeuvre, weather-beaten and grimy: small wonder it was hard to get a handle on tropical hues.

Clara and Mark – and sometimes Geraldine and Kim also – had made numerous visits to the Museum of Mankind. Of course they went to the V & A. Formerly awash with fire-hose water, Lisle Street became awash with dye again. On every floor. In every receptacle. Clara was mad to get Bethany's techniques sussed. When Mark undressed her at night, Clara's body was flecked with pink, green, orange, purple. Mark took to kissing wherever the dyes had stained. Sometimes Clara splashed certain areas accidentally-on-purpose.

The obvious thing would have been to have made contact with Bethany, but for a long while Clara was just too jumpy. The building might still be under surveillance. Their letters were being opened, perhaps. Maybe the phone was bugged. Bethany was evidently of the same opinion. After the postcard, communication had ceased. But then Calalu's general election took place. The party that had staged the coup was voted into power. The British government pronounced itself satisfied with the situation, and Calalu featured on a holiday prog. Geraldine Crowe had visited the island, after all. The odd long-distance and the odd airmail weren't so very suspicious, were they?

Bethany explained, advised, sent diagrams and instructions.

But she couldn't send summer. Conceivably that was the missing ingredient.

Muncher squeezed the van into a mini-spot on what felt like the fiftieth level.

'We are shaken but unharmed,' said Kim, emerging from the back. 'Though my nylons have sustained a ladder.'

'I was fighting nausea throughout,' proclaimed Geraldine.

'So *I* wasn't allowed to open the Thermos,' said Si.

'Hip flask's what you need for the wobblies,' said Muncher.

Mark squeezed Clara's arm. 'I'll get the suitcases.'

'My, my, my, Clara!' said Kim as Mark swung the luggage to the ground. 'Aren't you smart and matching!'

A lift. An escalator. The departure area. Glass and plastic. Gliding trolleys. Calm voices making announcements. Air Calalu Flight B120 up there on schedule. And all the shades and makes of the species present; as if this was a great human sorting-office.

Eventually Bethany had sent an invitation. Everyone insisted that Clara should go; there was just enough cash left to afford the fare. In person Clara would be able to learn from Bethany precisely how the batiks were done. The invitation was accepted. Bethany and her friends were jerking a whole pig to celebrate Clara's arrival. They would drink rum and sing calypsos, and all of Bethany's cousins planned to visit from their villages.

'Don't forget my present,' said Geraldine. She'd crocheted a doily. She gave Clara a bony hug and sniffed and snuffled. Clara pointed at the bag with the doily in it.

'Come back with a tan,' said Kim.

Clara winked.

'Have a nice time, luv,' said Muncher. 'And remember to buy some duty-frees.'

Clara nodded.

'Y'know what, Clara?' asked Si. Clara shook her head. 'I'm going to help out on the stall, then Maz and me'll get takeaways.'

Clara smiled.

'Going in an aeroplane is wonderful . . .' said Mark. Then he held her as tight as life itself for a minute before letting her go.

There were all sorts of nice aspects to air travel that nobody told you about. Above Clara's seat next to the window there wa nozzle you could twizzle and get different volumes of air out In the pocket in front of her seat was a free mag and a bag full of complimentaries: a pen with Air Calalu's logo on, a stethoscope thing you could plug into a socket for film sound and radio, a pair of socks that Clara decided to save for Muncher, and a little model of the aeroplane that would do for Si. The movies hadn't started yet, but the diddy screens were showing shots of tropical fish. There was a menu *with choices.*

The aeroplane hung around on the runway for a while; queuing, according to the pilot. When at last their turn came there was a pause during which the engines started going crazy. The plane seemed to take an almighty breath, and then it dashed along full pelt until there was nothing under the wheels and the airport was gliding away at an angle.

The fields really did look like patchwork. Clara watched them until the aeroplane entered cloud; journeying upward, upward, towards that place Mark had told her about where there was sunshine always. Guaranteed.